STORMY MONTANA SKY

BOOK THREE OF THE MONTANA SKY SERIES

1890'S MONTANA SKY SERIES

Wild Montana Sky
Starry Montana Sky
Stormy Montana Sky
Montana Sky Christmas: A Sweetwater
Springs Short Story Collection
Painted Montana Sky: A Sweetwater
Springs Novella

1886 MAIL-ORDER BRIDES OF THE WEST

Trudy

Look for future Montana Sky books,
novellas, and short stories

STORMY MONTANA SKY

BOOK THREE OF THE MONTANA SKY SERIES

By Debra Holland

Montlake
Romance

Printed in the United States of America

This edition published in 2013 by Montlake Romance, Seattle
www.apub.com

ISBN-13: 9781477817889
ISBN-10: 1477817883
Library of Congress Control Number: 2013916752

Cover design by Delle Jacobs

To Don Napolitano,
for all the years of support.

SWEETWATER SPRINGS, MONTANA

1893

PROLOGUE

Through the sheen of tears blurring her vision, Harriet Stanton watched the man she loved marry another woman. The amber rays of the late October sun gleamed through the plain glass windows of the church, gilding the pearl-studded lace veil covering Elizabeth Hamilton's blond hair. The light glistened over the lace and silk of her wedding dress, glittered the diamonds dangling from her ears and around her throat, and played over the bouquet of white roses and autumn leaves she carried. But even the sunshine couldn't best the radiant look on the Boston beauty's face as she gazed at her adoring bridegroom, Nick Sanders.

The moisture in Harriet's eyes beaded up, threatening to spill over. Pain squeezed her heart into a tight little ball. She lifted her chin to keep the betraying drops contained and clenched her fists until her nails dug crescents into her palms. No one must guess her secret pain. She wanted no pitying glances, no gossip to trail after her like a train of dust, smudging shame across her life.

Reverend Norton, in his rusty-black frock coat, stood in front of the couple and intoned the words of the marriage service. The minister's blue eyes beamed with obvious approval for the couple before him, softening the usual austerity of his white-bearded face.

Nick faced Elizabeth, hand-in-hand in front of an altar draped in white linen. His brown hair waved to the shoulders of the new navy-blue suit that had come from an expensive men's emporium in the East—a present from his bride. Even in profile, his obvious joy shone in his green eyes, and he smiled at Elizabeth without a trace of his usual shyness. Harriet had never seen him look so handsome . . . or so proud.

To Harriet's mortification, one tear welled out of her control, racing down her cheek. She made a furtive dab at her face with a lace-edged handkerchief, refusing to allow another to fall. Hopefully, anyone who noticed attributed the emotion to normal wedding sentimentality. Pride alone stiffened Harriet's back, kept the rest of the tears restrained, for if anyone here knew the heaviness of her heart, she would sink with embarrassment.

Beside her in the pew, the shopkeeper, Mrs. Cobb, nudged Harriet with one thick elbow. "Sinful waste of money, that dress. Ordered from Paris. Worth, a Frenchie designer." The woman sniffed, and the stuffed finch perched on her black bonnet bobbed forward. "Could have bought a dress from our mercantile. But no. The likes of us wasn't good enough for Miss Elizabeth Hamilton."

Harriet nodded that she'd heard. Luckily Mrs. Cobb didn't expect an answer. Nor did she seem to notice Harriet's pain. Even though Harriet boarded with the Cobbs, she wasn't close to the couple. For them to know of her feelings for Nick would be like scrubbing sand over an open wound.

She fingered the circle of gold leaves pinned to a froth of lace at the neck of her gray cashmere dress, twisting it back and forth. Her mother's brooch was usually a source of comfort. But not today.

Will this ceremony ever end?

Reverend Norton leaned forward, his white beard wagging. "Do you, Nicholas John Sanders, take…"

Harriet tried not to listen to the words that would rob her of her love.

Nick, my Nick.

She closed her eyes, clenching her teeth against the lie. *In truth, never mine.* Only in her heart had Nick belonged to her. She'd fallen in love with him when she'd first come to teach in Sweetwater Springs. In reality he'd never given her any encouragement. But Nick Sanders' shyness with women was legendary around town.

Some of their moments together had given her hope. She still treasured the time when she'd carried a load of books too big for her and some had fallen off the pile in her arms and landed on the dirt street. Nick had been riding by and had jumped off his horse, rapidly tethered the reins to a rail, and then had scooped up the fallen books. He brushed them off and insisted on taking the rest of the books to the schoolhouse for her. They'd actually had a conversation that day, finding they had favorite books in common.

From encounters like that, Harriet had spun dreams of Nick's green eyes glowing with love, that shy smile being directed at her. Creating a life together. Having a home. Babies.

She opened her eyes, looking anywhere but at the front of the church. Around her she could see only happy faces. The work-worn hands of husbands and wives slipped together in a shared renewal of memories. Rancher John Carter's thin face beamed with pride in the young man he'd brought up, while his wife, Pamela, grew misty-eyed watching her girlhood friend. Dr. Cameron and his wife, easily distinguished by their red hair, exchanged a reminiscing glance. Only old Abe Maguire, his craggy face turned to stone, sat with his arms crossed in front of him. He'd buried his wife three weeks ago. Like Harriet, he grieved his loss in silence, but only Harriet mourned in secret.

Until today she'd allowed herself to hope. She'd struggled, one part of her truly wishing Nick well—wishing him marital bliss—while the other wickedly hoped the engagement would end. She'd tried to banish that thought whenever it appeared, but the idea had kept burrowing through her mind like a gopher through a bed of bulbs.

Sometimes it helped that Harriet liked Elizabeth and, under other circumstances, would have wanted her friendship. At least Nick had chosen well, no, more than well. Each time she saw how the love flowed between the couple, she wished to rejoice in their happiness instead of ache from it.

Now the ache increased, expanding from her stomach into her throat until she could barely curb all the emotion in her body. She tried to swallow her feelings down, hold her jaw rigid.

Caught up in her misery, the rest of the service dragged on. By the time Reverend Norton pronounced Nick and Elizabeth man and wife, Harriet could only feel relieved that she'd survived the ceremony, her secret still intact.

Now she had only to endure the reception…and the emptiness of the rest of her life.

CHAPTER ONE

Nine Months Later

At the burst of artillery fire, Anthony Gordon ducked behind the remains of the brick storefront. His heartbeat pounded to the staccato burst of gunfire only a few streets away. He inhaled the acrid air, his breath ragged in his chest, impatient for the shelling to cease.

I should have known the count would try out his new cannons, attempting to win the feud with his neighbors. People will die over a dispute concerning a few acres of land.

He swiped sweat from his forehead with the sleeve of his coat. But he couldn't do anything about the moisture trickling down his back under the fine cotton of his shirt.

A momentary pause propelled him out of hiding. Shoulders hunched, he tried to block out the screams of panicked people fleeing in the opposite direction. He wove through the mass of terrorized citizens, seesawing around pushcarts and family groups, skittering past the ruins of the bakery, and skirting several fires. Smoke set him coughing, but he didn't dare stop.

Isabella, I must get to Isabella.

Several streets over, cannons pounded the buildings along the village square, raining destruction on the row of shops and taverns. Around him flying debris filled the air, blocking out the afternoon sun.

The closer Ant came to Isabella's cottage, the heavier his fear grew. Remorse squeezed through his terror. He shouldn't have left her alone for two days, all for what he'd thought was an important interview. He should have realized fighting could break out. Please, God may she have broken her promise to him to stay put.

He rounded the corner of a cottage and saw the boarding house. Without slowing, he breathed a sigh of relief when he realized the pristine whitewashed exterior, complete with flowering window-boxes, sat untouched.

He burst through the wooden door. "Isabella!"

No response.

Threading through the furniture of the parlor, he pushed open the dining room door, only to halt at the devastation before him. A cannonball must have caught the back of the house, collapsing the walls. The heavy oak dining table was pushed almost to the door; the bricks and wood from the walls draped over it and piled up around the rest of the room. The roof stood open to the sky.

"Isabella!" he yelled.

A faint moan reached him.

Ducking under the table, he crawled toward the caved-in kitchen. A shard of glass cut the palm of his hand. He cursed, but didn't slow, desperate to reach her. The wooden door was canted open. He pushed, but it refused to budge further. He squeezed himself sideways. His head and shoulders fit through, enough to see Isabella.

She lay in a crumpled heap, a heavy beam resting crossways over her body. Gray dust coated the lustrous dark tresses fanning out in tangles over the slate floor and turned her rose-colored dress a pale pink.

He angled the rest of the way into the kitchen and then crawled over to her. "Bella?"

Blood trickled out of the side of her mouth. She opened her eyes; pain blurred their brown depths. "My Antonio," she whispered, the words barely audible.

The familiar endearment cut to his heart. Even now, in all her pain, Isabella refused to use his nickname. He kissed her forehead. "I'm going to get you out of here."

Ant stood, reaching for the heavy beam. He could only pry it up a few inches, but it would be enough. He pushed some loose bricks under the wood with his foot, propping it up, and then dropped back to his knees.

She moaned.

Ant gathered Isabella's limp body to him, cradling her against his chest. "Bella, love."

Her dark eyelashes fluttered, then stilled. Her head lolled back.

A sword-thrust of agony stabbed through him. "Isabella," he whispered, feeling his heartbeat stop with hers. "No, Bella, no."

Pressing his ear to her soft breast, he begged to hear the familiar rhythm.

He found only a stillness so empty it echoed in his own chest cavity. His own traitorous organ thumped to life, pumping blood through his body, while his love lay dead in his arms.

The dream scene began to shift. A boy's plaintive voice called. "Uncle Ant. Uncle Ant."

Ant woke with a gasp, his arms wrapped around his chest. He sat up, fighting to stem the press of emotions clogging his throat and constricting his ribs.

Bella! Will you ever leave my dreams in peace?

A gentle breeze stirred the pine branches over his head, sending their spicy scent to chase away the remembered taste of dust and smoke. The faint blue-gray light of a

Montana dawn filtered through the shadows of the trees. A bird twittered in a nearby bush.

Ant pushed the red-and-gray Indian blanket off himself. He grabbed his boots and shook them before thrusting his stocking feet into the cold leather.

She's haunted me for too long.

He ran his hand over his eyes, pushing the hair from his face. At least this time, the scene with Isabella hadn't included the bloody body of his murdered sister, Emily.

Ant poured the pail of water over the embers of his campfire. Steam hissed. Too shaken to bother with breakfast, he gathered his gear and saddled up his black horse, Shadow, determined to leave the memories of his past behind with this campsite.

He needed to focus his mind on the task ahead. His goal was near. Once he'd found the boy and killed the father, maybe then he'd be able to sleep in peace.

◇

Harriet stood quiet and watchful in the front yard of the church, allowing the rest of the congregation to swirl around her. The colorful cotton or silk dresses of the women matched the cheerful mood she sensed among the people. The flow of the crowd eddied and swelled, catching in little pools as women stopped to chat with each other, and the men gathered in small groups.

She enjoyed the feel of the warm sun, while she waited for some of the prominent women of Sweetwater Springs to detach from their conversations. She had a mission for the summer. Today was the day to implement it.

Harriet caught a glimpse of Nick and Elizabeth Sanders talking with the Carters. Her heart crimped, and she turned away. For her own serenity, she always avoided looking at the two of them together. Even after nine months of marriage, they still looked the picture of joy.

She lifted her chin. She'd come to terms with her feelings for Nick, walled them tightly away where they'd been fading. Surely soon, they'd evaporate like rain puddles in the summer sunshine. If only Nick hadn't spent time at the school two weeks ago, helping rebuild the privy. Being around him had reawakened feelings that she'd strove to suppress all winter.

Overhead, a few puffy white clouds with gray underbellies moved in stately progress across the arching azure sky. Harriet reached up to adjust the straw bonnet shielding her face from the warm rays of the sun. Unlike last summer's punishing drought, this year, the season had alternated between the sunny and rainy days necessary for the growing of crops and acres of grass and hay. The hand of the Almighty had lavished the land with abundance. Behind her, she could hear a cluster of men already making hopeful guesses about the autumn harvest.

Like darting minnows, children scampered through the crowd making for the large oak tree next to the schoolhouse whose branches would shelter their games. The children celebrated their freedom after months of studies. Harriet watched them, feeling satisfaction as she looked at each child and remembered how much he or she had learned this past school year.

Seeing them play made her remember her plan. She wanted to travel to each outlying house, cabin, or soddy to find any children currently not in school and persuade their parents to send them. But she suspected some of the families might need some financial assistance in order to do so. So she wanted to form a committee of the most prosperous ladies of the community to help out. First she planned to talk to Pamela Carter, wife of the foremost rancher in the area. If Pamela agreed, the other women would follow.

Twin boys tumbled to a stop in front of her. "Howdy, Miss Stanton," the first one said, quickly echoed by the second. Jack, she thought, although she couldn't always tell; they looked so alike. But Jack was the outspoken one.

Harriet couldn't resist the twins' infectious grins, nor the way mischief brightened their gazes. She smoothed Jack's unruly brown hair, already springing out of Sunday neatness, and tapped Tim on the shoulder of his blue shirt. "You boys have done fine with your studies this week. I'm proud of you both. You'll be able to enjoy your summer off."

Their newly adoptive mother, Samantha Rodriguez, came up just in time to hear Harriet's remark. She dropped a casual arm around each boy's shoulders. "Those words are joy to a mother's ears." She hugged the twins toward her, and then released them. "Run along and play for a while."

"Yes, Mama," Jack said, flashing another grin at the women before running off, Tim at his heels.

Samantha's gaze followed the boys, pride banishing the drawn look she'd worn for the previous weeks.

Harriet took the moment to study the woman. Instead of the black widow's garb Samantha had constantly worn since she'd arrived from Argentina, today she shimmered in bright blue silk that brought out the color of her eyes. A straw bonnet, threaded through with the same blue ribbons, perched on top of her auburn hair, shading her smooth, pale skin.

Harriet smiled at the beautiful widow. "I'm so relieved the twins were exonerated for setting those fires. You'll never again have to worry about them being sent to an orphanage."

"It's all been an answer to my prayers." Tears misted in Samantha's eyes. "I can't believe those are the same two sullen boys that came to live with me three months ago. It does my heart good to see them happy."

Impulsively, Harriet grabbed Samantha's hand. "The boys aren't the only ones who are happy. You're glowing."

Samantha squeezed Harriet's hand. "It's the dress," she quipped, the fine lines around her eyes crinkling with laughter. "I'm afraid now that we're betrothed, Wyatt's taken to spoiling me. No more black." She cast a fond glance at her darkly handsome fiancé standing in the center of a group of men, who were obviously soliciting his opinions about ranching or some such important male topic.

"After all you've been through—almost losing the twins, your ranch—you deserve to be happy."

"Thank you, dear Miss Stanton. Let me say that I wish the same joy for you someday."

Harriet couldn't help the slide of her gaze toward Nick Sanders. As he and Elizabeth talked to the Carters, his hand rested protectively on the small of his wife's back. Elizabeth touched her hand to her stomach, smiled, and said something.

Pamela Carter let out a cry, then reached out and hugged first Elizabeth, then Nick. John Carter thumped Nick on the back, then kissed Elizabeth's cheek.

Cold shivers turned Harriet's body to ice and contracted her stomach into a painful knot. Dizziness waved across her vision and weakened her knees. She clenched her teeth, striving to maintain her composure, for, even without hearing the words, she knew: *Elizabeth Sanders was expecting.*

Harriet tore her gaze away from Elizabeth and Nick. Her vision constricted, graying the arching blue sky and dulling the bright colors of the ladies' dresses. Shock made her ribcage contract more tightly than the most restrictive corset. As she tried to banish the dizziness of her distress, the chatter of the church crowd stilled. Dimly, she could hear Samantha Rodriguez speaking to her.

Samantha touched Harriet's arm. "Miss Stanton, are you all right? You look pale."

Harriet hoped her mouth shaped a smile and not a grimace. "I'm fine," she managed to stammer out. "It's such a beautiful day, I'm contemplating taking a walk." There, she'd gotten words out. She hoped she sounded normal.

Samantha smiled, her blue eyes warm with understanding. "A peaceful walk sounds lovely."

Understanding? How can Samantha Rodriguez understand what she doesn't know?

Out of the corner of her eye, Harriet could see Nick and Elizabeth approaching them. Pretending not to see, she said to Samantha, "Mrs. Cobb is waving me over. Good-bye, Mrs. Rodriguez."

"Good-bye, Miss Stanton."

Harriet hastened away from the Sanders, diving into the crowd. She wiggled through the congregation, nodding and attempting to smile at anyone who greeted her. The Cobbs stood with their backs to her, engrossed in their conversation with Doctor Cameron and his wife. She veered away from them, away from the rest of the people, and headed toward the schoolhouse. If anyone saw her, they'd think she had gone there to do some work.

Once she reached the steps of the white-framed building, she walked past, rounding the corner and heading toward the back. She passed the lilac bushes screening the new privy. The stink mixed with the smoky smell left over from the fire Ben Grayson had set to the old outhouse last week. She didn't even glance at the tiny building. Just a few days ago, she'd watched Nick Sanders and Wyatt Thompson rebuild the privy and had secretly allowed herself to enjoy Nick's company.

Shame seized her, quickening her pace. Her feet carried her over the familiar path trod into the dust by the children who lived in the mountains.

Harriet could no longer avoid facing her feelings. She longed for a married man, a *happily* married man. She'd promised herself at Nick's wedding that she'd barricade away her love for him. And for months, she'd thought she'd succeeded. She'd even accepted the admiration of the local cowboys, although without encouraging their advances.

Harriet fingered the gold pin at her throat. Being around Nick last week had cracked her defenses, allowing her true feelings to seep back through her barriers and into her heart.

Today's news had been dynamite thrust into the chinks in her walls, exploding them to bits. Now the rubble lay shattered around her heart, leaving her raw, exposed.

She passed a stand of pine trees that stood between the town and the wilderness. Knowing no one would see,

Harriet hitched up her skirts, increasing the length of her stride. The heaviness in her chest forced her ever faster, uncaring of the branches that reached out to rake her straw bonnet and catch the material of her best Sunday dress. She ran a long way, feeling sobs building in waves, their intensity pressing against her throat.

The path forked. Harriet chose the left. A grassy glade beckoned, and she headed toward its shelter, ready to sink down and release her emotion.

Unseeing, she stumbled over a fallen branch, twisting as she fell. Pain shot up her ankle. The momentum carried her forward into the trunk of a tree.

Her head collided with the rough bark. Dark sparkles hazed her vision, and she collapsed into an unconscious heap at the base of the tree.

~

Harriet's consciousness returned in layers. Blackness faded to purple, then to gray, which in turn lightened to awareness. She vaguely realized she lay on the ground, half on her back, half on her side. The scent of soil and pine needles clogged her nose.

Without opening her eyes, she groped toward the ache in her forehead. When she touched the lump, the pain spread. She moaned and opened her eyes. One ray of sunlight, escaping the sheltering boughs of a pine tree, stabbed into her right eye. She turned her face to avoid the piercing light, only to have the ache in her head increase from the movement.

She made a sound of disgust. She'd have bruises to explain to the Cobbs, not to mention the ruin of her bonnet and Sunday dress. She'd been so careful with her salary, saving for a house of her own. Now she'd have to spend some of her precious funds for a new outfit. Annoyance blended with the pain in her head.

She tried again to shift her head and winced, a fresh wave of dizziness speckling her vision, and making her nauseous. Wooziness deadened her limbs and weighed down her thoughts. Harriet let herself drift for a long time without moving, hoping when she next awoke, she'd be better able to face her circumstances. The air chilled. She wrapped her arms around herself, refusing to stir.

Cold drops of water splashed on her face and brought her into full consciousness. The sunshine had given way to angry, dark shadows.

Gingerly Harriet sat up, her body sore all over. Even with a storm starting, she couldn't bring herself to move with any speed. She started to tuck her feet under her in order to rise; a spasm of pain racked her ankle. Gasping, she flopped her legs back down.

It can't be that bad, she told herself, trying to believe her own words. But still, she took the deepest breaths her corset would allow before she made the attempt again. Keeping her foot extended, she scooted closer to the tree. She braced both hands on the ground and lifted up her body. Using the trunk, she struggled to stand without putting weight on her foot. As she inched herself higher, the rough bark of the tree cut into her palm.

Once upright, she panted for air, trying to catch her breath. Her corset constrained her ribs. The lack of oxygen increased her dizziness, threatening to topple her to the ground.

Harriet slumped with her back against the tree, fighting to stay upright. Her head throbbed. Long moments passed before she nerved herself to take an experimental step.

The deluge increased, trickling through the pine branches. Her straw bonnet began to droop, and the gingham of her green dress quickly became saturated. A fresh rain scent sprang out of the grassy earth and trees. She shivered.

Her stays blocked another attempt to deeply inhale. A flash of frustration penetrated her growing fear. *When I return home, I'm burning this corset and never wearing one again.*

But first she'd have to get home somehow.

Harriet stepped forward with care. Fiery pangs shot through her ankle. She cried out, falling back against the trunk, almost fainting from pain. Frantically, she looked around for a stick to use as a crutch. But the only branch close by was the one she'd tripped over, and it was short and stubby.

She knew some families lived not too far away, surviving on hunting and small garden plots. They were probably snug in their cabins, but maybe someone else had been caught in the rain and was within earshot.

"Help, help," she called, the words little more than a croak. Harriet swallowed, trying to clear the helplessness clogging her throat.

She called again, louder. When no response came, she wanted to cry.

The wind whipped through the trees, scattering more drops across her body. One more time she called out. Only the sound of the storm answered.

Under another pine about twenty feet away, she could see some sticks. One of them looked as if it might be long enough. Harriet dropped to her knees and began to crawl, trying not to jar her ankle against the ground.

It seemed to take her hours to go inches. Every couple of yards, she collapsed, panting and dizzy, allowing the waves of pain to wash over her. Once she caught her breath, she forced herself onward. Fat raindrops pounded on her back, her skirt became sodden, seeming to develop a life of its own, tangling her legs. After a few feet, her skirt bunched up underneath her, trapping her in place. She rolled to her side and jerked the material above her knees, tucking the hem into the waistband. She inhaled a fortifying breath, trying to block out the pain, and then resumed her crawl.

Finally, she neared the tree. Flopping onto her stomach, she walked her fingers forward, straining to reach the nearest branch, which turned out to only be a few feet long. She tossed it aside, then slithered another few inches toward the next one. When she grabbed the wood, it crumbled to pieces, too decayed to use. The one closest to the tree looked the most likely. But when she picked the branch up, using it to help her stand, it snapped in two pieces, just as she rose to her feet. She cried out from the pain when her foot jarred against the ground.

Too exhausted and discouraged, Harriet sank back to the ground. She huddled against the trunk, her arms wrapped around her knees. Her head dropped to rest on her arms, and she began to pray.

Her wet, muddy garments weighed on her, little protection against the night. Her body numbed. By tomorrow, she knew the Cobbs would have people out searching for her. But rescue was long hours away.

I can't stay here. I might not be alive when they find me.

Just let me rest…gather my strength.

Harriet took a few bracing breaths. She uncurled her limbs and began to crawl down the mountain.

CHAPTER TWO

The path crested the mountain pass, and Ant reined in Shadow. The big black stallion tossed his head, seeming as eager as Ant to reach the town spread out below them. From this distance, Sweetwater Springs appeared storybook sweet. Tiny buildings, probably stores and other businesses, clustered along one main street, with some houses scattered behind. A steepled church looked to be one of the tallest buildings and was bound to mean there were several nearby saloons. A miniature train depot resided near railroad tracks thin as pins.

A glance at the thunderheads darkening the sky made him realize the storm that had been building up for the last several hours would soon break. He should find some shelter. But the impatience that had been brewing inside him didn't allow for that sensible choice.

Instead he urged Shadow forward. The sooner he arrived in Sweetwater Springs, the sooner he could reclaim David. He'd fulfill his vow, avenge his sister, and go home. The two-year quest would be over.

He could return to his former life, especially his newspaper reporting. The only difference would be in having a nephew to raise. And how difficult could that be? David had always been an obedient boy. Ant's many years spent covering news in Europe had precluded his spending much time with his nephew, but when he'd been home, they had a good relationship.

Ant headed down the trail, lost in memories of the childhood he'd spent with his sister, Emily. Always close, he and his gentle sister shared a love of literature and writing. Both children's early poems had showed promise, but their stepfather's taunts and beatings had driven any poetry out of Ant's soul. Emily, being a lowly female in his stepfather's eyes, had escaped the worst of his attentions, and she'd continued to write her poems and stories. Then she had married Lewis…. Ant thought of the book of poetry tucked at the bottom of his saddlebag. Emily's poems. Unopened since her murder.

The late afternoon gloom deepened. Sprinkles of raindrops scattered across his hands, bringing him back to the present.

Ant sighed and fastened the front of his slicker. *Best light the lantern before it gets much worse.* He halted the horse and slid off. He rummaged through his gear to find the lantern, his hands moving with the ease of long practice. Once he'd lit the lamp, he climbed back into the saddle.

The rain increased. Distant thunder rolled. A summer storm. Mild enough for the sustenance of growing crops, but not the chill rain of early spring which burrowed cold down to a man's bones.

Shadow flicked his ears, showing his displeasure.

Ant leaned over and patted the horse's damp neck. "I agree, old boy. Won't be much longer now. I promise you a dry stall and a bucket of warm mash."

Seeming to understand, Shadow nickered.

Ant tilted his head forward just enough for his wide-brimmed hat to keep the rain off his face and not far enough for water to drip down his neck.

A faint cry reached his ears. A human sound. He jerked his head up, listening. The call wasn't repeated. Came from down the path a ways. He raised the lantern up and slowed Shadow, not wanting to run over anyone. Narrowing his eyes against the gloom, he scanned with all his senses. Nothing. Just rain tapping through the trees.

A slight movement ahead and to his right caught his attention. He raised the lantern and saw a person crouched on hands and knees. *What the hell was anyone doing out on the mountain in the midst of a storm?* Concern seized him. The person must be hurt.

Ant guided Shadow in that direction. On closer inspection, he saw a sodden dress and drooping straw hat. A woman, a bedraggled one, not even a coat to keep her warm. She maneuvered to a sitting position, staring up at him.

His concern increased. If she didn't get to shelter soon, she could become ill.

"Howdy, ma'am." He rode close to her.

She gasped, scuttled back to press against a tree.

He dismounted and stepped forward, holding up the lantern so he could see the woman. "May I lend a hand, ma'am?"

She was small, he could tell that much. With her ruined hat sagging around her face, it was difficult to see her features. Except her eyes. The fright in their depths brought him up short. He'd once pulled a drowning kitten out of a pond. He remembered the terror in the big gray eyes, how the brown fur plastered to the thin little body, the weight of the rock tied around the skinny paw. The pity he'd felt for the scrawny creature had helped the animal wiggle her way into his heart.

Old compassion surfaced, urging he move toward the woman. But he kept his boots planted. His great height and dark features often intimidated females. He'd learned to use charm and humor to diffuse their apprehensions. But now, he cursed the necessity.

Ant made his tone light. "Anthony Gordon to your rescue." He swept off his hat and bowed. Rain splattered his hair and dripped down his neck. Had he thought the temperature was mild? He changed his mind, replacing his hat. "Knight errant to your damsel in distress." He waited for her response. She still looked shell-shocked, although he thought he could see her teeth chattering. "The answer to your prayers?" he quipped.

That did it. Her shoulders relaxed. A corner of her mouth pulled up. Not quite a half smile, but heading there.

He unstrapped his bedroll, pulling out a blanket. Moving with deliberate slowness, he approached her, trying to show with his gaze and movement that he was safe—that she was safe with him. Her body felt chilled. He'd touched dead bodies warmer than hers. Ant draped the blanket around her shoulders.

"I'll have to get you out of here." As he wrapped the blanket tight around her, the vulnerability in her gray eyes caught him in a tender heartspot.

Ant winced. He hadn't thought he had any softness left for a woman. He'd better be careful. Get her home and leave her be.

～

When the stranger on the big black horse loomed through the gathering darkness, Harriet had gasped. She'd never seen such a huge man, almost as if one of the surrounding trees had become human and mounted a mythical beast to gallop among the mountains. Clad in black from hat to boots, his sinister appearance spiked panic through her. Terrified, she wanted to flee for her life, for her virtue, but trapped by her injuries, all she could do was back away.

The dark man dismounted, the movement strong, yet fluid.

She scooted against a tree; the bark dug into her back. Everything in her hesitated, waiting.

The man stopped; the angular panes of his face stilled. In the lamplight, his wide-set brown eyes mesmerized—a snake charmer playing with his cobra. Then his right eyebrow peaked in an upside down *V*. He swept off his hat and bowed. Brown hair tangled the tops of his shoulders.

Pinned against the trunk by his menacing presence, Harriet barely registered what he'd said.

He replaced his hat. He spoke some more, then paused, waiting for her response.

Fear held her frozen.

"The answer to your prayers?" He held up the lantern in one hand, the other raised in supplication, fingers splaying wide as a dinner plate. That last line broke through her fear. He *was* the answer to her prayers. Just not quite what she had in mind when she prayed for a rescue.

The man's playful tone contrasting with his ominous appearance disarmed her. His voice sounded gravelly and deep as if he hadn't spoken much.

When he tucked the blanket around her, she shivered in relief.

"I think it's safe to talk to me. At least tell me what's wrong."

What's wrong? My whole life's what's wrong.

Harriet forced words through the paralysis in her throat. "I tripped and fell, hit my head against the tree, twisted my ankle."

"We need to get you to shelter." His voice took on an English lilt. "Good thing my noble steed, Shadow, can bear us both to yonder town."

The last vestiges of her fright fled. She doubted any man who deliberately tried to sound like a hero from a poorly written Arthurian novel would mean her harm. Even if he did seem bigger than a barn.

From somewhere inside herself, she found a bit of humor to match his. "Did you say your name was Gulliver?" She referenced her favorite book.

He grinned. "Only if your name is Lily."

"Lancelot perhaps?"

"Guinevere?"

"Ivanhoe?"

"My lady," he said, exasperation edging his humor. "Will you allow me to get you out of this wet?"

Harriet hesitated.

"I see I'll have to forcibly abduct you." He set the lantern down. Placing one arm under her knees and one behind her back, he scooped her up.

Harriet gasped and slipped one hand around his neck. A thrill shot up her backbone, setting butterflies to wing around her stomach and almost masking the pain of her ankle and head.

"Little bit of a kitten, aren't you?" he murmured.

With a lift, he set her sideways the saddle, making sure the blanket remained mummy-tight around her. He pulled the rest of his bedroll apart, spreading it like a cape over her. Picking up the lantern, he balanced it on her lap.

She lifted her blanket-shrouded hands to cup the base. Peering at him from under the hood created by the blanket, she said, "I'm sorry. I really didn't catch your name."

"Anthony Gordon. But everyone calls me Ant—a university nickname."

A laugh bubbled up, and she shook her head, not knowing what to make of this man. In the space of a few minutes, she'd gone from misery to fear to laughter. "Ant. I can see why."

"Resemble an insect, do I?" He grinned. He had one short eyetooth, which made his smile a little crooked. An endearing smile. One that invited her to share the humor.

She couldn't help smiling back. "Because you're as big as a house."

"Only a *small* house."

"Like a hut, then."

"And you're?"

"Harriet Stanton. I'm the schoolteacher."

"The teacher, eh?" He swung into the saddle and settled himself behind her.

She winced as her ankle bumped against the horse, the throbbing reawakened by movement. But then his arms settled around her, giving her something new to focus on.

He urged the horse back to the trail.

Harriet sat as rigidly as possible within the shelter of Ant's arms. He smelled of wet horse and leather and maleness, a not-unfamiliar aroma, but somehow made more intimate by his body enveloping hers.

As the giant stallion picked his way down the trail, the rhythm of the horse's gait soon seduced her into relaxing against Ant's broad chest. The rain ceased. After a time, the warmth of the blanket penetrated her numb body; drowsiness seeped through her limbs.

A memory hovered at the edge of her awareness, faint and tattered from age. She reached out to grasp a whisper of remembered sound. Papa's voice.... His lips on her forehead as he carried her to bed.... The scent of cigar and brandy. Snuggling against him, content, secure.... A feeling she'd lost with his death and had searched for ever since.

The faintest hint of tears brushed Harriet's eyes. She hadn't remembered her father who died when she was just three. Never had a paternal remembrance to call her own. Now like a gift, one had drifted into her heart.

Ant's gift.

Like a child, Harriet nestled closer into his arms. *I'm safe.*

≈

Like the kitten he'd named her, the woman curled into Ant's embrace. Her smallness unnerved him somehow. Usually he liked his women tall and well-endowed, so he didn't have to strain his back or crick his neck much to kiss them.

Yet this little one had showed spirit, bantering with him even when she'd been scared and in pain. During his years of reporting, he'd seen enough tragic situations to have experienced female bravery at its best—tight-lipped, head-held-high courage. But he couldn't recall a mite of a girl quipping her way through a frightening circumstance.

She said she was a schoolteacher. Maybe David's teacher. Hope stirred within him. The first in a long time. He refrained from rushing into questions. On horseback, during a storm wasn't the place to have that talk. But as soon as she rested up....

The trail leveled, joining with a dirt road. Ahead Ant could make out the shadowy outline of buildings, several showing amber light shining through the windows.

He leaned down to speak in her ear. "Where do you live, Miss? "

"I board with the Cobbs, who own the mercantile. Keep going a ways on this street and you'll get there."

They passed quiet houses and buildings. The lantern light didn't reach far enough for him to make out any details. Seemed like an ordinary enough town.

A burst of laughter and tinny piano music belted from a saloon; the sound followed them up the street. An ordinary town, all right.

"There." Harriet angled her chin to the left. "That's the mercantile. The front will be locked, so we'll need to go around the near side to the kitchen."

Guiding Shadow to a hitching post near a watering trough, Ant paused, reluctant to dismount. He knew he needed to get Harriet to shelter, but that would mean letting go of her. He hadn't held a woman since Isabella. His meaningless encounters with prostitutes were meant to satisfy a sexual itch, not lead to a physical connection. He'd forgotten the feeling of holding a woman in his arms—the powerful protective instinct a female could evoke in a man.

Or maybe it was because this one was so slight. Maybe it was a fatherly instinct. Yes, that was it. As soon as Ant grabbed for the idea, the thought whisked away. There was nothing fatherly about the control he'd been trying to exercise on certain parts of his anatomy for the last hour.

Best get her indoors and be done with her. "I have to dismount. I'll try not to hurt you."

She sat up, which did not help matters.

Ant eased one leg over Shadow and jumped down. "Now, relax and lean over." He reached one arm around her back and the other under her knees. "Heave ho, matey."

She giggled, and then gasped with pain.

He continued teasing, trying to keep her mind off her injuries. "At least I made you laugh before I hurt you."

Even though her face was drawn with pain, she managed that quarter smile.

To avoid the tick of response in his heart, he quickened his pace toward the door. "You'll have to do the knocking. My hands are full."

The light from a lace-curtained window illuminated the entry. Harriet untangled one arm from the blankets, reaching out to knock.

Just before her hand connected, Ant had a sudden thought and, half in jest, half in concern, swung her away. "Mr. Cobb won't be greeting me with a gun will he? As you can see, I'm in no position to defend myself."

CHAPTER THREE

David March stared out the single cracked window of the shack he and his father had called home for the last three months, watching the rain track wiggly trails through the grime. Behind him, his father sprawled on a filthy pallet; his drunken snores shook the tottery one-room building.

The storm trapped him inside with Pa. Usually, during the warmer nights of summer, David could escape and sleep in the lean-to with the mule. Safer there. Pa often woke up with a fierce temper and a heavy hand. If David made a morning appearance before Pa started drinking again, there'd be hell to pay. Or maybe, he thought bitterly, more hell than usual to pay.

Even with his father asleep, shivers of fear burned under David's skin. He wanted to escape. Run fast and far, back to....

Gray hazed with black speckles slid between then and now. His drifty place. David let his vision move out of focus, until all he saw was the slick surface in front of him. As if half-asleep, he tapped on the glass along with the rhythm of his father's snores.

Snort. Tap. *Whistle.* Scratch with a fingernail. *Pause.* Hold the pad of his finger over a bead of water. *Snuffle.* Draw his knuckle in a half circle.

In his drifty place, his body numbed, and his mind stayed gray. But at least he didn't feel the cramp of hunger in his belly, nor the tightness and tatters of two-year-old clothes.

Best of all, he couldn't feel any pain, for he didn't feel anything, anything at all.

∼

The side door yanked open so fast Ant thought the nails might fly from their hinges. A man's anxious face peered out, bulbous red nose twitching. Behind the man, Ant could hear a woman shrill, "Is that Miss Stanton?" The woman ducked under her husband's arm, holding up a glass lamp. "Miss Stanton! The Lord be thanked. What happened? Are you injured?"

"I'm all right, Mrs. Cobb. Just bruised. But I twisted my ankle."

"Come in. Come in. Don't just stand there. Isaiah, move over." She nudged her husband out of the way with one wide hip.

Ant turned sideways, careful to keep Harriet's feet from hitting the frame, and squeezed through the door into the kitchen. His first impression was welcomed warmth and the bitter fragrance of willow bark tea brewing. The Cobbs must have expected some trouble. But the tea should help ease Harriet's pain.

A quick scan of the room showed a rectangular table surrounded by six wooden chairs and covered with a

red-and-white checked cloth. A large cast iron stove provided the warmth. He strode over to the nearest chair.
Hooking the leg with his foot, he pulled the chair over to
the stove and deposited Harriet on it.

Mrs. Cobb stared up at Ant. Her close-set brown eyes
bulged in apparent shock—a not uncommon reaction to his
great height. Her mouth opened and closed like a fresh-
caught catfish, showing pointed eyeteeth.

Her husband stretched himself to his full length, another
common reaction to Ant's size. Isaiah Cobb had an ordinary
tall frame, which meant he reached to Ant's chin. The red
nose led Ant to think the man might have been drinking,
only there was no aroma of alcohol on his breath. A fringe
of gray-and-brown hair circled his bald head.

Mrs. Cobb emerged from her trance. "Well, and who
might you be?" she said acidly.

Harriet untied the remains of her bonnet, revealing
chestnut brown hair, fine gray eyes, a pert nose, and pink
lips. *Kissable lips.* She waved a hand to him. "My rescuer,
Mr. Anthony Gordon."

"But, my dear Miss Stanton, whatever happened to you?"

"I went for a walk. The day was so beautiful that I wandered farther up the mountain than I thought. I tripped
and hit my head against a tree. I was knocked unconscious.
When I awoke, I found I had sprained my ankle and couldn't
move. The storm began. I called for help, and Mr. Gordon
appeared." Her fingers explored the lump on her head.

Mr. Cobb leaned closer to examine Harriet's bump.
"Nasty bruise you have there. Better go for Doc Cameron."

Harriet's hand dropped to her lap. "No. Don't disturb
him."

"Disturb him." Mrs. Cobb's voice rose. "Why, we are all disturbed. Hunted all over town for you. It's not like you, Miss Stanton, to take off like that without telling anyone. Very inconsiderate. Dr. Cameron is half-expecting a summons."

Harriet brushed a hand over her eyes. "I'm sorry for all the trouble I caused." Her voice shook.

As Ant listened to the conversation, his ire rose. Instead of sympathy and prompt treatment, these people were blaming Harriet. "If you'll tell me where the doctor is, I'll go fetch him." In spite of his annoyance, Ant kept his voice even. "In the meantime, perhaps Miss Stanton can take a hot bath. She's chilled and muddy."

Mrs. Cobb bristled. "I don't believe we need a stranger to tell us how to take care of our Miss Stanton."

Apparently you do.

Miss Stanton fluttered a trembling hand. "Mrs. Cobb, Mr. Gordon's been very kind. I believe he saved my life." She fisted her fingers, dropping her hand to her lap, obviously trying to mask her weakness.

Mr. Cobb rubbed his nose with one thick-fingered hand. "Now, Hortense, we have to be grateful to Mr. Gordon. The Lord sent him as an answer to our prayers for Miss Stanton's safe deliverance." He patted his wife's shoulder. "You go heat up some water, while I give Mr. Gordon, here, the directions to Doc's house."

Ant wasn't fooled by Cobb's hearty tone. He could see the man would far rather stay inside than ride through a storm for the doctor. But he hid his scorn. He didn't much like these people, but for Miss Stanton's sake he'd be polite. Plus, he needed information about Lewis and

David. He couldn't alienate the Cobbs until he had what he needed.

~

Harriet wanted the smooth planks of the wooden floor to open up beneath her, preferably onto a fat featherbed. That way, she could disappear *and* not have to deal with getting up to her room. She hated arguments, hated seeing the Cobbs act almost rude to a man who'd been so kind.

The conversation shriveled her up inside, but she couldn't allow Ant to ride for Doctor Cameron. She wasn't injured enough to warrant disturbing the physician, nor did she need the burden of paying for medical expenses. "Mr. Gordon, you've done enough for me," she said, putting all the schoolmarm firmness she could manage into her tone. "I refuse to have you summon Doctor Cameron. I think a bath and some sleep should take care of me. You, yourself, need to get settled and dry."

"My slicker's kept me fairly dry. It's you I'm concerned about." Ant's eyes peered into hers, seeming to assess the truth of her words. Finally, he nodded. Turning to Mr. Cobb, he asked, "Is there a hotel in town?"

"No. Banker Livingston has plans to build one. Widow Murphy takes boarders, though. You can put your horse up at the livery stable."

"If you'll direct me, I'll take my gear to Widow Murphy's, stable Shadow, then return here. I think Miss Stanton will need to be carried to her bed."

"Mr. Gordon!" Mrs. Cobb dramatically clapped one hand over her ample bosom.

Harriet refrained from rolling her eyes. You'd think Ant had offered to ravish her.

He raised one eyebrow, giving the woman a quelling look. "Do you plan to carry her yourself, or do you expect her to crawl?" His gravelly voice took on an ominous tone. "I've been carrying her around already for the last hour. You can follow right behind us, so Miss Stanton will be well chaperoned."

Mrs. Cobb huffed, but wisdom prevailed, and she chose not to say anything. She turned toward the sink, grabbed a teakettle and filled it under the pump. She motioned toward a large copper pot sitting on the edge of a shelf of pots and pans. "Isaiah, fill that for me. We need to boil hot water. Then bring the tub in."

Exhaustion hit, almost knocking Harriet off her chair. A headache hammered at her forehead. In spite of her tiredness, she forced herself to act politely. "I thank you for all your help, Mr. Gordon."

He nodded. "My pleasure, my lady." The teasing lilt returned to his voice.

She made an effort to respond in kind. "My lord, the livery stable is across the street and to the right. Then there's the blacksmith shop, then the bathhouse. Mrs. Murphy's boarding house is across the street."

"I'll take my time, give you a chance to soak in a warm bath. Stop those shivers."

She unwrapped the blankets, her movements heavy, as though her body contained only sand.

He reached out to help, taking the burden from her. Balling up the bedroll, he nodded. "I'll return soon." He turned and strode out, taking the warmth of concern with him.

Mr. Cobb wrestled the tub in from the pantry tacked on to the kitchen, setting it next to Harriet's chair. He grabbed a bucket from next to the door and proceeded to pump some water into the pail to carry to the tub. After several trips, he lifted the big copper pot off the stove, pouring the steaming water into the basin, and then filling the pot again to heat up.

In uncharacteristic silence, Mrs. Cobb added the boiling water from the teakettle, and then refilled it. She waved her hands, shooing her husband from the room. "Go wait in the parlor until we're done. Then you can chip some ice off the block in the icebox to place on Miss Stanton's ankle."

Harriet balanced on one foot, clutching the back of the chair, and allowed Mrs. Cobb to undress her. The subdued air the woman wore from being chastised by Ant soon wore off. She began to cluck at the condition of Harriet's sodden clothes and chatter about the day's gossip. "Did you hear the news? Mrs. Sanders is expecting a baby come Christmas."

Harriet closed her eyes, wishing she could also shut her ears. Her stomach cramped. For the first time since Ant had miraculously appeared in the darkness, Harriet remembered Nick Sanders. *How could I have forgotten?* Fleeing to the mountains had been foolish. All she'd done was bring her more pain and trouble. She couldn't run away from reality. She was doomed to live with Nick and Elizabeth's happiness.

∽

The next day, Harriet perched on the brown velvet sofa in the parlor, her foot wrapped in a tight bandage and propped on a footstool in front of her. The Cobbs' sitting room was crammed with too much ornate furniture and all the little luxuries Mrs. Cobb thought necessary to display both the Cobbs' merchandise and their monetary success. Vases, pictures, porcelain statues, and several music boxes vied for space on the marble-topped tables. Tufted and fringed pillows overflowed the settee and chairs. The décor was the epitome of bad taste.

Just being in the room twisted Harriet's stomach and set her on edge. At least the Cobbs weren't present, and she had some quiet time. She tried to work on her poetry, but with the ever-present throb of her ankle distracting her, everything that came to her mind sounded like drivel. She'd given up in disgust.

Then she indulged in mentally consigning most of the expensive clutter to the shop, simplifying the decor. *When I have my own home someday....* But even her favorite day-dream about her own little house failed to lift her spirits or ease the ache in her ankle.

A cup of willow bark tea was close at hand on a marble-topped side table. Harriet took a reluctant sip. Mrs. Cobb had been pouring the bitter brew down Harriet's throat all morning, and she was sick of the drink, tired of being in pain, and bored. Even perusing the pages of *Gulliver's Travels,* normally a pleasant occupation, couldn't hold her attention. She would have even welcomed papers to grade and lesson plans to formulate.

A sigh escaped. Her long-awaited summer vacation was off to a most unpleasant start. *I haven't even begun on my project yet.*

Everyone was at church, listening to a visiting politician, who was breezing through town on his way to the bigger votes of the city. Mrs. Cobb had stayed behind to mind the store and monitor Harriet. She suspected that as soon as the speech ended, a horde of visitors would descend on her. She didn't know which was worse, boredom or having to tell her embarrassing story to the curious and endure their scrutiny of her bruised head.

Thoughts of a dark giant continued to loom in her mind almost as strongly as Anthony Gordon had done in person. She tried to shove the images away, but they slithered just out of reach, dancing around the edges of her brain, taunting her with memories of being held in his arms. The recollection alone evoked a feverish feeling in her body. Although she kept chiding herself for her weakness, the memories refused to properly confine themselves to the past. Her experience yesterday and her injuries today must be contributing to her failure.

As she remembered Ant carrying her to bed the previous evening, her cheeks flushed. After settling his affairs, he'd swooped into the Cobbs' kitchen like a dark knight, scooping her up from the chair where she'd been brushing out her damp hair before Mrs. Cobb could even protest. Harriet had smothered a laugh at the horrified look on Mrs. Cobb's face.

Then she had flushed with embarrassment, yet, being clad only in her sleeping attire—night shift and robe—had made the experience more exciting. A sensual awareness had penetrated her exhaustion and pain. The intimacy of being in his arms had even managed to drown out the sound of Mrs. Cobb's scandalized clucking as she labored up the stairway behind them.

Will Ant call on me today?

In response to her thoughts, a knock on the door connecting the parlor to the store heralded the first of her visitors. She smoothed down the skirt of her second-best summer dress, a gray calico scattered with tiny pink rosebuds, and made sure her bandaged ankle was covered.

Anthony Gordon ducked through the door. In the light of day, he appeared clean and dry, but no less imposing. He'd slicked his shoulder-length brown hair into a neat tail and wore a leather vest over a crisp white shirt tucked into black pants. He held his black hat in one big hand, a book in the other. Broad shoulders, slim waist, wider hips, long muscular legs....

Harriet realized she'd cataloged him in the same way as one of her nature specimens, and heat rose in her cheeks. For heaven's sake, he wasn't a butterfly or a pinecone. Her gaze darted away, before returning, fascinated by the sheer magnitude of the man. By her estimation, he must be about six-foot, five inches. No, certainly not a butterfly.

Ant trod across the room, a slight hitch in his gait, and held out the book. The worn leather cover testified to the volume being well read. "I thought instead of flowers you'd prefer something more...stimulating." His right eyebrow crooked in that wicked upside down *v*. A half-smile pulled up to match.

Her answering grin started in her chest and bloomed on her face. "You've judged rightly, Mr. Gordon."

He handed her the book. "Call me Ant. After all we've been through in our short acquaintance, I don't think we need to stand on ceremony."

"Then you must call me Harriet." She turned away from his gaze, smoothing her finger over the faded gold letters of the title. *The Count of Monte Cristo.* A sudden burst of joy cut through her low spirits. She paused, allowing some of her happiness at the gift to ease enough to talk. "What a delightful gift, Mr. Gordon, I mean, Ant. I feel like it's Christmas."

He pulled at his bare chin. "And I look just like Saint Nicholas."

She laughed. "I wouldn't go that far." She traced her fingers over the letters again. "I've always wanted to read this book. No one in town has it though."

His gravelly voice softened. "Now you do."

"A book is a present beyond price. I must tell you, my small personal library is one of the pleasures of my life." *Pleasures. I'm discussing pleasures with this man.* She tried to rein in the conversation to a logical pace, lest her feelings run away from her like a bolting horse. Who knew what else she'd blurt out? "Are you fond of other writings of Alexandre Dumas?"

"At home I have all of the three Musketeers novels."

"I envy you. John Carter, one of our ranchers, has those books. He's allowed me to borrow them."

"I couldn't help noticing the shelf of books in your room." He shifted his weight, speech hurrying on. "Not that I was studying your room, just that books always catch my eye."

The heat returned to her cheeks. She hoped he couldn't tell. She rushed into conversation to cover herself. "Only a small collection. I'm like Abraham Lincoln. I've borrowed books from everyone in town. I doubt there's one I've missed.... Well, not Doctor Cameron's medical texts, or Reverend Norton's religious treatises." She was babbling worse than a brook. She made herself dam up the flow of words, change the subject. "I'm forgetting my manners." She waved at a wing chair covered in crocheted doilies and placed at right angles to the sofa. "Won't you please sit down?"

He nodded, giving her his crooked smile. "You have quite a spectacular bruise on your head. How are you feeling?"

She wrinkled her nose. "I've always taken the ability to walk for granted. Today, I've had to remind myself to thank the good Lord for the usual soundness of my limbs, and that this is only a temporary affliction."

The twinkle in his eyes vanished. "I'm afraid we take life and health for granted."

Harriet discerned a touch of bitterness in Ant's voice. She wanted to ask more, but didn't want to presume on their short acquaintance, no matter how intimate.

Ant reached into his vest and pulled out a small leather folder. "I'm afraid I have an additional purpose in calling on you." He opened the folder, which she could see contained a photograph, seemed to hesitate, then reached over and placed it in her lap.

She picked up the photograph. A fashionably dressed woman sat on a wide bench, her sweeping skirt a backdrop for a boy—perhaps five years old—standing beside her. Without needing to be told, Harriet knew the boy was Ant's son. The child possessed the same big dark eyes, prominent cheekbones, and wide mouth. Although he held the stiff pose required by the photographer, something about the unnatural posture of his small body made her think the minute the sitting was finished, he took off to do handsprings or some other boyish activity.

Harriet couldn't help a pang of disappointment that the only other man besides Nick who'd drawn her interest was married. She transferred her attention to the woman in the photograph. Tall, shapely, and dramatically beautiful, with brown hair and eyes and dressed in the height of elegance; she made Harriet feel dowdy in comparison.

Why is he showing this to me? Does he think I was throwing myself at him?

Perhaps he wanted a tactful way to tell me he was married. The thought stung her pride, making her want to throw out quick words, distancing herself from him, from any idea that she might be thinking romantic thoughts of him. *If he only realized my heart belongs to another, he wouldn't think I was being forward.*

Caught in her embarrassed dilemma, Harriet could only pretend to examine the photograph. The only way to preserve her dignity would be to somehow hint that her affections were already engaged. *But I can't tell him. My love for Nick is my shameful secret.*

∾

Ant watched Harriet Stanton scrutinize the photograph, hoping for a sign of recognition to cross her pretty face. While he waited, he drummed his fingers on his knee.

The walls of the over-furnished parlor threatened to close in on him, and he resisted the compulsion to retract his arms and legs like a turtle, lest he knock over some of the bric-a-brac crowding the room. Nor did he give in to the mischievous urge to make a face at the trio of portraits—two unattractive couples and one elderly gentleman—who glared at him from the oval frames over the settee. He was a thirty-three-year-old man, not a boy David's age.

Instead, as Harriet studied the picture, he studied her. She'd attempted to hide the bruise on her forehead with a few artful curls of her chestnut-colored hair. But he could still see the purple-green lump marring the pale skin above her arching brown brows.

With her hair pulled back in a bun, instead of straggling in wet strands around her heart-shaped face, she appeared demure. Yet, he sensed an interesting woman lay beneath her conventional appearance.

His fingers tapped out a beat. To his disappointment, Harriet didn't seem to recognize David. Her expression remained serene. Then, as if a painter dipped a brush in the faintest of rose colors and brushed the tip across her face, she blushed. She looked up at him, her gray eyes troubled.

Hope uncurled in his heart. He prompted her. "As the schoolteacher, I thought you might know my nephew, David."

"Your nephew." She looked down at the photograph; her lashes lowered to hide her eyes. "Oh, I thought perhaps he was your son."

"He looks very much like I did at that age. That was taken four years ago. Of course, my sister, Emily, and I have the same coloring."

"Your sister is very attractive." Harriet handed the photograph back to him.

He could see the question in her eyes. Why had he showed her a picture of his sister and her son? Not the usual way to begin a new acquaintance. "You don't recognize him?"

Her brow creased. "No."

He released his breath in a long sigh, settling back in his chair. "I've been searching for David and his father for two years."

"That's a long time."

"Very," he said in a wry tone. "I was in New York when my sister...died. Her husband, Lewis, took David and left before I returned home. My sister and I were...very close. I want to have contact with my nephew, to be part of his life. When I'd heard they'd...settled in Sweetwater Springs, and then that you were the schoolteacher, I hoped you would know David."

"I'm sorry, I can't help you. Perhaps his father is tutoring him at home."

"Lewis was never one for education." *That's an understatement.*

"If the children don't come to school, or the families to church...I don't really get a chance to know people who don't live in town. It's one of my goals this summer." She gave her ankle a rueful glance. "I want to travel around to meet some of the families—encourage them to send their children to school."

"An admirable goal."

"But you can ask the Cobbs if they've seen David. They know everyone who frequents the mercantile. I can assure you that they never forget a face."

"They're next on my list."

"Reverend Norton and Doctor Cameron travel around to the homesteads in the mountains and to the various ranches. They'd be able to tell you more."

"Then perhaps you can tell me where to find them."

While Harriet gave him directions, an odd reluctance to leave her presence tethered Ant to the seat of the wingchair. He had an urge to confide in her, tell her the whole sordid story of Emily and Lewis.

Lest he find himself softening, he stood. Harriet had given him some good leads. He had a search to conduct, a nephew to find.

A brother-in-law to kill.

Tangling with this schoolmarm, no matter how winsome she was, would only slow him down.

CHAPTER FOUR

Three days later, Ant found his footsteps taking him toward the mercantile. While he walked, the dust of the main street puffed around his boots, and he was conscious of fatigue of body and soul weighing him down. The brilliant sun directly overhead had him squinting against a bit of a headache. He tilted back his hat, rubbing his forehead.

He'd spent the last three days questioning everyone in town and riding out to the Carter, Sanders, Payne, Dunn, Addison, and Thompson ranches. No one knew of David. Now he needed to start tackling the isolated homesteads scattered across the mountains. He didn't think Lewis would hide on the prairie. Too exposed. Yet, there might be one possibility on a farm he should check out.

From his search, he'd compiled a list of probable places. He'd told himself that maybe the schoolteacher could shed some light on the most likely ones to check out.

He strode up the steps of the mercantile and pushed open the door. He inhaled the scent of pickles in the crock by the entrance, overlaid with the earthy smell from the bins of potatoes, turnips, and carrots. Bags of sugar and flour beckoned to eager bakers. He eyed the jars of candy on the oak counter, wondering which was Harriet's favorite.

Mrs. Cobb looked up from behind the counter and gave him a smile that didn't reflect any warmth in her squinty brown eyes. She straightened a stack of jam jars that were already perfectly aligned. "Good afternoon, Mr. Gordon."

"Afternoon, Mrs. Cobb."

She fingered a gold foil box in front of her. "We've just received a shipment of chocolate from Europe. I set aside several boxes for Wyatt Thompson. I believe you rode out to his ranch yesterday. His fiancé was raised in Germany and fancies their chocolate."

Ant smiled, willing to charm, even though he didn't like the woman. He stepped closer to the counter, enjoying the aroma of coffee from the bags of beans stacked next to the grinder. "I've spent time there myself. Candy, pastries, nothing better."

She sniffed. "Then you haven't tried some decent American cooking. Many women in this town have a light hand with cakes and pies."

Put his boot right into that one. Best shy away from the subject. "I'll take a box." He pointed to some peppermint sticks. "And several of those."

She harrumphed, but tore off a piece of brown paper to wrap around the peppermint sticks.

"How's Miss Stanton doing? Has she recovered from her accident?"

"Bruise still looks nasty. She can walk though. Hobbles around holding on to the furniture." The shopkeeper jerked her head toward the door to the living quarters; the loose skin on her fleshy cheeks fluttered with the movement. "She's in there. Holding court."

Ant grabbed the box of chocolates and the parcel of peppermint sticks. "Then I'll just step inside and pay my regards."

Mrs. Cobb shrugged. "Makes no difference to me."

As he opened the door, he could hear the murmur of feminine voices. He recognized the two women sitting on the sofa, each holding a cup and saucer patterned with roses. Elizabeth Sanders and Pamela Carter. After his forays around town and to the neighboring ranches, Ant reckoned he already knew half the population. Too many people knowing his business.

To Ant's practiced eye, both women's silk dresses appeared to be the latest fashion, not that he'd paid much attention to such things in the last few years. Chasing Lewis and David across the country had rubbed some of the sophisticated edges off him. But he couldn't miss how the sapphire of Elizabeth Sander's dress made her eyes bluer than the sky outside, while Pamela Carter's maroon shirtwaist lent some color to her plump-cheeked, plain face.

Across from them, Harriet perched on the edge of the wingchair. As he entered, she looked up. A smile crossed her face, but he could detect signs of strain in her gray eyes. The bruise on her forehead had faded from purple to a greeny-yellow, but was still too vivid to hide.

"Mr. Gordon. How nice to see you."

He removed his hat. "Miss Stanton." He nodded at the other two ladies. "Mrs. Sanders. Mrs. Carter. Good afternoon."

He handed Harriet the box of candy. "To help speed the rest of your recovery."

Pink floated into her cheeks; a glow replaced the strained look in her eyes. "Why, Mr. Gordon. I don't believe anyone has ever given me chocolate. This is a rare treat. Thank you so very much."

Pride swelled in Ant's chest. His gift had made her happy. He backed off from the feeling, striving for deflation. "I always brought candy for my sister." He gestured toward the box. "She loved European chocolate."

Elizabeth Sanders' blue eyes sparkled with interest. "Your sister was very lucky. I wish my brother had been half so attentive," she said, speaking in a Boston accent.

Pamela Carter exchanged a reminiscing glance with her. "My brothers weren't so thoughtful, either." She too had a Boston accent, although not as strong as Mrs. Sanders'.

Mrs. Sanders laughed. "More tormenting than thoughtful."

Half with humor, half sadness, Ant remembered some of his more mischievous moments with Emily. "I believe that's the job of brothers—to torment their sisters."

Harriet waved to a straight-back wooden chair. "Won't you please be seated, Mr. Gordon. Would you like some tea?"

He would, but didn't see an extra teacup, and he didn't want to send Harriet hobbling off to the kitchen after one. "No thank you." He eased himself into a hardback chair. Hardly comfortable, but just sitting quietly out of the sun, released some of the tension in his head.

Harriet shifted in the wingchair as if in pain. "I see you already know my visitors."

"Had the honor of meeting them yesterday."

"You've covered a great deal of territory in your search for David."

Mrs. Sanders set her cup and saucer down on the marble-topped table next to her. "Is there any more news about your nephew, Mr. Gordon?"

"I'm afraid not."

Mrs. Carter leaned forward, worry shading in her brown eyes. "For the last two days, I've been trying to think of any place else your brother-in-law could be. I'm afraid I haven't had any success."

The warm concern in Mrs. Carter's gaze managed to penetrate the shell he'd encased himself in since Emily's death. Ant doubted the women would be so eager to help if they knew what he intended to do to Lewis when he found the bastard. "I've narrowed the possibilities to four places. With your permission, ladies, I'd like to run them by you and get your opinion."

They all nodded eagerly.

"On the mountain, near the edge of the Thompson and Rodriguez ranches, is a run-down cabin. One of Thompson's ranch hands mentioned he'd noticed signs of life there, but hadn't time to check it out. Thompson seemed a bit put out that his hand hadn't reported this before."

Mrs. Carter tucked a wisp of mouse-brown hair behind her ear. "Our Mr. Thompson has always been a very vigilant man. I'm surprised he didn't notice the cabin's inhabitants himself."

Mrs. Sanders smiled. A dimple played about the right corner of her mouth. "Being in love might have distracted him a bit."

The other two women laughed.

He cleared his throat to bring their attention back to the topic that kept him up at night. Even now, thinking of confronting Lewis had his gut tightening. "I had to persuade him to let me check it out first. I've promised to report back to him."

Mrs. Sanders nodded. "Wyatt Thompson is mighty protective of his family, but for the same reason, he'll want to help you."

"Appreciate that." Ant gave her a brief smile he didn't feel. "There's a family by the name of Crooks with several children living near where Shiny Stone Creek flows into the Blue River. According to Doc Cameron, the family size seems to vary from time to time. Do you know them?"

Mrs. Carter shrugged. More tendrils of hair slipped from the knot at the back of her head to wave around her plump cheeks. "I don't." She glanced across at Harriet. "Do you?"

Harriet shook her head. "Their children certainly don't attend school. When I can walk again, I'll have to pay a visit to see if I can enroll them."

Although disappointed, Ant continued with the possibilities. "There a deserted homestead about five miles south and two miles west. A creek runs through it."

The women shook their heads in unison.

"The last place is up the Hutter path. One of the cowboys I spoke to in town mentioned seeing lights at a former miner's shack one evening when he rode by. Looked like someone had done some work on it."

Mrs. Carter sighed. "That doesn't give you many places."

"I only need one—the one where David is." *And soon, if I am to have any chance of molding my nephew into a decent man.* He hoped it wasn't already too late.

With a quick sideways glance, Mrs. Sanders signaled Mrs. Carter.

Ant sensed an unspoken exchange between the two, but didn't quite pick up the meaning. *Damn.* Was he losing some of his astuteness in reading women? If so, when he returned to being a reporter, he'd have some sharpening up to do.

Mrs. Sanders rose to her feet with practiced grace. "We must be going. I do hope your ankle will be better soon, Miss Stanton."

Mrs. Carter stood up, "Speedy recovery, my dear."

"Thank you." Harriet made as if to move, than stopped. "Please give Mark and Sara my regards. And Lizzy too."

Mrs. Carter touched Harriet's shoulder. "They'll be so relieved you're feeling better. Lizzy, especially, becomes upset when she knows someone's in pain."

Harriet's face brightened. "She's such a little angel. I'm so looking forward to having her as a pupil when school starts up again."

Ant unfolded to his feet, while the ladies exchanged good-byes. After they left, he resumed his seat. Silence settled for a minute. He turned his hat in his hands. "Mrs. Cobb tells me that you are managing to walk, but not well."

Harriet wrinkled her nose. "I'm getting around with the aid of the furniture." Her gaze swept the room. "I always have something to hold onto."

He waved at the over-crowded room, "I see that."

Her mouth pulled up into a partial smile.

Ah, that quarter smile again. This time not an exhausted attempt to respond to his humor, but an I-agree-with-you-but-am-too-ladylike-to-say partial smile. "I came here to ask your advice about which place to pursue first."

She wrinkled her brow. "If you check out the cabin near the Thompson ranch, you'll save him the trouble of sending one of his hands."

Good thought. Just seeing Thompson's cowboys could be enough to make Lewis bolt. "There's still time to ride out there today. Tomorrow I'll visit the farm."

"The day after that, if you choose the family to visit, I'd like to come with you."

"No." He spit the word out more sharply than he intended.

Harriet reared up in her chair. Anger sparked in her eyes. Her jaw tightened as if she held back a cutting response.

Ant almost laughed. He'd bet that under her refined schoolmarm exterior this kitten possessed sharp claws. He was about to apologize, then stopped. Firmness was important. He didn't want her anywhere near Lewis.

"You haven't heard my reasons, Mr. Gordon."

He was back to Mister was he? Just as well. "I'm sorry, *Miss* Stanton. You've been injured and are in no condition to be traipsing up the mountain."

She lifted her chin. "I'll be perfectly able to ride by then."

I hope not.

"Mr. Cobb keeps a horse at the livery, which I'm allowed to ride when he doesn't need it."

"Your ankle needs more time to heal."

"My ankle is better every day. By tomorrow I should be able to walk without groping for the furniture."

A shaft of humor penetrated his protectiveness. Darn if he didn't like the woman, but he didn't dare let it show.

"I want to speak to that family about sending their children to school. Now that I know about them, I certainly intend to visit. If you won't escort me, I'll ride there alone."

Ant's stomach tightened, and he clenched his fingers around the arms of his chair. *Damn stubborn woman.* Although he remained planted, he wanted to pace the room, think through his response. But knocking over the furniture and bric-a-brac wouldn't help him clear his thoughts. The obdurate schoolmarm had him over a barrel. There was no way in this world he'd allow her to go anywhere near Lewis without being right at her side.

Uncurling his fingers, he looked at her, keeping his face stern. "Very well. But only if you promise to be careful."

"Of course." Her answering smile could charm the spots off an Appaloosa.

Ant dug deep inside for the strength to resist a growing attraction. He succeeded, but barely. And only because the fear in his belly weighed down any inclination to smile.

∼

Two days later, dressed in a brown divided skirt, a tan long-sleeved boy's shirt, with one of Mr. Cobb's leather hats shading her face, Harriet sat to one side of the steps leading to the mercantile. Resting on her lap, a burlap bag held enough ham sandwiches and oatmeal cookies to feed an army, plus a large jar of lemonade. She could barely heft the package, but judging from Ant's size, she figured this was about the amount of food needed to provision him.

Anticipation for a day with Ant made her restless. If her ankle had felt entirely sound, she would have paced back and forth in front of the store. But a thread of worry about the dull ache in her ankle kept Harriet seated. The rest of the day would put enough strain on her limb, and her pride would not permit her to show the least hint of pain. Not when she'd insisted on accompanying Ant against his inclination.

The early morning sun already hinted of summer heat, and around her the sleepy town stirred to life. Across the street at the trough in front of the livery stable, Pepe, the Mexican stable hand, pumped water into a bucket—the first of many trips.

Red Charlie slid open the doors that bisected the entire front of his blacksmith shop. A fire was already burning, and he bent to his work. As the clang of hammer on metal echoed across to her, she could see tiny orange sparks flying around the Blackfoot man.

On the porch of the white frame church, Mary Norton, the minister's wife, chatted with Hester Arden. Mrs. Arden usually cleaned the church on Saturday, but judging by the broom in her hands, had chosen today instead.

Helga Mueller trudged up the street toting two large wicker baskets containing the fragrant bread she baked every day for the mercantile. Apple-cheeked with thick graying-blond hair pulled into a coronet, the plump woman arrived, stopped to catch her breath, and greeted Harriet in German-accented broken English. "Iss a beutiful morning, Miss Stanton. Your foos besser iss?"

"Yes, much better, Mrs. Mueller. I'm able to walk now.

"Das iss goot."

"Thank you so much for the strudel you sent me. I certainly enjoyed it."

The woman beamed. "Haffy am I to hear zhat." She gave Harriet a motherly pat on the shoulder before climbing the steps and opening the door to the mercantile. The smell of the yeasty bread followed her through the entrance.

The rosebush beside the stairs that Harriet had coaxed Mr. Cobb to plant last autumn had just yesterday burst forth with three velvety red flowers. Their sweet scent stirred Harriet's longing for a garden of her own, full of every kind of flower. In her dreams, a white picket fence with climbing red roses surrounded her little house. She had only to walk by Dr. and Mrs. Cameron's house on the outskirts of town to see her vision a reality. Mrs. Cameron had already promised Harriet cuttings from her lavish yard, whenever she wanted them.

Further down the road, Harriet saw Ant emerge from Widow Murphy's house. He looked toward the mercantile, paused, then clapped his hat on his head and strode toward her.

The power of Anthony Gordon's presence filled the street. He wore a black shirt, vest, and pants, and a black hat shaded his features. His long stride covered the distance between them. He walked with a wide swing of the hips, as if he owned the town; one of his hands hovered above his gunbelt, seeming ready to draw at the least sign of provocation.

Early shoppers stopped to watch his progress, turning their heads to track him. Ceasing to pump water, Pepe mopped his face with a red kerchief and stared, mouth agape. Red Charlie stopped his hammer mid-swing to nod at Ant. Mrs. Norton and Mrs. Arden leaned their heads together, no doubt discussing the man.

Some of the initial fear she'd felt upon seeing him reappeared, and she shivered. Even in the morning sunlight, Harriet imagined ominous shadows surrounding him. She searched his angular face, trying to read his mood from his expression. His dark eyes showed no hint of the twinkle she'd seen before, nor did his mouth quirk into a crooked smile of greeting. Within herself she shrank back, although she didn't allow her expression to betray her apprehension.

He halted. Dust puffed around his worn black boots. Touching the brim of his hat, he said, "Good morning, Miss Stanton."

His gravelly voice sounded unused this morning. He probably hadn't dared say a word to Mrs. Murphy for fear of starting a conversation, during which the woman would unloose all the criticisms she harbored about the world of Sweetwater Springs. Once someone wound up the widow, she could spew for hours. Few dared provoke her. Harriet kept her contact with the woman to as little as possible. She wasn't sure even Ant's formidable presence would stay Widow Murphy's bitter tongue.

He stared at her boot-encased feet. "Ankle better?"

"Almost as good as new," she exaggerated.

He leaned over and plucked the bag from her lap. As he hefted the burlap sack, his eyebrow peaked, and his eyes softened with humor. "What do you have in here? Rocks?"

"Provisions." Relief relaxed her spine. He wasn't angry with her.

"Expect we'll be gone for a week, do you?"

"Just lunch," Harriet said with pretend matter-of-factness. "Man of your size must need some feeding. I kept a hungry elephant in mind when I packed the food."

He grinned. Three lines bracketed each side of his mouth. "Hope your generous…provisions will fit in my saddle bags."

"I'll just wait here for you," she said sweetly.

Ant lowered the sack to the step next to her. "Best not tote this around. Might strain my back. I'll wait until I have Shadow saddled up. He can do the work."

"Mr. Cobb is lending me his horse, Brown Boy. He's a brown gelding with a white front foreleg. Usually Mack keeps him in the last stall."

"I'll saddle him up for you."

Ant sauntered back up the street. As before, he drew all eyes, but this time he didn't seem so menacing. Maybe because he had more of a spring in his step. He sauntered toward the livery stable and disappeared inside.

Only a few minutes passed before Ant reappeared. He led both horses toward her, halting at the foot of the steps. Handing her the reins, he reached for the bag and rummaged around inside. He pulled out the jar holding the lemonade. One of his hands spanned the sides of the glass. "Plan on being thirsty, do you?"

Harriet wrinkled her nose at him. She'd needed both hands and some muscle to lift that jar.

"What else is in here?" He pulled out the paper package of oatmeal cookies, tied into a neat string bundle.

"Oatmeal cookies. Mrs. Cobb made them last night."

He removed two larger paper-wrapped packages. "And these?"

"Ham sandwiches."

"Must be awfully big sandwiches."

"I made ten."

"Ten." Ant's jaw dropped; he looked like a Christmas nutcracker.

She couldn't help but laugh at the resemblance.

He grinned; his eyebrow lifted in a wicked peak. "Guess we won't go hungry." He tucked the food into the saddle-bags. Then he reached over to give her a hand up.

Harriet slid her hand into his calloused palm. He folded his fingers around hers, easing her to her feet. Warmth flooded into her palm, flowing throughout her body. Her cheeks flushed; she hoped he didn't notice.

Ant held Brown Boy, while Harriet placed her good foot in the stirrup and mounted, compressing her lips to keep an exclamation of pain locked away. Once in the saddle, she pretended all was well, reaching down and petting the horse's neck.

Ant mounted and led the way out of town. They rode in silence, although Harriet occasionally waved at anyone who stopped to watch the two of them together. At the base of the mountain, Ant urged Shadow ahead on the narrow trail. They rode through strands of fragrant ponderosa pine and shivery aspen. Hidden birds called, and a snow-shoe hare, wearing its summer gray coat, hopped across her path. Brown Boy tossed his head but continued his plodding walk.

Several hours later, they crossed a stream to reach a clearing. Two lean-tos, the wood still unweathered, propped up a rickety old cabin, with an outhouse crouched a few steps away. The drying pelts of different animals were nailed to the eaves of a shed to stretch and dry out. Harriet averted her eyes, glancing over to where a straggly vegetable garden sprouted on one side of the house.

A gaggle of barefoot girls poured out the door, all dressed in faded, too-small frocks and patched aprons. But their faces shone with cleanliness, and all had their fair hair neatly braided in two long tails. Their blue eyes showed eager curiosity, although they remained silent. The oldest carried a toddler on her hip. "Ma," she shrilled. "Comp'ny."

Harriet counted five stair-stepping daughters plus the little one. Three of them looked old enough to attend school.

A woman appeared in the doorway, wiping her hands on her apron. Like her children, she had blond hair, although her braid wrapped around her head several times. She glanced warily at Ant, then Harriet. The sight of another woman must have reassured her, for she relaxed and smiled, showing a trace of prettiness in her careworn face.

Harriet leaned forward. "I'm Miss Stanton, the school teacher." She waved a hand at Ant. "This is Mr. Anthony Gordon. He's searching for his nephew, David."

The woman looked amused. "As you can see, we have only girls here. I'm Mrs. Swensen."

Ant shifted in his saddle. "Have you seen a nine-year old boy around?" He pulled out the photograph and held it out.

The next oldest girl darted forward and looked at it. "No, sir." She stepped back.

Mrs. Swensen waved at her daughter. "Inga's my rambler. Can't keep her inside unless it's raining or snowing. The rest of us stay close to home. My man might know, but he's hunting."

Ant returned the photograph to his pocket. "Thank you."

Inga scrunched her face, obviously thinking. "I'll keep a lookout for ya."

"Have a care," he warned.

The girl frowned, clearly uncertain of his meaning.

"If you do see David, don't approach him or, especially, his Pa. He's not…fond of little girls. You come find me, instead. They'll know at the livery stable where I am."

Ant looked at Harriet, one eyebrow peaked in inquiry.

She answered his unspoken question. "Yes, that's a good idea. Mack Taylor usually knows everyone's business. Everyone with a horse, that is."

Ant touched his hat. "Thank you, Miss Inga." He fished in his pocket and tossed her a silver coin, which she caught. "That's for your trouble." He snuck a quick look at Mrs. Swensen. "I'm hiring her, if that's all right with you?"

The girl giggled, glanced at the coin, then at her mother, who smiled back at her, nodding in approval.

Although Harriet would have liked to dismount so she looked less imposing, she didn't dare put weight on her ankle unless she had to. Not after her fib to Ant about being able to walk. "Mrs. Swensen, the other reason I'm here is to invite your daughters to attend school."

The woman's face lost her smile, and she rubbed her hands down her apron. "My man, he's Swedish. He…."

I'll bet he doesn't believe in education for women. Harriet felt anger burn in her stomach at the thought.

Mrs. Swensen glanced at her daughters. "He's proud. Thinks they shouldn't go to school unless they have shoes. Nice dresses, too. I teach them their letters, though. Inga, she's nine and can read and cipher."

Harriet thought rapidly. She knew Pamela Carter and Samantha Thompson would be willing to donate their girls' outgrown clothes. "I know some mothers whose daughters have outgrown their dresses and shoes. We could bring them to you."

The woman twisted her hands in her apron. "We don't like to be beholden." She shook her head. "My man, he won't stand for it."

Harriet understood how some people had difficulty with taking charity, yet she wanted these girls in her schoolroom come autumn.

The older girls didn't say anything, but Harriet could see the pleading in their eyes as they glanced from their mother to her.

Somehow, she had to make the woman think she wasn't accepting charity. "Actually, Mrs. Swensen, if your husband could see his way through to send the girls to school, I would appreciate it. Most of my pupils are boys. Must be something about our spring water in the valley that makes for more boys being born. You know how girls," she smiled at the children, "especially pretty ones, have a civilizing influence on boys. Having your girls in my classroom would make my job a whole lot easier. So you can see, I'd be beholden to you."

Ant sent her a sardonic glance; his eyebrow crooked, and a corner of his mouth pulled up.

Mrs. Swensen didn't appear convinced.

What else can I come up with? "I think Pamela Carter would be downright grateful to you. Her five-year-old, Lizzy, almost died a year ago. She's very frail. And there's no other girl her age. Lizzy starts school next term." *True.* "I know Mrs. Carter worries about her not having friends." *Not true. Everyone adores Lizzy.* "She can't always play the more boisterous games." *Partly true.* "Someone she could play quietly with would be a blessing and would ease Mrs. Carter's mind."

Mrs. Swensen's tight expression eased. "I'd like to think we could help her. My Krista is about her age."

"That's settled then. Sometime this summer, we'll pay you a visit again and bring clothes and shoes."

Ant nodded farewell and turned Shadow toward the path that led up the mountain.

Harriet waved goodbye at everyone and had to smile at the enthusiastic way the girls echoed her. A surge of optimism flooded through her. Somehow, she knew the older children would be sitting in her schoolhouse when the next term began.

As Ant passed her, his face impassive, Harriet caught a look of sadness in his eyes, and her good spirits dimmed. She'd gotten what she'd wanted—new pupils. But Ant hadn't found his nephew.

CHAPTER FIVE

Ant rode up the path, his senses alert. He listened to the breeze through the trees, the sounds of birds, and an occasional chittering red squirrel that ran overhead, and then jumped from branch to branch. Most of all, he listened to the clip clop of the horse behind him, the rhythmic beat a reassurance that the schoolmarm was doing all right. From time to time he twisted to look back at her—just checking up. Each time he turned, she rewarded him with a sweet smile.

That smile always tugged at him, but Ant tried not to let his thoughts dwell on her, instead focusing on his need to find his nephew. Were Lewis and David in this area, as he'd heard months ago?

Ant had to contain the impatience urging him to go faster. Speed would only tire the horses and perhaps distress his little schoolteacher. He took a deep breath of the pine-scented air. They'd get to the next place when they got there. Another hour, more or less, wouldn't make a difference.

After a while, they reached a clearing, where a snug log cabin with a narrow front porch nestled among the trees. Two hens pecked at the ground in front of the house. A boy looked out an open window, then pelted through the front door, scattering the chickens, and heading straight toward them.

Reining in, Ant placed a steadying hand on Shadow's neck. Miss Stanton pulled up next to him.

The boy didn't stop. Running to them, he grabbed Ant's leg, a pleading expression on his face. "My Ma and Pa are real sick! So are some of the young uns. Will ya help us? Please!" Still holding on, anguish on his face, he looked back and forth between them.

Harriet leaned over to touch the boy's forehead, apparently to check for fever. "Of course we will. What's your name?"

"Jimmy, ma'am. Jimmy Crooks."

Ant studied the boy. Dirty brown hair, green eyes, freckles, a painfully thin body in worn out clothes. He'd be about David's age, around nine or so. The thought of his nephew in such circumstances made his stomach clench, although something in his gut told him they'd not find David here.

"Back up a bit, son, so we can get down." He shot a look at Miss Stanton. "Don't move until I can help you."

Ant swung down, handed the reins to Jimmy, and then reached up for the schoolteacher, spanning his hands around her waist. He helped her down, careful to lower her gently to the ground, where she landed on her good foot. He made sure she was steady before he released her.

He dropped his hand on Jimmy's shoulder. "You think you can water the horses, son? We'll go on in the house."

Jimmy straightened his thin shoulders. "Yes, sir."

Ant crooked his arm for Miss Stanton. No matter what she'd said, he suspected that ankle wasn't as sound as she claimed.

She hesitated, then slipped her arm through his, leaning on him as she took her first tentative steps, slowly. "I'm a bit stiff," she murmured.

She probably didn't have much chance to get out on a horse. "Take it slow," he said.

They climbed the steps to the porch. A long plank bench for sitting was propped against the house.

"Mr. Crooks, Mrs. Crooks," Harriet called. "We've come to help."

Ant stepped into the dim room lit only by the open door and a window. Harriet followed. Two beds were set against the far wall. One held the parents, and the other several children. All seemed to be sleeping. Even the open window and door couldn't cut the stench of feces and vomit. "Oh, my," Harriet whispered.

Ant held his breath and ventured near the children's bed. A quick scan told him that his nephew wasn't there. He didn't know whether to feel disappointed or relieved.

A little girl about hip high jumped down from the table where she'd been sitting, playing with a worn rag doll. She, too, was scrawny and dirty, but her big green eyes lit up, and she threw herself across the room and into Miss Stanton's arms. "Hello, I'm Martha. Who are you?"

Miss Stanton smoothed back the child's tangled hair. "I'm Miss Stanton, the school teacher. And this is Mr. Gordon."

"Everyone's sick but Jimmy and me. I'm hungry."

Miss Stanton gave him a glance that told him to go get the food out of the saddlebags.

Ant nodded his understanding, thankful to escape the foul-smelling cabin into the fresh air. Once he'd moved away from the house, he took a deep breath, feeling compassion for the people inside and gratitude he was healthy. He'd had food poisoning a couple of times, and had been sicker than a dog. Made you just want to die and be out of your misery. *Nope, wouldn't want to be in their position.* The family definitely needed a helping hand, though. Good thing he'd brought Miss Stanton along.

He took stock of the situation. Jimmy had the horses near a trough, obviously just having watered them. Ant walked over, took their reins, and tied them to a tree that had some grass growing underneath, then opened his saddlebag. Good thing Miss Stanton had packed so much food. They'd need it all.

Miss Stanton stepped out of the house, carrying a slop bucket with both hands, her face scrunched up. She looked around for the outhouse and then headed toward it, limping.

Not a job he would relish. He took a few steps toward her. "Let me take that, Harriet."

She shook her head, a stubborn look on her face.

He'd already learned to pick his battles when the schoolmarm wore that expression. Ant looked down at the boy. "Come on, Jimmy. We've brought food. Let's get you and your sister washed up so you can have something to eat."

The worried expression vanished from Jimmy's face, and his eyes got big.

Ant had to laugh at his expression. "Miss Stanton brought sandwiches, lemonade, and cookies." He took the heavy saddlebags off the horses.

"Cookies!" The boy flashed him a big grin, then grabbed Ant's hand and tugged him to the house.

Miss Stanton had already gone back inside for the chamber pot near the parents' bed and hauled it outside. Ant could only be grateful she'd taken care of those tasks right away. He put the food on the porch bench. Better they eat outside.

"You have soap anywhere here, boy?"

Jimmy nodded.

"Fetch your sister then and wash up. Face *and* hands."

Ant strode inside. Already the place smelled better. Still bad, but better. But he opened the only other window to get more air in.

There was a stir from the bed. The man propped himself up on an elbow and squinted at Ant.

Ant moved a little closer. "I'm Anthony Gordon, Mr. Crooks. The schoolteacher, Miss Stanton, and I are here to help."

The man nodded, then rolled over to check on his wife, who continued to sleep. He felt her forehead, then, apparently satisfied, pushed back the covers and, clad in his union suit, set his feet on the floor. The act seemed to make him dizzy, and he put both hands on the bed to steady himself. "Much obliged," he said in a rusty voice.

Ant held up a hand to stop the man. "How 'bout you stay right there. Maybe sit up in bed for a while."

The man looked mulish, and then shook his head, obviously giving in. "I'm as weak as a babe." He slid his legs back on the bed, plumped the pillow, set it behind him and leaned against the bed. "I was so sick I wanted to die. Wife, children, too. But I think the worst has passed. Haven't heard no one throw up for a while." He seemed to think. "Yah, a while."

"You need me to ride for Doc Cameron?"

Crooks shook his head. "Got no money for the doctor. He looked over at his children. I think the worst is over. They're all alive, thank the Lord."

Miss Stanton came in, shaking her wet hands, followed by the children. "Soap, but no clean towels." She lowered her voice. "Ant, we can't leave them this way."

"We won't. Checking out the other place can wait."

"Good. Can you pump some water and cut some firewood? I need to start cleaning them up. That is, after I feed Jimmy and Martha."

Thankful to be given the easier task, Ant walked out the door. He sent up a quick prayer that David wasn't ill and neglected somewhere... that Lewis was taking good care of him.

∾

After checking to see the children's faces and hands were clean, Harriet handed them each a sandwich, telling them to take small bites and chew slowly. They bit ravenously into the sandwiches. "You're gulping," she reminded them. She let them take a second bite before asking, "When did you last eat?"

Jimmy tilted his head at the hens in the yard. "Git an egg a day each. Boil it." He took another bite, swallowed, and then looked anxious. "Ma said not to bother with feeding anyone who was sick. Wouldn't keep it down anyway."

"You've just had one egg a day? For how long?"

"Three days, ma'am."

"No wonder you're so hungry. Well, we have plenty of sandwiches." Harriet went into the house to look for glasses or cups. *Three days without food. How awful! What would have happened if we hadn't come here?* She gave a quick prayer of thanks that Ant's search had led them to this family.

In a wooden cupboard nailed to the wall in the kitchen area, she found a stack of tin cups and took several of them outside with her. She poured the children some lemonade, and then watched the delight on their faces as they drank it. *I wonder if they've ever had lemonade before.* "Not too fast, now," she warned. "I'm only giving you a little. I think we need to save the rest for your family." She went back inside to tackle the next chore.

Ant walked in, carrying the bucket from the pump. He took it to the stove and poured the water in a big pot on the stove. He opened up the stove and looked inside it. "I'll bring wood in. More water, too."

After he left, Harriet leaned out the door to check on the children. They'd both finished their sandwiches and looked longingly at the bag of food. But neither had moved to take any.

She stepped outside. Ant wasn't in sight, but she could hear the sound of the axe splitting wood.

"Can I have a cookie, Ma'am?" Martha piped. "Please?"

"Yes, dear. Jimmy, do you want another sandwich first? Or at least a half?"

The boy gave her several quick nods. "Yes'm. What about my family?"

"I think it's best to wait and see how they feel. I'll make a little broth and see if they can keep it down. As for you, sandwich first, then a cookie." She handed both to him, then gave a cookie to Martha. "When you're finished, I'll need your help inside."

Ant rounded the corner of the cabin, one arm full of wood, a bucket of water in his other hand. He eyed the children eating, and he gave them his crooked smile. "Guess you found the cookies." He kept going into the house.

Watching him made Harriet's heart beat faster. There was something about the tall, dark man, she didn't know what, which caught her attention and kept it in a way that previously only Nick had.

To her surprise, Harriet realized that she hadn't thought of Nick all day. *Not once.* She waited for the familiar pang of pain to hit her, but it didn't. *Well!* She tucked that thought away to ponder later and followed Ant into the cabin.

He'd already lit the fire in the stove and stacked the rest of the wood in the box next to it. "I'll go see to the livestock. I noticed a shed round back. See what they have that needs tendin'."

The children wandered in.

"I want to bathe your folks, change the bedding, and put them in clean nightclothes, she told the children." *Please, please may there be a second set of everything they need.* "Do you have other sheets and night clothes?"

"The company sheets. Ma only brought them out when my grandma used to visit." The boy pointed to a wooden chest, the nicest piece of furniture in the home. *Probably Mrs. Crooks's hope chest.*

She lifted the lid, relieved to find sheets and pillowcases, nicer ones, with tatting on the edges, another nightgown with lace on the collar and sleeves, and a clean union suit. There were also several child's shifts and nightshirts. She lifted them all out, uncertain which would fit.

The water on the stove started to boil. She had Jimmy bring a washtub outside, and she poured the water into it, before sending the boy to get another bucket of water. She straightened and tucked an errant strand of hair behind her ear, took a deep breath, and headed back into the house. It was going to be a big chore to get everyone and everything clean. Not one she looked forward to.

～

At the end of the day, feeling weary in body and mind, Ant saddled up the horses, listening as the teacher called her final goodbyes to the children. He couldn't help but feel some pride in all they'd accomplished today. They were leaving behind clean sheets and clothes, hanging on the clothesline. The animals were taken care of. The ill family members had managed to keep bread and some lemonade in their stomachs, and Martha and Jimmy had stuffed themselves to the gills on sandwich fillings and cookies. Everyone was scrubbed and sweet smelling, including Crooks. And darned if his little schoolmarm hadn't convinced the parents to send the children to school.

Harriet walked out the front door, a concerned look on her face. She limped over to him. The hard work she'd done today had obviously taken a toll on her ankle.

"What's wrong?"

"I hate to leave them, Ant."

"You could move in."

The corners of her lips turned up, but there was no humor in her smile. "Ant, they have no food. Mr. Crooks hasn't been able to hunt. Only two chickens. What will they do? They won't take more charity than we've given today. Why do they have to be so prideful?"

"Sometimes for the poorest people, pride is all they have."

"And if their children starve?" Distress darkened her eyes.

Ant couldn't resist. He leaned over, way over, and dropped a light kiss on her lips. "I'll find a way to help them. Don't worry."

Harriet's wide eyes, and the blush creeping into her cheeks, tickled his fancy, and he wanted to give her another kiss. A longer one this time. But mindful of his priorities, he pulled away. Jerking his head toward the horses, he said. "Up you go. We'll be racing daylight as it is."

He helped her onto the saddle. Then he mounted Shadow and turned him downhill.

Ant settled into the ride. One more day gone by without finding David. One more day when his nephew might be suffering—hungry, cold, beaten, or neglected. As good as he felt about helping the Crooks, and he felt mighty good about that indeed, his guilt and worry over David wouldn't let up.

Tomorrow, he'd check out the last cabin. Maybe by tomorrow the long search would be over. He could only hope.

What will I do if he's not there?

CHAPTER SIX

As Ant pushed open the unsecured door and walked into the entry of his sister's house, the scent caught him first—the coppery smell of blood, familiar from his years as a reporter. His gut tightened. "Emily!"

On the left side of the dark paneled entry was Lewis' so-called library, on the other, the parlor. Following his nose, Ant strode into the parlor.

He saw a crumpled heap in a blue dress lying half behind the settee, black button boots sprawled. "Em!" Ant rushed around the furniture, then halted.

His sister lay in a pool of blood that soaked into the Aubusson carpet and spread onto the wooden floor. A diagonal slash ripped across her throat, and her eyes stared sightlessly at the ceiling.

I'm too late.

Ant didn't have to drop to his knees, feel for her pulse. He'd seen enough dead bodies. He forced down the emotion that wanted to boil out of his throat into a roar of grief and rage, and made himself study the scene like the reporter he was.

The blood was dark, congealing. Two small footsteps scuffed the edges of the stain next to a big one.

"David!" Ant whirled, studying the room. He pulled a chair aside to make sure his nephew wasn't behind it.

"David!" He raced up the staircase and down the hall to the boy's room, and burst through the door. When he didn't see a dead body on the unmade bed, his first feeling was relief. Then he realized the room had been ransacked. Drawers of the bureau pulled open, the clothes inside rumpled. A stocking dangled over one edge.

In the corner, a sailboat propped against the wall reminded him of David's last birthday. He'd given the boy the sailboat, then taken him to the park to try it out. Emily had written a poem about the day for David. Sadness choked Ant's throat.

He turned and hurried to the master of the house's room. If he found Lewis, he'd strangle him. But even as the rage and fear propelled him down the hall, he knew what he'd find. Sure enough, the room bore evidence of a hurried departure.

Just to be sure, he systematically searched the house, but couldn't find his nephew. Lewis had killed his wife and taken his son. Now David was on the run with a murderer.

But not for long, David, I promise. I'll find you and revenge your mother. This I swear!

Ant held out his hands as if squeezing the life out of Lewis, only to see them covered with blood. He could feel the stickiness on his skin.

David called to him *"Uncle Ant, help me!"*

"David? Where are you?"

Ant woke with a gasp, his hands raised a few inches, pushing against the bedding. It took a few breaths before he realized he was in his room at Widow Murphy's, not in Emily's townhouse. *Another nightmare.*

If it's not Isabella haunting me, then it's Emily.

He rubbed his hands over his face, willing them to stop shaking.

You'd think I'd be used to the nightmares by now.

~

David awoke early, when the sun was lightening the dark cabin to shades of gray. He glanced over at the neighboring pallet. Didn't look like a day his pa would bestir himself. The man sprawled on his back, one hand stretched out, fingertips touching an empty whiskey bottle. The stench of sweat and booze clung to him. His honking snores seemed to shake the flimsy walls.

David allowed himself a sigh of relief. This morning, he wouldn't be dragged from his bed and set to do his pa's bidding, the orders accompanied by blows. From the look and sound of his pa, he could escape for the day.

A rumbling in his stomach made him toss aside the thin blanket and roll to his feet. He debated carving off a chunk of the rock-hard bread in the crate in the corner of the room, but he knew if his pa wanted food later, and there wasn't enough, there'd be hell to pay. *My hell.*

His pa snorted.

David froze, heart thumping, waiting to see if his pa moved. When nothing happened, he tucked his slingshot in his pocket along with a knife. He could pick some berries for breakfast. Maybe, after he hobbled the mule on that thin patch of grass near the trees, he'd get lucky and bring down a squirrel or rabbit—something he could roast over a fire and fill his belly with.

David slipped outside the door and inhaled the pine-scented air, feeling an unexpected and almost forgotten feeling of excitement. *Yes, maybe today I'll get lucky.*

～

Riding through the trees, Ant glanced at the sun overhead. *Almost mid-morning.* Later than he'd hoped. But he'd been weary after yesterday, and he knew that Miss Stanton would need extra rest. She'd protested last night when he'd told her so, but he'd held firm.

He'd considered riding out without her, but after seeing how she was with the children yesterday—caring and efficient, putting them at ease with strangers—he'd decided she might help him when he found David. His nephew might instinctively trust her, making it easier for them to spirit him away. Plus, Ant had a suspicion that the stubborn schoolmarm might just light on after him.

Now, however, he wondered if he'd made the right decision. It had taken them longer than he'd thought to reach the clearing; they'd headed up the wrong path for a while. But according to Mack Taylor's directions, he and Harriet should soon be at the cabin.

He glanced behind him at the little teacher. Before she caught him looking at her, he could see her face was pinched in pain. Her thighs must be sore from all their riding. *Not that she'd admit it to me,* he thought in admiration. *She's a tough kitten. I guess she'd have to be to handle some of those rowdy boys she's mentioned.* Harriet lifted her gaze, saw Ant watching her, and straightened in the saddle, sending him a tight smile that didn't fool him one bit.

He grinned back, enjoying the hint of pink that crept into her cheeks. Then he faced forward again. *Please God, may David soon be one of her rowdy boys.*

A few more minutes of riding brought them to the edge of a rocky clearing, an almost-falling-down small shack in the center, and a bony mule hobbled near a lean-to. The sorry-looking animal raised its head and let out a raw whinny.

Ant held up his hand to stop Harriet, then, with a backward-shooing motion, indicated he wanted Harriet to back her horse.

Ant moved them into the pines at the edge of the clearing, until he was sure they couldn't be seen from the shack. Then he swung down from Shadow. Holding the reins, he moved close enough to say to her in a low voice, "I'm going to sneak around back. See what I can see. I don't want to alert Lewis that we're here. Don't want him to make off with the boy again."

Harriet parted her lips, looking as if she was about to protest, then seemed to change her mind and nodded instead.

"Hold onto Shadow's reins. Turn the horses around so we can have a quick getaway if we need to."

"Why would we need a quick getaway?"

He tipped his head in the direction of the shack. "You never know who's holed up in there. Could even be outlaws."

"I think we would have heard if there were any outlaws in the area."

He mentally shook his head at her naiveté. "I'd rather be careful."

"And if it's not outlaws, not David, but there is another child?"

"I'll come get you, and you can do the schoolteacher thing."

She rolled her eyes, and then reached out a hand for Shadow's reins. He handed them over and watched her maneuver the horses around until they were faced away.

I shouldn't have let her come.

How could I have stopped her?

Ant strode through the trees and circled around until he could approach the shack from behind. From that vantage point, he could see one cracked window, glass miraculously still in place. Hand propped on his gun, he watched from the woods for a few minutes, then took quick steps to the building, and, sliding to the side, peered through the grimy window. He could barely make out one body on the bed. But the snores filtering through the gaps in the plank wall told him it might be safe to venture inside.

The area below the window wasn't visible. He darted another glance around him, then slunk around the side and up the two almost rotted stairs. His heart rate picked up. Easing the door open, he caught a pungent whiff of unwashed male and alcohol and held his breath.

The snoring man didn't stir. He was clad in dirty clothes, even had worn boots on. Lewis, all right, although Ant had to take a long look to find the familiar features of his brother-in-law in the bloated face. Another small-size pallet with a rumpled blanket told Ant what he needed to know. He sagged against the doorframe in relief. In the past two years, he hadn't allowed himself to think that David might be dead. But the niggling fear had always been there.

He quietly closed the door. No telling where David was. *I'll come back early in the morning, when I don't have a schoolteacher to deal with.*

Once in the shadow of the trees, Ant hurried to Harriet, flashing her a big grin. "My brother-in-law is in there sawing logs so loud, I though the place might collapse. Didn't even wake when I looked in the door."

"David?"

Ant shook his head. "Not there. Saw where he slept though." He took her gloved hand and squeezed. "Until I saw that small pallet and realized David's alive..." He shook his head. "Harriet, I can't describe the feeling." He took a breath to get away from the emotion, forcing teasing into his tone. "Thought I might faint away like a debutant with her corset tied too tight."

Harriet giggled. "Ant." She made a token protest.

Ant couldn't help but grin; she looked so sweet with her eyes alight with laughter.

Still holding his hand, she playfully shook it. "You've found him. How wonderful!"

He sobered. "Until I see David face to face, give him a hug, have him say, 'Hello, Uncle Ant,' I won't rest easy. I need those things, Harriet. I need David."

She squeezed his hand in reassurance. "You'll have him, Ant. You will. Shall we go wake up your brother-in-law?"

Hell no.

"It's a small room, Harriet. Lewis is definitely not dressed to receive visitors. Plus, from the smell in the place, he tied one on last night and waking him will be like waking a grizzly bear."

"I can wait outside, while you..."

"No, Harriet. I won't subject you to that. I'll come back. Lewis will be more presentable tomorrow when he's had a chance to recover and clean up."

She opened her mouth to protest.

Ant dropped a kiss on her parted lips to shut her up. However, when he tasted her sweetness, it was he that was floored into mindlessness. He held the kiss for a few seconds before breaking it off and stepping away.

Harriet's eyes were wide and starry. "Oh," was all she said.

Oh is right. "Let me help you mount the horse." *If I don't get her out of here, she'll be in more danger from me than from Lewis.*

～

Harriet woke early, eager to begin her secret mission. She gingerly put her sore foot to the floor and stood, relieved to only feel a twinge of pain, not the stabbing agony of the earlier days. She quickly dressed in her riding habit, scooped up the peppermint sticks she'd bought from the Cobbs the night before, and put them in her reticule.

Quietly humming, Harriet made her way down the steps outside. She swung her reticule, thoughts of the surprise she had in store for Ant lightening the arduous journey down the stairs.

In the dim kitchen, she grabbed the packet of food she'd made up the night before, and then let herself out of the house. Walking over to the livery stable with barely a limp, Harriet watched the sun rise over the distant mountains. The purple night shadows grayed; a hint of the orange sun peeked over Pete's Mountain, named for an old prospector who used to work a claim there.

As early as she was, the livery stable doors were already wide open. Pepe walked outside and started pumping water into the trough. As she approached, he gave Harriet a shy nod and a quiet, *"Buenos días."*

Glad not to have to explain herself to Mack Taylor, she stopped before the man. "Is Brown Boy fed and watered?'

Pepe nodded.

"Then I'd like you to saddle him for me." *And hurry before Mack comes out.* The stable owner might refuse to let her take the horse on her own to go up the mountain—at least until he cleared it with the Cobbs—something she'd rather not have happen because she'd allowed the Cobbs to think she was riding with Ant again today. Her conscience pricked her, but she reminded herself that it wasn't precisely a lie; she just hadn't corrected their assumption.

How could she explain to the Cobbs the compulsion she felt to find David? She had a fantasy of presenting Ant with the nephew he longed for. To witness their reunion and bask in his gratitude…

A shake of Pepe's head brought Harriet back to the here and now.

"What?"

An uncertain look crossed the man's round, brown face. "No Señor Gordon?"

"No Señor Gordon," she echoed in a firm tone.

"You wait, Señorita Stanton," he said, his Spanish accent so strong she could barely understand him. "I'll finish." He motioned to the bucket of water near the trough. "I'll go with you."

"No, thank you, Pepe. I'll be fine."

Reluctance showed in his stiff shoulders, but he went inside. A few minutes later, he emerged with Brown Boy and helped her into the saddle.

Harriet arranged her divided skirt and draped the strings of her reticule over the saddle horn. Then she gave Pepe a smile in farewell and urged Brown Boy forward. Yet, as she rode away, the unhappy look on Pepe's face stayed with her, and, for some reason, she shivered, as if a goose had walked over her grave.

~

Ant ran from Isabella's body to Emily's and back. No matter what, he couldn't prevent their deaths, but he kept trying in an endless cycle. Helplessness and rage coursed through his body. Surely he could prevent the women he loved from dying, if he could just get there in time.

But he never could.

Ant awoke, his arms in a death grip around his pillow. He could feel moisture on his cheeks, and his throat ached. With some relieved part of his brain, he realized he'd had a nightmare and hoped he hadn't scared Widow Murphy awake. But the rest of him shivered with horror.

He shifted and winced. His body felt stiff and sore as if he'd been dragged behind the back of a horse. Exhaustion dragged his eyelids down. He'd worked so hard in the nightmare. It didn't feel as if he'd actually slept. *I can't lie about. I need to find David.*

The thought of his nephew helped draw Ant from the remnants of the nightmare. He glanced out the small window at the foot of the bed. Dawn cast a dim light in the room. He tossed the pillow aside and sat up. *Time to go after Lewis and bring David home.*

CHAPTER SEVEN

Ant walked through the doors of the livery stable, feeling the weight of the gun holstered in the belt around his hips.

Mack, the livery owner, straightened from cleaning the left hoof of a Pinto horse and gave Ant a sideways glance out of rheumy green eyes. "Missed your schoolteacher by about fifteen minutes."

"What's that?"

"She went riding off this morning."

Mack's words felt like a shot to Ant's gut. *No, she didn't go after David!* But he had a bad feeling that she had. "Did Miss Stanton say where she was going?"

"No, and that's not like her." Mack paused, rubbed his gray-stubbled chin. "When she takes Brown Boy out, she always says where she's going."

His stomach fisting in a knot, Ant took long strides to Shadow, not bothering with the morning greeting and head rub. He threw on the blanket and the saddle, cinching it up.

He slipped the bridle over the horse's head, centering the bit in Shadow's mouth. Taking the reins, he led the horse outside, mounted, and kneed Shadow to a canter, resisting the urge to gallop down the street. Harriet wasn't that far ahead of him. He'd catch her in time.

~

Harriet reached the clearing and paused Brown Boy, looking around her. The early morning sun shone golden rays through the trees. Birds chirped, and a red squirrel scampered across the open ground, jumped to the top of a rock, and then kept on going out of sight around the shack. The bony mule dozed under the lean-to.

No one stirred, and she wondered uneasily if David and his father still slept. It might be awkward if she woke them.

Harriet dismounted, led Brown Boy to a scraggly patch of grass, and looped the reins over a dead pine branch. She untied her reticule from the saddle horn, hearing two peppermint sticks inside click together, and slipped the strings over her wrist.

She hiked across the clearing, feeling the tension in her stomach and her heart tap tap against her chest. She trod up the rotted steps. Knocking on the rickety door, Harriet called out, "Mr. March, I'm Miss Stanton, the schoolteacher." She paused, listening for the noise of a presence, before knocking again. "Hello, is anyone home?"

Harriet waited for a while, and then slowly pushed open the door, wrinkling her nose at the stale odor. *No one here.* From the looks of the rumpled, dirty bedding on the two pallets, father and son were out in the woods somewhere.

Backing out of the house, Harriet pivoted, trying to see any sign of where they might have gone. On the upper edge of the clearing, she could see a faint path. Too narrow for the horse to navigate, but a boy could squeeze through. *And so can I.*

~

The closer Ant came to the clearing, the more fear for Harriet weighed in his gut. As he rode, he cursed himself dozens of times for not telling Harriet the whole story about Lewis March and what he'd done to Emily. Partly from old habit—he didn't share the family pain and shame with anyone—and partly because he'd wanted to protect Harriet from the horror of the whole sordid tale. But in so doing, he'd endangered her.

Not to mention that her presence was going to make it harder to kill Lewis. He didn't want her to think he was murdering the man in cold blood. Well he was, but Ant knew he was really meting out justice to a murderer.

What will Harriet think of me? Will she understand?

Does it matter? Right now all he wanted was to find her and David and get them to safety. He would deal with Lewis later.

Almost there. Ant kneed Shadow to a faster pace. As he rode, he battled thoughts of what might happen to Harriet if she reached Lewis before he caught up with her. His little schoolmarm had no idea she was heading into the lair of a murderer.

~

David sat at the edge of the cliff, legs dangling, drumming his heels against the side of the overhang, his favorite secret place. Behind him, woods grew to a few paces from the edge of the cliff, leaving a narrow swath of grass, dotted with a few boulders that ran alongside the edge.

Far below him, the river flowed by, frothing over rocks. He loved to watch the water as it rushed down the mountain. Sometimes he considered jumping, angling toward the pool cupped between some rocks, then floating downstream to freedom. *One way or the other, dead or alive, I'll have escaped you, Pa.*

"David!" A woman's voice called behind him.

Fear prickled through him. He pulled up his legs and scrambled to his feet, dodging behind the shelter of a nearby boulder. Peering out, he saw a brown-haired woman wearing a divided skirt, staring at him with a look of concern on her pretty face. He'd never seen her before.

How does she know my name?

David prepared to sidle to the other side of the boulder and vanish into the woods, but something held him in place. His body canted toward the safety of the trees, and, from the corner of his eye, he gauged the distance from the lady to him.

"David, I'm Miss Stanton. I'm the schoolteacher in Sweetwater Springs."

Paused on the verge of escaping, he waited.

"I'm a friend of your Uncle Ant."

Who? David shook his head.

She stepped closer.

He edged away.

The lady held out a hand. "Don't go. I've brought you candy."

Candy. He remembered candy. It had been a long time though. Not since... His stomach knotted, and his thoughts shied away from the memory.

She untied the strings of a little bag, hanging from her wrist.

He lingered, wary but curious.

She pulled out two red and white sticks.

Peppermint. With a sudden bite of memory, the taste of cool sweetness made his mouth water.

"They're for you."

For me?

She held the peppermint sticks out to him, taking a few careful steps closer.

He debated whether to come out from behind the boulder, snatch them from her, and run off, but instead decided to wait.

"Your Uncle Ant has been trying to find you."

This time the name rang a vague bell in his brain. He could sense the memory clanging against the painful place where he kept everything locked away.

"He's been looking for you for a long time. I can tell he loves you very much."

The woman's words skittered over him like ants on his skin. Too uncomfortable to let in the meaning of what she was saying, he concentrated on the candy.

"Won't you have a piece, David?" She stepped closer.

He leaned forward over the top of the boulder and took one stick between his thumb and forefinger, then slowly slid it out of her hand. All the while, he kept an eye on the lady in case she decided to do something to him. Although he didn't know what such a small woman could do, he just didn't want to find out.

"Good," she said, satisfaction in her voice.

David risked a full glance at her face, and saw her smiling and looking misty-eyed. That look relaxed the tightness in his chest a bit. He dropped his gaze and popped the end of the candy stick into his mouth, giving a long pulling suck. When the sweet flavor hit his tongue, he breathed in the pleasure of it, the scent of peppermint lingering in his nostrils.

The woman stood quietly watching him. Somehow her scrutiny didn't make him uncomfortable. She had kind gray eyes and a warmth about her that reminded him of…His thoughts jumped away. But, before he could settle again into his enjoyment of the candy, David saw movement in the bushes around the faint path he'd made in his walks to the cliff.

CHAPTER EIGHT

Feeling as though she was trying to coax a bird to eat out of her hand, Harriet held her breath lest a sudden movement frighten the boy away. He was skinny and dirty, dressed in too-small rags that barely resembled a shirt and pants. Yet he had Ant's brown eyes and hair, and his angled cheekbones. Watching him caused an unexpected surge of maternal emotion to seize her heart. When he'd taken a peppermint stick, she'd wanted to cheer and cry at the same time.

David looked past her, and his expression changed from wary to terrified. His body stiffened. He pointed behind her, jabbing his finger in a *look out* gesture. Then he ducked behind the rock.

Imagining a grizzly, Harriet whirled around, but instead saw a man, squeezing between the last two trees and bursting into the clearing. He was big with a balled stomach, yet barely any flesh on the rest of his heavy frame. His puffy features looked unhealthy.

Before her racing heart could slow, Harriet realized from the narrow-eyed look on his face, and the hands clenched into meaty fists in front of his body, that she might be in as much trouble from this man as from a bear.

"Mr. March…" She started to greet him, but before she could get a whole word out, he took two running steps and grabbed her shoulders.

"What have we here?" The man wrenched the remaining peppermint stick out of her hand. "Trying to entice my boy, eh?" He kept one hand on her shoulder, digging his fingers into her skin, while he shoved the candy in his pocket with the other hand. "Pretty little girly, aren't you?"

Fear shot through her.

His free hand squeezed her breast, hard enough to hurt.

Shocked at the violation, she cried out and swung hard.

He caught her wrist. "Scream away, girly. There's no one to hear you." His leering face lowered to hers.

The stench of his breath made her gag and turn her head. She struggled to get away, shoving and twisting. Her hat tumbled off her head and sailed off the cliff. Her elbow caught him is his ribcage.

He let out an "ummff" and slapped her face.

Pain radiated across her cheek. Dazed, she collapsed backward, pulling him off balance.

He fell on top of her. His weight was heavy, his breath foul.

Harriet screamed, pushed.

He reared back, propped up by one hand and pinned her arm with another.

Harriet could see David peer around the boulder, his eyes wide as he stared at them.

Gasping, she tried to shift out from under the man. She got one leg free and kicked at him, but her skirt hampered her, and her foot barely tapped his shin.

He growled, then grabbed the top of her shirtwaist and ripped it to her stomach.

Harriet fought through her terror to stay conscious... to try to wrestle away from him. Her fingers strained toward a rock, but she couldn't quite grab it. She reached. Just another inch.

∾

Ant rode into the clearing and saw Brown Boy tied to a tree but no sign of Harriet. With a curse, he dismounted, looping the reins around a tree limb, then started toward the shack.

A scream cut through the trees on the opposite side of the clearing. *Harriet!*

He broke into a run, leaping over rocks in his race across the clearing. He saw a faint path between two trees. He squeezed through sideways, and then dodged around trees, when the path became too narrow. The woods seemed to come alive like a nightmarish Grimm's fairytale. They reached out skeletal limbs to grab him. He thrashed through the forest muttering curses and inarticulate prayers. It seemed to take hours, but was probably only seconds before he could see though the last of the trees where Harriet lay pinned underneath Lewis as he tore the front of her dress.

Rage crashed through Ant, and he barreled through the trees that tried to confine him.

From behind a boulder, a boy rose, his hand cocked back to throw a rock. *David!*

Lewis saw David poised to attack and leaped to his feet. "No you don't, boy," he snarled, lunging toward David.

Ant let out a roar and burst into the open.

Startled, Lewis glanced over at him, his eyes widening. He lurched to his feet.

Harriet grabbed the man's ankle and hung on.

David let the rock fly, smashing into his father's face.

Lewis tottered sideways.

Ant bounded toward Lewis, his fist raised to drive into the man. Then he realized that the small clearing was really the edge of a cliff, and Harriet still clung to Lewis's leg. *They'll both go over.*

Seeing Ant charging toward him made Lewis shift his weight backward, only to find no purchace for his feet. He tottered, arms windmilling, eyes bugging out, then toppled back off the cliff.

"Let go!" Ant dove for Harriet. He tackled her just as she started to slide off the edge. A few more inches....

She released Lewis' leg.

Lewis kept flailing his arms. He let out a cry of fear, and then dropped from sight.

Ant could feel Harriet's forward momentum slide over the edge. With all his strength, he rolled backward, whipping her over the top of him to his other side. They tumbled together, until he ended up on top of her.

Ant's face rested on Harriet's stomach. He felt the heat of her and the rise and fall of her gasping breaths. *Thank you, Lord. Thank you, thank you, Lord!*

On his elbows, he scooted up until they were face to face. Harriet's gray eyes were full of fear.

"You're safe, Harriet."

A red mark marred her pale cheek.

"He hit you," he murmured, gently kissing the bruise. "If he wasn't dead, I'd kill him for that."

Harriet searched his face, as if needing reassurance. "He's dead?"

"We'll check to be sure. But dead, or near dead, he won't hurt you again."

Tears welled up in her eyes.

"Harriet, sweetheart." He slid his arm under her neck and gathered her to him. He could feel the rapid beat of her heart against his chest, and knew she could feel his. He buried his face in her hair, inhaling the scent of her.

Harriet sobbed in his arms, her face turned to his shoulder.

Helpless, all he could do was hold her and make soothing noises as she wept. After a few minutes, to his great relief, she gave a few sniffs, and then pulled away.

He kissed her forehead. "You all right now, Kitten?"

"Yes, I..." Her eyes widened, and she struggled to sit up. "David!"

David. The boy was leaning over the rock watching them. Untangling himself from Harriet, Ant stood, and helped her to her feet.

Harriet clutched the torn shirtwaist to her chest.

David straightened and tensed to run.

Ant strode to him, hoping to forestall his escape.

David bolted toward the trees on the other side of the boulder.

Where's he going? Ant took off after him and caught his nephew just as he reached the woods. He grabbed David by the shoulders, meaning to gently turn him around, but the boy exploded in a frenzy of kicking and hitting. Ant held David away from him, but a kick to his shin made him pull the boy close into a bear hug, and he hooked one leg around David's knees. From there, no matter how David struggled, he couldn't get free, nor could he inflict damage on his uncle. "Davy, Davy boy. It's all right. I'm your Uncle Ant."

David didn't cease his frantic struggles.

Ant held him in a firm hug, squishing the boy to him just enough to contain him, but not enough to hurt.

Harriet hurried over. "David, David, you're safe."

Ant could see that she wanted to move closer. But afraid she might get kicked, he warned her off with a sharp look.

She obeyed, staying put, arms crossed against her chest.

All of a sudden, David went limp. Wary, lest it be a trick, Ant gradually loosened his hold, but not enough to let go. "Davy, boy. It's Uncle Ant. Remember the sailboat I brought you the last time I visited? Remember how we sailed it across the pond, and then it sank in the middle? Remember how you cried, and I promised you another one?"

David didn't move. Nor did he turn his head to look at his uncle. Instead, he angled his gaze at Harriet.

Ant nodded for her to come closer. Maybe she could get through to the boy.

Harriet stepped forward and ran a gentle hand across David's head, brushing the long matted hair back from his head. "David, you saved me," she said, her voice gentle. "You threw that rock..." her voice caught. She leaned over and kissed his forehead. "Thank you."

Ant dared to release the boy, but kept a hand on David's shoulder just in case. "I've been looking for you, David, ever since your father took you away. I've never forgotten you, never stopped searching. You're safe now, son." He cupped his hand under David's chin and angled the boy's face to see his eyes.

Instead of the fear or anger he expected to see, there was only blankness in David's eyes. He stood unresponsive like a puppet.

Uneasy, Ant brushed his knuckles across David's dirty cheek. "I'm going to leave you here with Harriet, while I check on what happened to your pa. You both stay here." He punctuated his words with a commanding glance at his schoolteacher.

She hesitated before nodding and taking David's hand.

Bracing himself for what he might see, Ant strode over to the edge of the cliff and looked down.

Lewis' body lay below, a tiny rag doll, sprawled on his back, three quarters of his body in the stream.

Ant eyed the cliff. No easy way to get down, even if he had wanted to leave David and Harriet to go make sure the man was dead. He'd get them home and come back for the body.

He glanced over to see the two of them hand-in-hand, and didn't like the anxious look on Harriet's bruised face and how she held her shirtwaist together with her other hand, nor the empty look in David's eyes. No. He'd send some men for the body. He wasn't about to leave them alone anytime soon.

~

Riding through town next to Ant and David on Shadow, leading the poor, weak mule, Harriet felt every ache in her body. For part of the way, silent tears had spilled down her cheeks, tears she didn't dare wipe away because then Ant, who was behind her, would know she was blubbering. But the memory of Lewis assaulting her, of him toppling off the cliff, kept coming back to her, no matter how hard she tried to banish the memory. She had to fight the shakes and worked hard to stay upright in the saddle.

The tears had finally dried up. When she went around a sharp bend and out of sight for a moment, she'd taken her handkerchief from her sleeve to mop her eyes and blow her nose. She longed for a hot bath where she could scrub away the feeling of Lewis' hands on her body and the privacy where she could reflect on the day's happenings—not something she was likely to find at the Cobbs. There were many times in the last few years she'd wished for her own home where she could be alone, but never more than today.

At the outskirts of town, the street seemed mostly deserted, thank goodness. *No one to see me riding hatless, with a torn shirtwaist.* Although she was too exhausted and achy to care if anyone did see her.

Toward the middle of town the Nortons strolled down the street. The couple saw them and stopped. Mrs. Norton, her white hair in a tight bun, waved and angled over to them. Reverend Norton, wearing his old black frock coat, followed behind her. As Mrs. Norton came close she cried out, "You found your nephew, praise the Lord." Then her gaze sharpened when she saw Harriet's face and the torn shirtwaist, which she'd tried to tuck into some decency with the couple of pins she'd had in her reticule. "Miss Stanton, what has happened!"

Reverend Norton hurried up. "My dear Miss Stanton, has someone done you harm?"

Harriet shook her head, too weary to explain. "I'm sore, but all right. But I wouldn't have been if it weren't for Mr. Gordon. He *and* his nephew saved me."

Ant urged his horse forward. "It's a long story, Reverend. As you can see, Miss Stanton and my nephew, David... Gordon are in need of care."

Mrs. Norton placed her hand on Harriet's leg. "Dear girl, I'll go for Dr. Cameron."

Harriet was about to demur, but Ant cut through the beginning of her protests. "Yes, please, Mrs. Norton. I want the doctor to examine David and see to Harriet's face." He shot a don't-argue-with-me look at her. "Of course, I'll pay for it."

Harriet was too worn out to object.

Ant leaned closer to Reverend Norton. "Reverend, my nephew's father was a murderous criminal. Right now, I won't go into what he's done before, but he attacked Miss Stanton. Through her efforts to free herself and those of my nephew, David, here—" he patted the boy on the leg "—to help her, Lewis ended up stumbling off the cliff, just as I arrived on the scene. Could you send some men to retrieve the body?"

Reverend Norton nodded. As the two men discussed logistics, Harriet felt herself sway in the saddle. She dropped the mule's lead. *I'm so tired!*

Ant must have seen, for he lifted David off the horse, and thrust him into the startled minister's arms. "Don't let him go." He hastily dismounted, took two steps to Harriet's horse, and then reached his hands up to her waist. "Come, Harriet."

She leaned into his hands, and felt herself lifted over the saddle and off the horse. Once on the ground, he held her firmly, which was good because her legs wobbled.

They had attracted more attention. Pepe appeared from the stable, followed by Mack, who seemed to take in the situation without the need for an explanation. "I'll take the horses and that sorry-lookin' mule, Mr. Gordon," Mack said. He picked up the lead from the ground and reached for Brown Boy's reins, jerking his head to indicate to Pepe to take hold of Shadow. "We'll git 'em rubbed down and watered. That ole mule needs seeing to. We'll take care of everything." He rubbed Brown Boy's nose. "Maybe a treat, eh, ole boy?"

Vaguely, she heard Mrs. Norton order Artie Sloan to run for Doctor Cameron and ask Helga Mueller to hold onto David. Then the minister's wife came over to them. "I'll help her to the Cobbs', Mr. Gordon. You see to your nephew."

Harriet could feel Ant's reluctance to release her. Even if she wanted to cling to the shelter of his arms, his nephew's needs were his priority. "Yes, Ant, you need to see to David. I'll be in good hands." *Hopefully, I won't bowl Mrs. Norton over if I collapse in the street.*

Ant eased away from her, allowing Mrs. Norton to put her arm around Harriet's shoulders.

Mrs. Cobb must have been watching from the store because she rushed out and hurried over to them. "Miss Stanton, what have you gotten yourself into this time? Oh, your dress, it's torn. Oh, dear." A judgmental look crossed her face.

"Hortense Cobb, not another word," said gentle Mary Norton in an unusually sharp voice. "Miss Stanton was attacked, but saved by Mr. Gordon and the boy before the worst happened, thank the good Lord."

Mrs. Cobb's face turned red, and she sputtered, obviously collecting her wits. "Thank the good Lord, indeed, Mrs. Norton," she echoed in a pious tone of voice.

"Miss Stanton will be in need of a bath, Hortense," Mrs. Norton said pointedly.

"Yes, of course. I'll see to it." Mrs. Cobb turned and hurried away.

Harriet and Mrs. Norton followed more slowly. Harriet tried not to lean on frail Mrs. Norton.

"I know you don't have it easy, boarding with the Cobbs, Miss Stanton. I've often wished the parsonage was bigger so we could take you in."

Even through her daze, Harriet couldn't help feeling some wry amusement at Mrs. Norton's words. The Nortons often filled their tiny parsonage with those down-on-their-luck individuals in need of a hot meal and place to rest for the night. If their house had a spare bedroom, Harriet would love to be another one of their strays.

Making her slow, painful way to the Cobbs, Harriet worried about David. He was obviously traumatized. Ever since he'd thrown the rock to save her, all her maternal instincts had awoken. Her connection to him felt deeper—more natural even than her feelings for her students. She wanted to be there to look after him, see that he was cleaned up and well fed.

His father's a murderous criminal. Ant's words finally penetrated her foggy brain. She'd unknowingly gone after a murderous criminal today because Ant hadn't told her about the dangers. Anger built inside her.

"Almost there, dear," Mrs. Norton said with an encouraging lilt to her voice.

The anger swirling though Harriet's body gave her a burst of energy. *Just wait until I give you a piece of my mind, Anthony Gordon. You just wait!*

Anthony Gordon had kept his secrets close to his chest, and Harriet couldn't help wondering what others might lie in his dark past.

CHAPTER NINE

David stayed in his drifty place. Even curiosity about the town, which he'd only seen once when he and Pa had rode through to buy some provisions, didn't pull him out. He remained vaguely aware of a group of people surrounding him, of the big man handing him off to an old man before he was passed to a fat woman, who cushioned him against her soft body and smelled of bread and cinnamon.

The big man came for him. "Thank you, Mrs. Mueller," he said, laying a strong hand on David's shoulder, though the grip wasn't hurtful like Pa's.

"Iss goot, Mr. Gordon. You bring the *bube* to visit me." She pinched David's cheek. "Ve give you some *kuchen*. Fatten you up. You vill like, *nicht wahr?*"

The big man gave the cinnamon woman a weary smile. Something about his crooked grin stirred something inside David, but before he could examine it, the man nudged him to a square house set back from the street. "Come, David. It's time for a bath and some food."

The thought of food penetrated, and he reluctantly followed the big man to the door of the house. The man knocked, and the door flew open.

Inside an older woman glared at them. She had a sharp nose, thin lips, and skin hanging from under her neck like a rooster. "Found him, did ya?" Her lips pursed in disapproval. "Dirty. I'm not letting him in the house in that state."

The big man sighed. "Mrs. Murphy, do you expect David to bathe in the middle of the street?"

Her expression didn't change.

"I think Mrs. Norton will be over soon to check on him."

An uneasy look crossed her sour face.

"I'll pay extra."

That seemed to work because she moved aside from the door, reluctance oozing from her very bones.

David's feet remained planted on the wooden steps, reluctant to enter the house. The big man stood next to him, a firm hand the size of a tin plate still resting on his shoulder. The hand propelled him forward, not with a shove like his pa would have done, but still strong enough to make his feet move in spite of their reluctance.

They followed the rooster-woman to a kitchen, big and clean, with the smell of baking bread from the loaf resting on the table in the center and a rich meaty aroma coming from a pot on the big black stove. His stomach contracted, aching with hunger pangs.

The widow pointed at a chair. "Sit. Don't touch anything. I'll start heating water." She pointed out a back door and shot a look at the big man. "Tub's in the lean-to."

David sat frozen in the chair, wondering if he could make a break for it before the big man caught him. *But where would I go? What would I eat?*

The man nodded, then moved over to the washbasin, wet his hands, soaped them and rinsed, then dried them on a towel. He walked over to the stove, picked up the loaf and tore off a chunk.

Mrs. Murphy squawked in protest.

He shot her a look that clammed her up. Then he handed the bread to David. "Something to tide you over."

David held the warm chunk in his hand, fighting the need to gobble it down.

"Go ahead, David. Take a bite."

David waited until the big man they called Mister Gordon turned away to go into the lean-to. Then he took a quick bite. The bread melted in his mouth, leaving only the chewy crust. David's eyes watered—from what, he didn't know. He gulped down the rest of the bite.

After Mister Gordon brought in the tub, setting it next to the black cast-iron stove, he looked over at David. "Do you think you could wash yourself, while I go to the mercantile and buy you some new clothes?"

David nodded, not sure what he was agreeing to.

The big man gave him a crooked smile and brushed a hand over David's hair. "Goin' to need a haircut." He cocked his head toward the door. "It won't take me long."

David could tell from the man's tone that he meant to be reassuring. As scary as the stranger was, he didn't hold a candle to the old biddy. *Don't leave me.* But the words didn't come out of the place in his throat that had frozen a long time ago.

~

David looked so lost sitting in the chair. He reminded Ant of a captured bird paralyzed with fear. For a minute the blankness left David's eyes, and he gave Ant a look of appeal. *The boy has Emily's eyes.*

Ant's gut knotted, and he could feel an unfamiliar prickling behind his eyes. He rallied behind a teasing tone. "You'll be all right here, David. Can't have you walking about as naked as a scrawny jaybird." He nodded to the rooster-woman. "Beg pardon, Miz Murphy." And to David: "Eat your bread to tide you over until we can have a meal."

David looked down, breaking their eye contact.

"Need anything from the store?" he asked Widow Murphy, and then waited impatiently while she reeled off a list.

He nodded good-bye, then left the house, leaving behind an odd feeling of oppression. As he strode down the street, he couldn't help feeling guilty about needing to escape. But the boy reminded Ant too much of his sister, something he hadn't thought would bother him at all. Actually, the problem had never occurred to him. If he *had* thought about it, he would have assumed that the boy would be a welcome reminder of Emily.

Added to his pain were the obvious physical and emotional scars the boy carried from his abuse…Familiar guilt weighed Ant down. If only he hadn't argued with that scoundrel Lewis the night before that terrible event…threatened to take Emily and David away from him. If only he'd gone to Emily's house a few hours earlier the next day. Hell, if only he'd stopped the wedding in the first place. But he'd been out of the country having fallen into love with Isabella…had assumed his sister had chosen a better man than their stepfather. His whole life seemed one long chain of regrets.

The boy didn't talk. Not one word. Even on the horse, seated in front of him, David's thin body had remained rigid. Had never relaxed. In response to David's silence and misery, a lump had seized Ant's throat like a fist. He hadn't known what to say to the stiff young stranger in his arms. Ever since the kidnapping, he'd fantasized about the conversations he'd have with his nephew. He had two years of words stored up. Yet when the time had come to say some of them, he'd choked.

I may not be cut out to be raising that boy.

Dressed in a gray calico gown, Harriet sat by the stove in the Cobbs' kitchen, combing out her hair. Between brushing, she sipped a cup of tea and nibbled on some sugar cookies. She'd settled for a sponge bath instead of a soak, eager to escape to the privacy of her room.

Mrs. Cobb bustled around, setting the kitchen to rights. The woman had alternated between scolding Harriet and punishing silences, even while she'd made tea and set out cookies. While they'd been in Mrs. Norton's presence, Mrs. Cobb had acted solicitous and thanked God Harriet was safe. But that caring behavior had vanished when the minister's wife left.

For a while, Harriet had remained silent, too tired and numb to even listen. She'd allowed the scold to sail over her head, something she'd become good at since living with the Cobbs. But, once she was clean and changed, and after drinking some tea, it was harder to shut out the woman's words.

"A good reputation is so important to a school teacher, Miss Stanton. I don't know what the school board is going to think about this incident."

That statement sucked her into the discussion. "They'll probably be grateful to have another student. I'm sure Mr. Gordon will be a fine contributor to the school."

"I mean about *you*, Miss Stanton." With angry energy, Mrs. Cobb balled up one of the wet towels.

Anger began to uncurl in Harriet's stomach. "What are you implying, Mrs. Cobb?"

The woman sniffed. "I'm not saying you're a fallen woman, Miss Stanton…"

Harriet tried for some levity. "I almost was. I was halfway off the cliff before Mr. Gordon grabbed me. If he hadn't, I wouldn't just be a fallen woman, Mrs. Cobb. I'd be a dead one!"

Even that didn't deter the woman. "It's *not* funny, Miss Stanton. I'm talking about how your shirtwaist was ripped through."

Should have known that wouldn't work. The woman has no sense of humor.

Harriet sobered. "That was the most frightening moment of my life. Thank you for being concerned."

The woman's bosom swelled with indignation. "It's indecent, I say. In front of Mr. Gordon. Parading that way through the town!"

The anger uncoiled. Harriet held onto her temper, but it was like trying to dam a flooded river. Any moment the dam was going to breach. "You're talking as if I was exposing myself, Mrs. Cobb. I was completely covered."

"It's indecent!"

107

A knock on the door to the shop interrupted the tart reply Harriet had on the tip of her tongue.

"Come in," Mrs. Cobb called.

Mr. Cobb stuck his head in the room. His bulbous nose twitched. "Mr. Gordon is in the store. He wants to know if Miss Stanton will join him and his nephew at Widow Murphy's for supper."

Widow Murphy was even worse than Mrs. Cobb. *Surely Ant's presence will keep her in hand.* "Tell him I'll be delighted. Actually, if he doesn't mind waiting, I'll join him in a few minutes."

Mrs. Cobb sputtered something about resting.

Harriet wanted a nap, but even more she wanted to see David. Freshening up and having the tea and cookies had restored her. "Nonsense, Mrs. Cobb. I'm fine." *Please, please stop talking before I throttle you.* She began braiding her hair.

"Miss Stanton, you're spending entirely too much time with Mr. Gordon. It isn't seemly."

Harriet's hold on her temper broke. "How dare you be so judgmental! You are *not* the arbitrator of what is right and proper. I've been helping Mr. Gordon find his kidnapped, abused nephew, an act of *kindness* and *charity*, two virtues you seem to lack!"

Mrs. Cobb drew herself up. "Well!" she harrumphed. "This behavior after all we've done for you. Boarded you. Fed you."

"I *pay* you for that."

"Yes, and where would you have been, missy, if we hadn't? Some miner's shack?"

"Perhaps. But at least it would have offered more congenial company!"

Mrs. Cobb's face turned puce. She made some gabbling noises. Failing to find words she pointed at the door. "Leave," she choked out.

Harriet tilted her chin proudly. "Gladly." Without taking the time to pin her braid up, she hurried out the door, slamming it behind her.

Over at the counter, both Mr. Cobb and Ant looked at her in astonishment. Ant had a twinkle in his eye, while Mr. Cobb looked reproving.

Ant walked over to the milliner's shelf, studied several bonnets, and selected a straw one with green velvet ribbons. He brought it to the counter and held it up to Mr. Cobb. "Add this to my bill." He set the hat on Harriet's head.

She stared up at him too astonished to say anything.

"To replace the one you lost today. And I owe you a shirtwaist too. I'll leave money for it, and you can pick it out later."

"Mr. Gordon," she protested, conscious of Mr. Cobb's avid curiosity. "That was an old straw hat, not a bonnet."

He tapped the brim. "This is what you need now."

Half chagrined, half delighted, Harriet tied the velvet ribbons under her chin.

Ant placed some money on the counter. "This should cover everything, including Miss Stanton's new shirtwaist. Keep the change for my account." He gathered up the brown paper-wrapped packages, holding one out to her. "Miss Stanton, if you'll help me carry things, I believe I'll only need to make one trip."

Conscious of the new hat, Harriet walked forward, trying not to limp, and took the parcel Ant held out. He piled two more in her arms, then swept up an armful and picked up the handle of a basket with his other hand. "Thanks for the loan of the basket, Cobb."

The man eyed Harriet as if she was a rabid dog. Without taking his gaze off her, he nodded an acknowledgment to Ant.

Ant faced the door, waiting for her to precede him.

"Come, Miss Stanton. Let's go see what David looks like clean."

Harriet marched down the aisle, ignoring the merchandise that she usually enjoyed inspecting.

Before she reached the door, Ant stepped in front of her, set down the basket, and opened it. "After you, milady."

Out in the sunlight, Harriet blinked, realizing under her new hat, her hair was trailing in a braid down her back like a girl's. *Oh, well.* She stiffened her spine, hoping she wouldn't see many people on her way to Widow Murphy's.

Ant extended his arm to her. "My lady. Shall I escort you to Mrs. Murphy's?"

Harriet blushed and set her hand in the crook of his arm.

They fell into step. Although Ant was far taller than any man she had ever walked with, he courteously kept his arm at an angle that was comfortable for her. Her sore ankle made her grateful for his support.

"Some fireworks back there."

Harriet looked up at him to see Ant's crooked grin, peaked eyebrow, and teasing brown eyes. "Oh, dear, you heard."

Ant chuckled. "I would have paid money to see the look on Mrs. Cobb's face."

"Puce and puckered."

Ant laughed again. "What a vision."

"It was, indeed," Harriet admitted ruefully. "Your invitation offered a welcome escape."

"I don't think Widow Murphy's is going to be much of an escape."

She couldn't help laughing. "My thoughts, exactly. But for right now, better than the Cobbs'."

"And later?"

She sobered. "I'll worry about later...later."

They'd reached Widow Murphy's house and went around the side to the kitchen door. Once again, Ant set down the basket so he could open the door for her.

In the middle of the kitchen, Widow Murphy sat in a chair next to the wooden tub. David crouched in the tub, his legs drawn up, arms wrapped around his knees, as the woman attacked his back with a scrub brush. He whimpered in pain, tears rolling down his face.

A wave of anger carried Harriet over the threshold, Ant close on her heels. She tossed the parcels on the table, stormed over to Widow Murphy, and grabbed the scrub brush out of her hands. "He's not the kitchen floor. You're hurting him!"

"That boy has years of ground in dirt. He needs to be scrubbed off."

"You're scrubbing off his skin along with the dirt! It's cruel."

"How dare you!" Mrs. Murphy puffed up like a rooster.

Ant came up behind them. He placed a quieting hand on Harriet's back before kneeling down next to the tub and brushing the stringy wet hair out of David's reddened eyes. "I'm sorry, David. I didn't mean for this to happen. I shouldn't have left you."

Harriet heard a whole wealth of pain in Ant's words, and her heart twisted in sympathy. "Why don't we finish giving him the bath," she said to him. "We can be *gentle.*" She shot a sharp look at the Widow.

The woman's body trembled with rage. She shook her head, and her wattle jiggled. "Don't you order me around in my own house."

Ant rose to his feet, his dark length towering over both of them. "Mrs. Murphy," he said in a firm tone. "Let's talk in the parlor."

Harriet took off her new bonnet and set it on the table. She grabbed the towel from the washstand and dipped one end in the water, then gently wiped David's tearstained face.

He scrunched his eyes shut and turned his face away, making a noise of protest.

"I know, dear. This is uncomfortable. Let's get you clean so you can get out of the bath."

He didn't turn his head.

Harriet kept up a flow of soothing one-way conversation, but to no avail. David wasn't responding. She needed to try something else.

Harriet started to hum. She soaped the towel, then ran it down David's arm.

He flinched, but didn't protest.

She glanced at his face, but was disconcerted to see how his eyes stared into nothing. She increased the level of her humming, gently washing the cloth down his body. Gradually his muscles relaxed.

The water in the tub turned darker. She needed to change it but didn't want to stop. She worried how David would react if they made him get out of the tub while they emptied and filled it again.

"David, I'm going to wash your hair. I want you to keep your head tilted back and your eyes closed."

Harriet reached over to a bowl on the table and grabbed the handle of a ladle. She dipped it in the dirty water, and then sprinkled it over his head, smoothing his hair back with the palm of her hand so no soap would drip into his eyes. Once his hair was wet, she took the bar of soap and rubbed it over his head, then worked it through the long strands. Then she rinsed the soap out.

David started to shiver.

He probably needed another soaping and rinsing, but he was clean enough. He could always take another bath tomorrow.

With a pang, she realized she wouldn't be here to give him one. Maybe she should have Ant take him to the bathhouse, although from the rumors she'd heard about the place, maybe that wasn't a good idea either. Ant would just have to do the bathing himself.

CHAPTER TEN

Knowing he was leaving his nephew in good hands, Ant led Mrs. Murphy into the painfully clean parlor, as sparsely decorated as the Cobbs' was ornate. He turned to face her, holding onto his temper as if damming up a stream.

Charm, Gordon. Use charm. Once, he'd possessed that ability in abundance. Overabundance, actually, considering some of the escapades he'd engaged in during his younger years. Just that thought was enough to lighten his anger. Not much, but a little.

"Mrs. Murphy," he said in a manner so smooth you could skid on it. "I know—"

"Don't you try to bamboozle me, Mr. Gordon. I don't run a lodging house for boys."

So much for my charm.

"David's been through a horrible experience. Actually, several years of abuse. I appeal to your sense of Christian charity, Mrs. Murphy. The boy needs food and shelter. It will only be a few days, while I figure out what to do."

Her expression remained mulish.

So much for Christian charity.

"I'll make it worth your while, Mrs. Murphy. Just for a few days."

"Three, Mr. Gordon. Three days. And I want *triple* my regular room and board."

"Then we have an agreement. You will be...." He was going to say *kind,* but didn't think the woman had any caring blood running through her veins. "You'll be... *accommodating* to David."

She gave a sharp nod that bounced her wattle. "I'll be in the garden until you finish bathing the boy," she said, each word sharp. "Then I'll git the meal together. I've got venison stew cooking on the stove. Bread's baked, although," she grimaced, "it's no longer a whole loaf. I've already made a lemon cake from California lemons."

Ant gave her a slight bow. "I think your lemon cake will be a treat for David. One he hasn't had in several years. For that matter, it's been quite a while since *I've* had lemon cake, so I'll look forward to it."

Her face didn't soften, and she left the room.

Old besom. Ant took a moment to take several breaths and calm down. He and David had a reprieve. Hopefully, that would be enough.

∽

Widow Murphy stomped into the kitchen.

Ant followed her, hoping that Harriet had things well in control with David.

Without a word, the woman stormed to the door, took a battered straw hat from a peg on the wall, and plopped it on her head. Then she continued out the door.

Harriet, crouched down by the tub, looked up in inquiry at him.

"She's letting us stay here for three more days."

"How did you accomplish that?"

"Judicious bribery."

She laughed.

Seeing Harriet smile for the first time lightened a bit of the heaviness and guilt that Ant had carried with him all day.

Harriet tilted her head toward the stove. "We're going to need clean water. Check the temperature. If the water is too hot, add some cold."

Ant hurried to obey.

They worked together, sometimes fumbling, to get David cleaned, rinsed, dried, and dressed in his new clothes. He didn't help, just moved his limbs like a marionette whenever they told him to do something. Then Harriet combed out David's hair. "Maybe we can give him a haircut tomorrow," she said to Ant. "He's been through enough today."

Ant smiled at David. "That you have." He handed him another hunk of bread.

The boy slowly nibbled at the chunk, still staring vacantly out the window.

"Tomorrow's good." Ant tried to force some optimism into his tone. "Tomorrow will be a better day."

"Well, it certainly couldn't be worse," she retorted.

Shame coiled around his gut. Before he could say anything, a knock sounded on the door.

Ant opened it to see Dr. Cameron, dressed in a black Prince Albert coat, standing with a leather satchel in his hand. Ant had met the doctor during his quest to find David and had formed a good impression of the man. His blue eyes looked tired, but his cheerful smile with the crooked teeth banished the signs of fatigue.

"I'm told you've found your nephew and wanted me to examine him?" he said in a Scottish brogue.

"Please come in." As the doctor stepped inside, Ant continued, "I'd also like you to examine Miss Stanton, who was attacked today."

Harriet shot him a sharp look. "I'm fine!"

Doctor Cameron set his bag on the table next to Harriet's bonnet. He took his hat off, and then dropped it next to the bag. He ran his hand through his red hair. His curls sprang up. "How about I see to David first, Miss Stanton, and you can fill me in later on what happened and let me be the judge."

Harriet grudgingly acquiesced.

All this time, David sat in the chair, like a stick figure, staring out the window. Only the tenseness of his posture betrayed any emotion.

Dr. Cameron fished a hard candy out of his sagging pocket, walked over and crouched down in front of David, eye level to the boy. "David, laddie. I'm Doctor Cameron." He held the sweet up to David's face. "I'm here to see how you're doing. Can you tell me if anything hurts?"

David didn't move. Nor did he look at the doctor.

Dr. Cameron pressed the candy into David's hand. "You can eat that later."

The boy's fingers closed around it.

Ant gestured to David. "He's been like that the whole time. Hasn't said a word."

The doctor ran his hands over David's arms and down his torso.

David winced.

"He has a bruise there," Harriet offered. "I saw it when I bathed him."

The doctor unbuttoned David's shirt, and he visually examined the bruise. "I'm going to press on you there, David. It will hurt, but I need to know if you have broken ribs." The doctor followed his words with his fingers.

David shrank away, giving a little mew of pain.

"Not broken," Dr. Cameron said in a cheerful tone. "Now for your legs." He ran his hands down David's legs." He peered into David's eyes, and took a metal tongue depressor out of his bag and looked down his throat. Standing, he ran his hands over David's scalp. He patted David on the head before turning to Ant.

The doctor pointed to the parlor door. "Why don't we talk in there? Miss Stanton, if you'd keep an eye on the boy?"

Harriet sent David a warm smile. "Both eyes."

The men went into the other room, and Dr. Cameron lost his cheerful air. "That laddie's been dreadfully abused." The doctor's accent thickened. "If that father of his wasn't dead, I'd be tempted to take my buggy whip to him."

"I believe the first honors would have gone to me, Doctor."

"Tell me what happened."

Ant related the story. Even the retelling was enough to make his muscles tight.

Dr. Cameron reached up and clasped Ant's shoulder. "It's hard for a parent when something happens to his child."

"I'm not his parent."

"You are now."

Ant digested that thought. It formed a lump in his stomach.

"He's obviously malnourished. He's been mistreated, but physically, with some good food in him, he'll fill out."

"What about talking?"

The doctor hesitated. "David's been through a lot, but I don't find a bump on his head to indicate an injury. I believe it will take time. Perhaps when he feels safe, he'll come around."

"You're sure?"

Dr. Cameron gave him a wry glance. "Like I said. Give him time." The doctor dropped his hand from Ant's shoulder.

"I do na advise moving him though. The laddie's been through enough."

"I wanted to take him back to New York."

"Nor do I advise travel and a big city life for the lad. At least not for a while. Let him get his bearings, then we'll see."

Ant clenched his fist at the news, and then relaxed it.

"As for Miss Stanton," the doctor continued. "It doesn't seem as if she's injured. So I won't push to examine her."

"She's a stubborn woman. A little mule."

The doctor laughed. "That she is. However, our Miss Stanton needs every bit of that stubbornness to be a good schoolteacher."

"Then she must be an exceptional one," Ant said wryly.

"Oh, yes. The very best." Dr. Cameron tilted his head toward the door. "Shall we join them?" He walked to the door.

Once inside the kitchen, the doctor gave Harriet another opportunity to talk to him, which she rejected, careful not to look at Ant.

Stubborn little mule.

"How's Mrs. Cameron doing?" Harriet asked the doctor, obviously trying to switch his attention elsewhere.

The man's tired face lit up. "She's in the time of bending over the chamber pot in the morning. But as far as I can tell, she's healthy."

"That's wonderful. I'll have to go visit her."

"She'll love the company."

The doctor glanced at Ant. "This is our miracle baby. We've been married nigh on ten years, and like Abraham and Sarah, had given up hope."

Ant felt a twinge of jealousy, which surprised him. He'd never before thought of having babies. *Is life passing me by while I gather the ruined shards of my past?*

Harriet picked up the doctor's hat and held it out to him. "Do you want a girl or boy?"

"A healthy babe is all we pray for. And a safe delivery." He took the hat from her. "However, I think we'll have a boy. I have six brothers and Mrs. Cameron has five. Nary a sister in the bunch. No nieces. Only nephews."

Harriet shook her head. "Your mother must have had her hands full."

"That she did. I was the eldest, so I had my hands full too."

"I can't imagine having brothers. I just have one sister." Her expression turned wistful. "She married and moved with her husband to Kentucky." She shrugged. "At least we exchange letters."

"We do, too." Doctor Cameron placed his hat on his head. "My youngest brother has recently finished medical school in Edinburgh. He'll be joining me in Sweetwater Springs."

Ant's interest quickened. If the town could support two doctors it was far larger than he'd suspected. "Do you have a big enough practice for both of you to make a living?"

Dr. Cameron shrugged. "Probably not. I know we could help more people, though. It will do Angus good to practice frontier medicine, although I'm sure he'll be shoving all sorts of new-fangled medical notions my way."

Ant handed Dr. Cameron some money.

The doctor tucked the money into his pocket and shot a knowing glance at Harriet. "You come on by if you need to see me...or to talk."

"I will." She opened the door for him. When it closed, she leaned her back against the wood, and gave Ant a wary glance.

"I wish you would have let him examine you."

Harriet huffed in exacerbation. "I'm *quite* well. And that's my last word." She walked over to David.

Ant held up his hands in surrender.

The door flew open, and in stomped the widow, her dirty hands full of carrots. She dumped them in a basket on the shelf near the washbasin, and then proceeded to wash and dry her hands, although she had to hunt around for a fresh towel, scolding under her breath.

Briskly she directed them to help her set out the food. A general couldn't have commanded his troops better. Harriet lifted down white china plates from a plain wooden china cabinet. Ant took food out of the icebox and pie safe. Mrs. Murphy did the rest. Soon, they were sitting down to the meal.

Ant had been prepared to keep David from wolfing down his food, but instead, the boy ate like a mannequin, not seeming to taste anything. Although once, from the corner of his eye, Ant thought he'd seen a look of satisfaction cross David's face, but the expression passed so quickly he couldn't be sure.

After a few attempts at conversation on Harriet's part, they lapsed into awkward silence. The food was good. Ant had to give the widow credit for her cooking and house-keeping skills, the only favorable things about her. After a small slice of cake, Ant finally surrendered to the uncomfortable feeling building within him. He needed a few quiet minutes to think.

Knowing he was acting rudely, he excused himself by saying he needed to check on Shadow and left David and the women to finish the widow's lemon cake. He only took a few steps outside and stopped under the window of Widow Murphy's parlor.

Overhead, an almost-full moon gave off enough light to see vague details of the town. The breeze carried a faint whiff of horse manure and dust from the street. He turned to the back of the house, looking past the garden and the street behind. He spared a glance for the tall, dark shape of Banker Livingston's house, downstairs windows alight, set back from the street and towering over the rest of the homes in the area. Then, he stared blankly off into the darkness, trying to wrap his mind around the idea that his life had changed today, and not the way he'd expected it to.

For two years, Ant had focused exclusively on his quest to find David. He thought recovering his nephew and revenging Emily would release the knot of anger that had settled in his stomach after his sister's murder. He'd rescue David and all would be well. Perhaps not well, he amended. Not with David orphaned in the worst possible way. But uncle and nephew would be reunited—a joyful scene that he'd imagined too many times to count.

Now, instead of the happy ending he'd assumed he'd find when he'd accomplished his goal, and a speedy return to his old life, he had a whole new set of problems. *And no answers.*

He heard the door open. Quiet footsteps and the silent swish of a skirt told him one of the women had followed him outside. He didn't have to turn to know his schoolmarm had joined him, but he did anyway, surprised by the feeling of comfort her presence brought him.

Harriet had draped a shawl she must have borrowed from Mrs. Murphy over her shoulders, and stood hugging the ends around her body, as if uncertain about her welcome. "Widow Murphy gave David another piece of cake. Guess she figures as long as you're paying for it, she can be generous."

"That's the first sharp thing I've ever heard you say about anyone."

"I'm still angry with her for how she treated some of my students a few weeks ago. She caused great pain to them and their family and friends. I know I'll have to work on forgiving her, but I'm not quite there yet. But that's a story for another time." She stepped closer. "Actually, I'm also angry at you."

"Me?"

"For not telling me the truth about Lewis."

"I didn't think you'd go hightailin' after him alone," he chided, dropping his hands on her shoulders. "Good God, woman, what were you thinking? That man would have taken advantage of you, then murdered you like he did my sister. He would have tossed your body over the cliff without giving two thoughts to it."

In the moonlight, he could see the blood drain from her face and cursed his loose tongue.

"He murdered your sister? David's mother?"

"Yes."

"Why didn't you tell me?"

Hoping not to answer the question, he barreled on with the story. "Then Lewis took David and fled before he could be arrested. You can see why it was so important to get my nephew back before his father harmed him or he became steeped in vice from growing up with that blackguard."

"Oh, that poor boy."

"I think David witnessed the murder. Or at least saw his mother's body. There were small bloody footprints next to Lewis' big ones."

"What he's been through," she whispered. Then her voice sharpened. "But that doesn't excuse you not telling me."

Ant took a long, drawn breath and ran his hand over his head. "You're right. I've kept as close to the ground as possible for someone as big as me. It's a salacious tale. I learned early on that if I told one person, it often spread through the town. Lewis would hear word of it and light out with David before I even knew he was there."

"But you could have trusted me," she said, disappointment in her voice.

"It wasn't you, Harriet. I couldn't take a chance on David's life. I wouldn't put it past Lewis to kill David, just to keep him out of my hands."

124

Her hand flew to cover her mouth. She stood there, obviously taking in what he'd said. "What an *evil* man. My feelings about his death were all mixed up before this, but now I'm relieved that neither David nor anyone else will ever be harmed by him."

The fierceness in her voice caused a wave of emotion to flood through him. He half turned away from her and glanced at the moon.

"Ant, are you all right?"

No, I'm not all right. Not that I would admit it. "Harriet, I don't know what to do. David's so…" He spread his hands in a helpless gesture. "It never occurred to me that my own nephew wouldn't recognize me. Instead see me as a stranger and a threat."

"Today was upsetting for you both."

Upsetting wasn't the word. David's rejection caused a pain deep in his gut. What his nephew must have been through to withdraw inside that frozen shell.

Just thinking about what the boy had experienced send a surge of anger through him. If his brother-in-law were standing in front of him, he'd take pleasure from grabbing the man by the throat and slowly choking the life out of him.

Harriet placed a reassuring hand on his arm.

Ant tried to shake off his anger and form words to describe his concern for his nephew. He wanted her opinion, for he certainly didn't know anything about children, especially damaged ones. "David hasn't said one word yet. To me. To anyone. And the look in his eyes is positively eerie. He seems like he's gone away within himself."

She squeezed his arm. "My uncle fought for the North in the Civil War and liked to tell us stories. He and his boyhood friend, Jimmy, signed up in the very beginning. As he put it, 'two still-wet-behind-the-ears boys barely old enough to squeak past enlistment age.'"

Ant nodded for her to go on.

"They were so proud of their ill-fitting new uniforms. Bragged about what they'd do to Jonnie Reb. Until their first battle. Bull Run. They'd never been so scared in their lives."

"I'm sure that was just the first time."

She grimaced. "Yes. Uncle Ed said that battles became more familiar, but never less scary."

"Go on."

"After Bull Run, Uncle Ed saw a blank look on Jimmy's face. His eyes looked empty. He became uncharacteristically quiet. Wasn't the same. My Uncle described him as looking as if his soul had fled from his body. Uncle Ed thought it would wear off but it didn't."

"What happened?"

"When Jimmy did talk, he kept saying he wanted to go home. But Uncle Ed knew that would make him a deserter. He'd be in worse trouble. So my uncle persuaded him to stay. He died in the next battle. Uncle Ed always blamed himself for that."

Ant stroked his chin. "So you're saying fear from the experiences David's been through has caused that empty expression, and that it might not go away?"

She nodded. "Or at least will take some time to heal. But you'll give him the security he needs, Ant."

"Will I?"

"You sound doubtful."

"I am...ill-equipped...."

"What did you expect to do with David after you found him?"

"You mean after I killed his father?"

She frowned at him. "I didn't quite mean that."

"I'm serious, Harriet. That was the plan." He held his breath, waiting for her reaction.

She pursed her lips. "I never thought I'd feel this way about another living soul, but I think I would make the same decision if I had to protect that child from his father."

Relieved, Ant released his breath. "Now to answer your question...I planned to spend a couple of months with David and then send him to boarding school. While he was in school, I could travel where I needed and still report for the paper. Come home at school breaks."

"I don't think your plan's going to work, Ant."

"I realize that now."

"David won't be ready for boarding school for a long time...if ever. He'll need to be around you...become acquainted with you again." She stretched her arm to indicate the town. "Stay in familiar territory. Learn that he's safe."

Ant rubbed a hand over his face. "I'll have to give up reporting."

"Maybe give up being a foreign correspondent, but couldn't you write from here?"

"About what?" Ant said, an edge in his tone. "The latest saloon brawl?"

Harriet looked as if he had slapped her, but before he could apologize, she snapped back. "Write a book!"

The kitten had her claws out. In the light of the moon, he could see how annoyance brought a becoming flush to her cheeks and sparked her eyes. *She's pretty when she's angry. Fighting with her would definitely have some benefits.* The thought mellowed Ant's ill-humor. He grinned at her. "I was a dashing war correspondent. I hate to give that up."

She narrowed her eyes at him.

He held up his hands in a placating gesture. "All right. Maybe not a *war* correspondent because officially they weren't *wars*. Clashes actually."

Harriet raised her brows. "You were the dashing clashes correspondent?"

"Yes, indeed. The skirmishes were not important to anyone but those involved. Some noble would get greedy and try to annex his neighbor, who wouldn't be pleased at the idea of relinquishing part of his land. I'd write a long story and the paper would maybe print an inch, if that. Actually, Europe during the last few years has been remarkably peaceful. I had better luck writing about the news in the capital cities. Americans love to read about nobility and royalty."

"Sounds interesting." Harriet's voice sounded wistful. "I still think you should write a book."

"Writing books is for fuddy-duddy college professors."

She playfully shook her head. "You're definitely not fuddy-duddy."

"At least you didn't say, I'm definitely not dashing."

She swatted his arm.

"Sorry, Harriet, I'm not interested in writing a book." Yet even as he said the words, a faint memory came to him, of the joy of creating stories and writing poetry before his stepfather had beaten that nonsense out of him. He wrenched his mind back to the here and now.

"Why don't you start a newspaper? We could certainly use one." She drew herself up. "I could contribute."

He seized on the idea as a way to get away from the thought of writing a book. "You could, could you?" He made his voice sound teasing. "What?"

"My poetry."

"No poetry!" Just the idea brought back bad memories.

Harriet shifted away from him, a look of fear on her face.

Ant cursed his sharpness. A man had violated her today. She needed gentleness from him. Instead he stomped on her suggestions like they were cockroaches. He wanted to reach out and take her shoulders, drawing her closer, but he didn't dare touch her. He couldn't bear to feel her flinch under his hands. "What if you wrote a column?" He made sure to keep his tone mild.

Curiosity banished the fear from her face. "Maybe the doings at the school?"

Ant shook his head. "I can see the headline now," he said, careful to sound teasing and not critical. He moved his hand through the air as if framing a headline. "Sweetwater Springs Students Recite Shakespeare."

Harriet placed her hands on her hips. "I'll write columns that will appeal to women."

Ant's amusement became genuine. He couldn't resist. "Housekeeping tips?"

She wrinkled her nose. "Perhaps, but women are interested in more than housekeeping, although keeping a family fed and clothed takes up most of a woman's time. Then there's shepherding the education, morals, and values of her youngsters. Making her home, no matter if it's a hut or a mansion as attractive as she can contrive, tending the garden and livestock—"

He reached out and tweaked her nose. "I'm sure you're quite capable of writing something that will appeal to my female readers."

"Then you'll do it? Start a newspaper?"

His expression sobered. "I'll do some thinking on it. See how it goes with David over the next days."

"Wonderful! I hope you give the school a free subscription. Perusing the newspaper may appeal to some of the students who aren't very interested in reading books."

Ant wanted nothing more than to saddle up Shadow and head the horse toward New York and his familiar life. Yet he'd given up that life two years ago to find David.

Harriet gave him an understanding smile.

He reached for her hand and brought it to his lips. "Thanks for being my wise counselor."

She slowly pulled her hand back, an adorable look of confusion on her face.

There might be some benefits of staying in Sweetwater Springs, after all.

"Anytime, Ant. Anytime."

She tucked her shawl tighter around her. "I'd better go say good-night to David and thank Mrs. Murphy for dinner."

As Ant escorted Harriet back into the house, he couldn't help wondering if he was considering staying in Sweetwater Springs because of David or because of one attractive schoolteacher?

CHAPTER ELEVEN

Ant awoke with a sharpness that took him from sleep to fully alert. *David!* He rolled over to check on his nephew, who slept between him and the wall. Last night David had scooted as far away from him as possible, resisting sleep to watch Ant with wide, wary eyes.

Ant had pretended to read a book by the lamplight, hoping that David would relax if he thought his uncle's attention was elsewhere. But it didn't work. The boy had fought to stay awake. His battle revealed as much to Ant as if David had begun talking and told him the whole story. Ant knew David hadn't slept in safety since his mother died, and, knowing how Lewis abused Emily when in a drunken rage, perhaps not even then.

Ant could only pray that Lewis had only used his hands on the boy. Just the thought of anything worse turned his stomach.

He raised himself on his elbow to better see David's face in the faint light of dawn. David was still tucked into the corner, his arms and legs tight together. His sleeping posture had changed from the little boy sprawl he remembered. Even while asleep, David had to protect himself. The ache in Ant's gut hardened.

David's face, relaxed in sleep, was still the one Ant remembered, although not as childish. The plump cheeks and rounded jaw of a seven-year-old had been replaced by those of a narrow high-cheekboned youth, even though David was only nine. *Aged before his time.* He wanted to brush the hair out of the boy's eyes, but didn't dare risk waking him.

Ant was so damned grateful he had found the boy and didn't have to murder Lewis. At the same time, he felt as if a huge burden had settled on his shoulders. Far greater than he'd expected.

Ant rolled to his back and stared at the beams of the ceiling, wondering what in the hell he was going to do now. Should he start a paper, as Harriet had suggested? He had the funds from the inheritance from his grandfather. Not the fortune it had been in his grandfather's day—thanks to his stepfather getting his greedy paws on some of it—but it was more than enough to establish himself in Sweetwater Springs. Although he would have to make the paper a going concern because the money wouldn't last forever.

His mind raced, puzzling out how to make it work, where they'd live. Dozens of important decisions.

Weighty decisions. Time to seek the advice of someone who must know this town inside and out—Reverend Norton. Ant had never been one for church-going, although he'd trailed Isabella to Mass because it made her happy. But, in Ant's opinion, that didn't count. A service in Latin, with the sermon in an unintelligible foreign language, wasn't the same as one in English—providing, of course, the sermon was a good one.

In spite of the Reverend Norton's Calvinist preacher looks, Ant suspected the minister wasn't the fire and brimstone type. At least that's what he hoped. He and David would be sitting in a pew every Sunday, regardless of how Ant felt about it. His nephew had to wash off the taint of his father. He wanted David to grow up to be a solid citizen. Religion should help that. Plus, social life in a small town often revolved around the church. He needed to be part of it all...for David's sake.

With an unhappy exhale, Ant inched back the covers and eased out of bed. David still slept like the proverbial log, no doubt worn out from yesterday, and would probably do so for several hours. He hoped Harriet also found comfort in sleep and wasn't tormented by nightmares.

Dressing in silence, except for his boots, Ant tiptoed out of the room, slowly closing the door behind him. He would have liked to leave a note saying where he was going and that he'd be back soon. David had learned to read a bit before his kidnapping, but how much the boy had retained was a mystery he'd solve later.

Ant tiptoed downstairs and into the kitchen. Although he wished he could linger in the quiet kitchen, boiling some coffee and toasting some bread, he wanted to be back before David woke up.

Yesterday in a brief after supper-visit, Reverend Norton had assured Ant that he was an early riser and had welcomed him to drop by whenever he felt the need. As Ant hiked down the street, he saw the town start to stir to life. A few people waved, and he realized how many names he already knew. Not that that was uncommon. He got acquainted right quick when he was turning a place upside down in his hunt for his nephew. But in this town, he felt more of a connection to the people he'd met, probably because this was where he'd found David, or because he thought the two of them might put roots down here.

Because you're sweet on a little schoolmarm, whispered a chiding voice in his head.

I'm not sweet on her, he argued. Then he reconsidered. *Well, maybe I am. But that doesn't mean anything. I've been attracted to women before.*

You're sweet on her. That's different.

Maybe a bit, he conceded. *But I'm not making a decision to stay here because of a kitten of a woman with fine gray eyes. I have to think about what's best for David.*

The argument had carried him down the street and around and behind the church to the tiny parsonage. With relief, he saw Mrs. Norton sweeping the front porch.

She noticed him coming and set aside her broom, wiping her hands down the apron covering most of her dark blue dress.

"Good morning, Mrs. Norton. I hope I'm not too early to call."

"Not at all, my dear Mr. Gordon." She beamed at him, making the wrinkles on her face crinkle. "I've been thinking of you and David. Woke me up early. Apparently Reverend Norton felt the same. We'd welcome a chance to talk to you further. Won't you come in?"

Ant stepped into a shallow hall.

"Come into the kitchen, Mr. Gordon." She waved a hand to the door on the right. "Mr. Norton is praying in his study. Let's just give him a couple more minutes."

"Of course."

"Would you like some coffee, Mr. Gordon?"

"I think that's an answer to my prayer, Mrs. Norton."

She swatted his arm. "I'm sure having *your nephew* safe is the answer to your prayer."

"Most definitely. Perhaps, I should say that coffee is the answer to the wish I made when I tiptoed through the kitchen this morning."

"A wish I am able to command."

They entered the small kitchen, dominated by the big black cast iron stove and a plank table. Ant didn't pay attention to his surroundings. His nose drew him to the scent of coffee and baking, and his stomach rumbled. He'd been too unsettled last night to do justice to Widow Murphy's stew. Embarrassed, he pretended he didn't have a drum beating in his middle.

"Would you like some hot biscuits to go with your coffee?" Mrs. Norton chirped.

"I think my stomach's given you the answer to that question, ma'am."

She looked amused, then deftly took the tin coffee pot and poured some coffee into a cup. She reached into a pie safe and took out a plate of biscuits. "Good thing I made an extra batch this morning. I had a feeling we'd need them. A man of your size will take some filling up."

"Don't worry about the fillin' up part, ma'am. Mrs. Murphy will have breakfast for me. Just something to take the edge off will be mighty fine."

Mrs. Norton handed him the cup and saucer, then motioned him to take a seat at the table. With deft motions, she slid the biscuits into a round Indian basket with a napkin inside, handed him a plate, utensils, and another napkin, and then set the basket in front of him, followed by a tiny crock of butter and a jar of some purple preserves.

"They're still warm. Eat up, Mr. Gordon."

He did just that. The preserves turned out to be saska-toon, and the light rolls, dripping with butter and preserves, went down with as much speed as was polite. He spared a thought for David and how the boy would probably like a similar breakfast, although, judging from the last few days, it would be porridge—filling, but not like this. He made a mental note to see if the mercantile carried honey. If not, he'd bring the widow some brown sugar.

He heard the sound of the study door opening, and then Reverend Norton walked into the kitchen. Clad in a worn gray sack coat and vest over a white shirt and black trousers, he seemed more approachable without his old frock coat on.

"Mr. Gordon." He shook hands with Ant. "I'm particu-larly glad to see you. You and your nephew have just figured into my prayers."

In spite of not being a church-going man, Ant couldn't help but feel a warmth in his gut at the preacher's words. For so long, he had been the only one concerned about David. And there was no family left who'd care about him either. He'd cut his ties with his friends and colleagues…not really cut so much as left them behind, assuming he would pick them up again when he returned to New York. Yet the genuine caring in the minister's voice unfurled a heart root that planted itself in the soil of Sweetwater Springs. Ant almost snorted at the fancy analogy. *Shades of Kathleen Pickering, the societal columnist. I never could abide the woman, and now I sound like her.*

"When you finish eating, why don't you come into my study, Mr. Gordon?"

Ant swallowed another bite. "Have you had anything to eat yet?"

The reverend gave his wife a loving smile. "My help-mate encouraged me to break my fast before my prayers. As always, I followed her wisdom."

Mrs. Norton's withered cheeks turned pink. She made a shooing motion. "Get along, you two. I'm sure Mr. Gordon is anxious to return to his nephew."

Reverend Norton nodded. "You finish your food, Mr. Gordon. I'll be in my study."

Ant swallowed the last few wonderful bites and thanked Mrs. Norton, then left the room. Inside the book-filled study, Ant found Reverend Norton sitting at a big wooden desk that took up much of the room, loose papers and some tracts scattered around him. He perused a paper that looked like a letter.

"I hope I'm not disturbing you, Reverend."

"Not at all." He folded the paper and set it under a book on his desk. "I was just reading a letter from my son. Until a few months ago, Joshua was a missionary in Cameroon. Then his wife died, and he and his son left to come back to America. They are presently visiting for a while with his wife's family in Nebraska, and then they will continue on to Sweetwater Springs."

"You must be excited."

"Most certainly. We've never met our grandson, Micah. He's David's age."

"After Cameroon, Sweetwater Springs will be quite different. Perhaps he and David can adjust together."

"They will both have their challenges."

"Will your son and grandson live with you?"

The minister gave a rueful glance around the small room. "Yes." He shrugged. "Somehow the Lord will provide.

But enough of my family." He gestured to a chair, laden with books. "Just set them on the floor and tell me how things are going with David."

"On the surface, well." Ant ticked off his fingers. "He's safe. He's clean. He's fed. He's clothed."

"Those are things that must be taken care of before you can see to his healing."

"The doc says he's malnourished, but otherwise he's well."

"I mean to his inner healing."

"That's why I'm here. Originally, I'd planned to take David back with me to New York. But he's in no condition to travel, to be thrust into city life."

"Why don't you two stay here in town?"

"I'm considering it."

"I think you'll be welcomed. It's a good community. I think both you and David will be able to put down roots."

Ant remembered the fanciful image he'd thought of earlier. "Perhaps," he said in a noncommittal manner.

"The town, like the people who reside in it, has its faults. I think you may have already encountered some of them."

"If you mean Widow Murphy and the Cobbs, I'll say yes."

Reverend Norton's expression didn't change, but his blue eyes twinkled. "In any town there are people who are our crosses to bear. But what we do have in Sweetwater Springs…"

"Even with your crosses?"

"Even with our crosses…. What we do have is grit and heart. Two things you and that boy of yours are going to need in full measure."

Ant let out a discouraged sigh and dropped into the chair. "I don't know that I have enough of either."

"Son, I don't know that anyone thinks they have enough. Both are qualities that take patience and persistence, especially during times of great difficulty."

"This seems like one of those times." Ant rose from his chair and paced the room. Four steps could take him from end to end. "Yet that notion also seems ridiculous. I have David. He's safe... Great difficulty was when I found my murdered sister's body and realized that David was gone. Great difficulty was times I had to endure in my two-year search for my nephew. This *shouldn't* be a time of great difficulty."

"But it is," the minister said, compassion in his voice. He waited a beat. "I'm sorry to hear about your sister. When a loved one is murdered, we feel a grave sense of injustice and anger.... Sometimes that anger can interfere with our mourning."

Ant felt himself close up. "The murderer, David's father, is dead. It's time to focus on the future, not the past."

Like a snowy owl, Reverend Norton watched him with wise eyes.

Ant almost came close to pouring out everything, but he settled for a brief statement. He rubbed his hands over his eyes. "I'm thinking of staying here. I'm just not sure that's the best thing."

Reverend Norton held up one bony hand. "Let me get my helpmate in here. When it comes to children, I value her advice." He paused. "When it comes to *anything*, I value her advice. Although, I'm told I frequently cut her off in my enthusiasm to voice my opinion." He shook his head, as if thinking. "We'll talk about it, then we'll pray about it. Hopefully, both will help you find your answers."

~

David awoke slowly, half conscious of the softness of the bed and the warmth of the coverings. In a moment his mother would come and urge him to get up but for now, he'd snuggle into... He went under again, and only later did he gradually float into wakefulness.

A sharp feeling of fear propelled him into alertness, and he bolted upright, fists raised in protection, looking for his pa, prepared for the blow that would knock him off the pallet if he hadn't scrambled off beforehand.

The unfamiliar room made him dizzy, and he glanced wildly around before the events of yesterday caught up with him. He wasn't on a hard pallet on the floor of the shack, but in a real bed.

Since he was alone in the room, David relaxed his fists and leaned a shoulder against the wall covered in little flowers. Tears choked his throat, and he tried to hold onto them. For a long time now, he'd managed to keep from crying, no matter what his pa did to him. But yesterday unsettled him somehow. That bath...remembering made him burn with embarrassment.

These tears were different. They wanted to come from a place deep inside himself. He thought if he let them up, he'd never stop crying. *Be a big baby.* He had himself two choices. He could drift away, or he could run.

Today, feeling stronger than he had yesterday...than he had in a long time...he chose to run.

Popping out of bed, David realized he was still clad in a man's white shirt that hung almost to his ankles. He lunged for his new clothes, folded neatly on a wooden chair backed against the wall at the foot of the bed. For a moment he paused, running his hand over the stiff new material. He brought the blue shirt to his face and sniffed the crispness, feeling a tingly bit of happy in the pit of his stomach.

Disconcerted by his reaction, David dropped the shirt back on the chair. He fumbled with the stiff buttons of the man's shirt, so different from the two that had remained on his old one, the thread holding them to the cloth so limp that the buttons sagged when pushed through the buttonhole.

David let the big man's shirt drop to the floor, and he scrambled into the new clothes. He debated about the boots. He'd gone barefoot ever since his shoes had worn out at the end of the winter, but the shiny brown leather convinced him to pull on thick socks without holes, then the boots.

Once dressed, David clomped down the stairs and through the kitchen. He would have stopped to snatch something to eat, but the old biddy set up a squawk when she saw him and flapped her apron at him, just like an angry chicken. So he kept on going. He ran into the street, avoiding the few people he saw. The dust puffed with each step.

David felt a slight regret for ruining the shininess of his boots, but even that didn't stop him. He kept on running.

∼

After an almost sleepless night, in which her mind refused to let go of the visions of her assault, Harriet dressed slowly. Her ankle ached, and she felt tired, sore, and reluctant to go downstairs and face the Cobbs, as well as everyone else. Even the treat of picking out a new shirtwaist wasn't enough to prod her through the door.

She wondered if anyone would miss her if she stayed in her room and read. *The Count of Monte Cristo* beckoned to her. After all, she hadn't touched that book since she'd joined forces with Ant to find David. It had been a tumultuous few days. *I deserve some solitude.*

Harriet almost sat down in the wooden chair by the window. She'd made a cushion for that chair in the first few days she'd lived with the Cobbs. It was her favorite place to read. Now she longed with all her heart to plop down, well, ladies didn't plop…gracefully seat herself…and shut out the world through reading a book.

But she doubted even revolutionary France would be enough of an escape from Sweetwater Springs. Even if she could immerse herself in the story, she'd still have to return to her surroundings when she stopped reading.

Besides, she wanted to know how David was doing. Not that she could go to Widow Murphy's to find out. After yesterday, with Mrs. Cobb's insinuations about her reputation, Harriet had to tread carefully. Continued close association with Ant might, indeed, cause gossip and jeopardize her job. Besides, news of David's condition would be all over town today. *The Cobbs probably already know. I won't need to go over there—won't need to see him…see them.* The thought hurt.

Her heart sank to her knees at the thought of interacting with the Cobbs. *How can I continue to live with them?* She'd wracked her brain much of the night, trying to come up with an alternative, but couldn't see one—except for leaving Sweetwater Springs, which she didn't want to do.

Single ladies had few respectable choices in a small town. Living with the Cobbs, paying only a small room and board, allowed her to save money for her eventual home. She should really count her blessings, instead of complaining. *Nothing good ever came of complaining.* One of her mother's favorite sayings, uttered far too often, whether Harriet had actually grumbled or just expressed a wish for something her mother couldn't afford.

Harriet braced herself and reluctantly descended the stairs. She took a deep breath and walked into the kitchen.

Mrs. Cobb stood at the stove, deftly turning bacon strips in the cast iron skillet. The smell made Harriet realize how hungry she was. Mr. Cobb was already seated at the table reading the day-old newspaper that had arrived on the train.

Neither greeted her, although Mr. Cobb made a grunting acknowledgement when Harriet took her place at the table. Mrs. Cobb bustled over, the towel-wrapped handle of the iron skillet in one hand, serving spoon in the other. She scooped some scrambled eggs onto Harriet's plate, followed by two strips of bacon and a piece of toast.

Harriet ate in silence. The Cobbs sometimes spoke to each other, but didn't include her in the conversation. Harriet didn't care. She tried to ignore them in the same way they ignored her.

The name *Elizabeth Sanders* caught her attention. Mrs. Cobb started complaining about Nick's wife shipping her family's possessions from Boston to Sweetwater Springs. Mrs. Cobb seemed to think it was a deliberate slight to them.

It wasn't as if the mercantile could stock the valuable items Elizabeth had reportedly lived with.

Harriet thought her spirits couldn't sink further. But at the thought of Nick and Elizabeth, they crashed to the floor at her feet. She kept her head down, slowly eating, although the food had lost its flavor.

"Six wagons, mind you. Six!" Mrs. Cobb exclaimed. "Three more than when Trudy Flanigan came here as a mail-order bride in '86."

Mr. Cobb looked up from his paper. "Who all's driving them wagons?"

She counted them on stubby fingers. "Nick Sanders, of course. Carter. Thompson. Mack Taylor. Payne. Dunn."

He snorted. "Be a regular parade. Probably have folks come just to gawk."

Mrs. Cobb perked up. "That's right. And since folks are here, they'll probably frequent the mercantile."

Harriet's mind was full of memories, pondering the foolishness of first love. The whole time Nick was building a house on his new ranch, Harriet had fantasized about living there with him. She'd even secretly ridden over there one afternoon, stopping at the edge of the woods nearby to observe the house. In her mind, she'd added a white picket fence with rose bushes trailing over it. She'd made curtains for the windows and planted a vegetable garden in the back. She had her own chicken house off to the side of the garden. She'd loved Nick's house as much as she'd loved him, and giving up the dream of both had been the hardest thing she'd ever done.

Harriet had forced herself to stop fantasizing once Nick and Elizabeth had married and moved into the little house.

Then the wealthy bride had commissioned a bigger house, using her funds to import carpenters and masons to build it on the hill overlooking a lake. When Harriet had heard the news, she'd felt outraged. She couldn't believe Elizabeth didn't appreciate the home Nick had built for her—one that Harriet would have given anything to have for her own. The workmen had just finished most of the new mansion, and the couple was in the process of moving in, leaving the smaller house available for their foreman and his family. Harriet wondered if anyone but her would appreciate the modest ranch house.

Mrs. Cobb sniffed. "Invited everyone to a party afterwards, too."

Harriet looked up at that comment.

Mrs. Cobb noticed and apparently condescended to talk to her. "You, too, Miss Stanton. Mrs. Sanders came by yesterday, while you were gallivanting on the mountain with Mr. Gordon."

Harriet didn't even have the heart to argue with her.

The woman gave her a sly look. "The party will be after they haul all that furniture and get it in the new house; dishes, bedding, and other things as well. I have a mind to see it." Her tone turned malicious. "Although I've heard that everything is *not* the latest style."

But I'm sure it's all in good taste.

Mr. Cobb cleared his throat. "No need for me to go. I'll stay here and mind the store."

Harriet heard what he wasn't saying. Mr. Cobb had no desire to be put to work lugging furniture.

"Then Miss Stanton and I will drive out in the buggy." Mrs. Cobb shot a spiteful glance at Harriet.

The food balled in Harriet's stomach. She didn't want to go to the party, and she certainly didn't want to travel there with Mrs. Cobb. And something else bothered her about Mrs. Cobb's intentions, although she couldn't identify what it was. She was used to the woman's critical nature, yet this felt like something more.... *It's obvious she's still angry with me, so why does she want me to go with her?*

CHAPTER TWELVE

A nt left the parsonage, strode around the church and into the street. He'd spent more time with the Nortons than he'd intended. *I hope David's still asleep. Widow Murphy will skewer me if he's anywhere near her.*

A man riding a brown Appaloosa saw him, hesitated, and then reined in. With one finger he shoved his black Stetson back a bit so Ant could see his face. "Mr. Gordon?"

"Yes." He studied the unfamiliar rider whom he didn't recognize. A younger man with green eyes, a slightly crooked nose, and freckles under his tan.

"Nick Sanders. You've met my wife, Elizabeth."

Ant recalled the beautiful blonde who'd helped him strategize where to look for David. "Pleased to meet you, Mr. Sanders. Rode out to your ranch the other day, but missed you. Met your wife, though." As Ant spoke, he wondered what there was about this man to appeal to the beautiful Elizabeth.

"Not in the habit of stopping strangers, but the word's out you've found your boy."

"Yes." Ant couldn't help but grin. "Sure did."

"We were mighty glad to hear the news."

What is it with small towns? Word of mouth spreads faster than a newspaper.

"Thank you. I appreciate your wife's help."

"You might not have heard... being so busy with your search. We're going to have a..."

A? Ant raised his eyebrow in inquiry.

"What feels like a circus is arriving tomorrow on the train."

Circus?

"But really it's the contents of my wife's former home. Almost lock, stock, and barrel. Her sister-in-law made a clean sweep." He grimaced. "My wife's happy about it though, and that makes me happy."

Ant laughed. "I'm sure it does."

Color crept up Nick's neck. "I've lined up a bunch of men with wagons to haul everything out. The wives want to get involved too." He shrugged. "The ladies have come up with the idea of an unpacking party."

And your point is?

"Afterwards food, music, dancing. You and your boy would be welcome."

Ah. Ant couldn't resist a little teasing. "So you saw me and thought, there's a fine, big fellow," he drawled. "Bet he could carry a lot. Make short work of the job so we could all get to partyin'."

Sanders flushed a little. "Yes. No," he stuttered to a stop.

Ant took pity on him. "I'll be glad to lend you my back."

"Doesn't sound neighborly, does it, to invite you to work before you even know us?"

"Sounds like the best part of neighborly, Sanders. I've seen enough of this town to know you already have plenty of people to help out. You don't need me. But the invitation is just what I need since I'm thinking of parking us in Sweetwater Springs."

The man smiled with shy charm. Ant could see how he might have won the fair Elizabeth.

"My wife will be pleased to hear you're coming."

"Sounds like your work party will be good for David."

"Guess he can carry some light packages."

Ant thought back to yesterday. Unless David had an overnight change, he wouldn't be helping. He gave a slow shake of his head. "I'd best find someone to watch him."

"I'm sure Miss Stanton will. If she's not up to it, I'm sure Mrs. Rodriguez will. She has a boy about your David's age, then went and adopted three more strays. Turned them into a good little family.

"I'll have to ask her advice. David's not comfortable with me yet. I wouldn't put it past him to hightail away."

Nick's gaze sharpened. He studied Ant as if seeing him with new eyes. "I think that might have already happened. Saw a boy heading out as I rode in." He pointed the direction. "Skinny. Looks a bit like you. Blue shirt. Didn't think anything of it. But now I realize I didn't know him, and I know most of the children hereabouts."

Ant bit off a curse. "My thanks."

He spun around, heading for the livery. Fear and anger drove him to quickly saddle Shadow, mount the horse and ride after David. Hopefully, the boy was headed for the shack he knew as home. For if he wasn't, Ant might have a hard time finding him again. And who knew what might befall a boy alone on the mountain?

∾

David had long since abandoned his socks and boots on the side of the trail. They'd rubbed blisters before he'd gone very far. Now he trotted up the trail, comfortable in bare feet, unless he stepped on a sharp rock or stick. But he had plenty of experience in picking out the smoothest ground.

He neared the clearing with the cabin he and his father had lived in, then through long practice, veered into the forest along the side, trotting up a faint game trail that he'd used on his explorations, for the first time realizing he didn't have to dread going "home." He had plenty of other things worryin' at him though, and he needed space to think—a place that didn't have big men, old biddies, and pretty schoolteachers anywhere around.

He came to the edge of the cliff, and, with a sigh of relief, set himself down, dangling his legs over the side. He studied the rocks below carefully, looking for his pa's body, half wanting to see him dead, half glad not to see any sign of him.

David allowed the sight of the water moving over rocks to calm him. As always, he came here to escape, even if he did have to eventually go back. He'd fantasized plenty about following that river and had come very close a time or two. He'd also come close to jumping, but something had always held him back. He didn't know what.

Despair settled on his shoulders, as heavy as a coat of rocks. At least with Pa, he'd known what to expect. Could avoid him most of the time. His pa rarely searched for him. He had a feeling the stranger wouldn't let him off so easy.

He needed to do something, and now was the time. For sure as shootin', the big man would find him if he stayed here long.

~

Ant stood back through the trees just far enough away to see David but not spook the boy. His hand rested on the rough bark of a pine tree. He didn't want a wrong move on his part to startle his nephew off the cliff. His heart pounded from the hurried climb from the shack to the top of the cliff and from the fear he felt just watching the skinny back of his nephew. One slip...

He made himself take some deep breaths to slow down his heart. David obviously was familiar with this spot, and he could move like a mountain goat. Charging after the boy might be the worst thing he could do. David had experienced enough anger and meanness from his father. From his uncle he'd need strength and patience.

Ant surveyed the pine needle strewn ground, searching for twigs that might snap under his feet. He had no illusions about getting into the open without David hearing him. Now would be a good time to be an Indian, wearing moccasins, able to move silently through the forest without leaving any sign of his presence. But he'd have to settle for giant feet in boots not meant for hiking.

Might as well make the attempt. By the time he reached the clearing, he knew David had heard him, but the boy didn't turn around, nor did he try to get up and run. Instead, his back stiffened, but that was the only sign that David sensed his uncle's presence.

Somehow that frightened Ant even more. *Is he thinking of going over the edge?*

Please, God. Ant wasn't a praying man. Hadn't been one since Isabella's death, but for the precious life of his nephew, he'd bargain with the Almighty.

He thought a moment. *What do I have to bargain with?* He'd already decided that he and David would be going to church on Sundays. He didn't know what else to give up. *Please, keep him rooted on that edge, and I promise I'll stay here in Sweetwater Springs.*

"David," he called softly. "It's Uncle Ant."

The boy flinched, but didn't turn.

Ant walked over until he stood next to David, then folded himself down to sit next to him. With an inward sigh, he eased his legs over the side of the cliff.

Now what?

A gentle breeze caressed his face. *Just sit here with him,* it seemed to say.

Not a bad thing to do.

Ant focused on the water far below. The scene from yesterday jumped into his mind...Lewis lying there, dead. He wondered what had become of the man's body. The searchers Mack had sent had found no sign of him. Maybe his body had washed away or a cougar dragged him off to feed her young. Ant particularly liked that idea.

An eagle soared off the cliff, not too far away from them. From the corner of his eye, he noticed David watching, but he didn't want to turn his head to see if there was any sign of life in the boy's eyes.

They sat in silence for a long time. Ant could feel his heartbeat slow and his breathing relax.

"I've been searching for you for two years, David." He made his voice gentle. "I never stopped. I'm only sorry it took me so long to find you."

David didn't say anything, but Ant felt him listening, which was a vast improvement from yesterday.

"Sometimes I just missed you and your father by days. Once…" Ant had to stop because something lodged in his throat, remembering the anger and despair he'd felt about coming so close, only to have Lewis evade him and slip out of town, stowing away, he'd later learned, in the boxcar on a train. "Once I almost had you."

David twitched a shoulder.

"I'd like you to make your home with me. I think you've already seen that you'll be well fed and have clothes. Go to school. Have friends."

The boy hunched his shoulders.

"We're going to stay here. The people are kind." He half laughed. "Well, maybe not Mrs. Murphy. But soon we'll have our own house and won't live with her. You'll even have a room all to yourself."

David's shoulders relaxed.

"I want to show you something." Ant reached in his pocket and pulled out the photograph of Emily and David." He handed it over. "Look inside."

David fingered the flap, before opening it and staring at the picture.

Ant watched him, trying to figure out what the boy was thinking.

David touched his forefinger to Emily's face.

"Your mother, Emily."

David pointed to himself in the photograph.

"That's you. You were about five."

David abruptly shut the flap and pushed the photograph at Ant.

Ant took it back. "Whenever you want to look at this, David, you let me know. Anytime you want."

The boy shook his head.

"David, you'll be safe with me. I promise."

The boy appeared to watch the river down below and didn't turn his head.

Ant suppressed a sigh. *Patience*, he reminded himself. His stomach rumbled, and he remembered the lack of breakfast.

"Bet you didn't eat before you ran off. You hungry?" Ant didn't wait for an answer. "I sure am. Let's go get us some food. I have some peppermint sticks for you. You can have them after breakfast."

David gave him a quick glance.

Ah, that got your attention.

Ant slid his backside away from the cliff and got to his feet, but he squatted down, ready to grab David if he so much as teetered. But the boy rose to his feet in a smooth motion that showed he had a lot of practice.

Ant tilted his head in the direction of the shack where he'd left Shadow. "Sooner we get going, the sooner we eat."

David nodded his understanding and led the way, his scrawny body fitting through gaps in the trees that Ant had to squeeze through or go around. As they walked across the clearing, Ant felt his stomach relax, as if a knot he hadn't known was there had untied. He'd just crossed a small bridge with David.

Just the first one, though. Just the first one.

CHAPTER THIRTEEN

Harriet stood with a group of women, elderly men, and children in the shade of the mercantile, David at her side, trying not to put weight on her bad ankle. They watched the men unload wooden crates from the train that held the possessions of Elizabeth Hamilton Sanders. An air of excitement buzzed through the crowd. Harriet doubted Sweetwater Springs had ever seen such a show. The women gossiped and kept an eye on the children so they didn't get underfoot.

Wyatt Thompson's wagon was parked on the street in front of the train depot, one of his ranch hands holding the reins of the team. Behind him and out of the way, five other wagons waited in a row. Men scurried like ants hauling crumbs, working to unload the train so it could take off.

The pile of boxes on the landing grew bigger. Harriet tried to shut out the sounds of the people around her speculating what might be in them. She didn't want to know.

"Look at the triangle shape of that box," Abe Maguire cackled. "Bet that's a piany."

Harriet wouldn't take the bet. She knew Elizabeth's family owned a piano and had no doubt that crate held it.

A frisson of envy shot through her. She'd always wanted a piano. The instrument had resided in her dream house. In her imaginings, she'd taught herself to play.

She watched Nick direct the men in what to do with the boxes. She'd never seen him in a leadership role before, and a part of her thrilled at the sight. Nor did Nick stint on doing the heavy work himself. He'd carted off so many boxes that he probably would be sore tomorrow. Elizabeth would be the lucky wife who'd rub liniment on his neck and shoulders.

Harriet's throat tightened. She forced her thoughts away from Nick and Elizabeth.

Ant appeared in the door of the boxcar, his arms around a crate. He glanced at the ramp to make sure of his footing and strode down. Instead of stopping and setting the crate with the others, he kept on going until he reached the first wagon. Then he lifted it over the side and shoved it against the seat.

There were some feminine murmurs of appreciation for his strength, and the gossip started flying. Half the women seemed frightened by his great height and dark looks. The other half tittered about his rescue of David and the rumor of his potential newspaper business. It wasn't lost on the young women and spinsters that an eligible bachelor was about to take up stakes in town. After a few remarks about Ant's husband potential, Harriet wasn't sure whether to cover her ears or David's.

She solved the problem by taking her charge and walking him across and down the street to sit by themselves on the steps of the school. They were farther away from the activity, but at least they had some peace.

Maybe by concentrating on David, she'd be able to get through this day with a minimum of heartache.

∾

Her first sight of Elizabeth's new kitchen struck Harriet speechless. The spacious interior was so much grander than she'd ever imagined, big black stove, a sink with a pump, a long, high counter, a rectangular table running down the middle, an ornate icebox and matching pie safe, and lots of cupboards. But it was the finishes—mahogany stain or clean white paint, shiny surfaces, gleaming metal as well as the sheer amount of space—that overwhelmed her. *I'd love to cook in this kitchen!*

Harriet wasn't allowed to remain awestruck for long. Pamela Carter and Samantha Rodriguez became twin whirlwinds of energy. Mrs. Carter tucked Harriet into a chair at the table to keep her off her feet, set another across from her to prop her foot on, and handed her dishes to wipe off with a dishtowel.

While the women worked, they chatted, sometimes stopping when men trudged in laden with the remaining crates. Whoever had packed them had done a good job, painting in big black letters what kind of items were inside. Unless there was *kitchen* or *dining room* written on the outside, the men kept right on going.

Much of what they carried would be stored in the attic or basement until the rest of the house was finished. Except for the kitchen, parlor, dining room, and one bedroom, much of the carved paneling and other finishing details still weren't installed. Apparently, much of the fine details such as mantelpieces and the stair rail were being made in Boston and would be shipped out and installed on site. Even the stair rail was just a crude length of wood. The focus had been to finish up the exterior before winter made working outside impossible.

Mrs. Carter unpacked the crates that the men had already pried open, and Samantha Thompson put the dishes that Harriet wiped clean into the glass-fronted cabinet in the pantry. Other women were scattered throughout the house, polishing the furniture the men unloaded, unpacking linens and making beds, cleaning the candlesticks, figurines, and other articles emerging from the boxes, and finding places to put them.

Elizabeth, who still managed to look elegant in an old blue dress, flitted back and forth throughout the house, scarcely able to take one thing out of a crate before someone called to her to come determine the placement of an article of furniture or the height she wanted a picture hung. Every time Nick entered the house, usually carrying something, he checked on his wife to make sure she wasn't lifting anything, because of her pregnancy.

At times, Harriet heard Mrs. Cobb's raised voice sounding like a general, directing her troops. Elizabeth would probably have to rearrange things after everyone left, otherwise she might end up with rooms that looked like the Cobbs' parlor.

Annie, Mrs. Carter's capable Chinese cook, had overseen the food with the help of the Carter's Indian maid, Dawn, and Millie, the wife of their foreman. Cloth-covered trestle tables creaked under the weight of platters and bowls. Between the lavish spread the Sanders had laid out and the food everyone else had brought, Harriet wondered if they shouldn't have telegraphed Fort Ellis and invited the army.

As Harriet unloaded and wiped down a beautiful set of silver, including utensils she'd never seen before and wouldn't have known how to use, serving pieces, and an elaborate tea and coffee set, she'd kept an eye on David sitting under a tree, watching the other children play a game of tag. She could see his face, and he looked so lost. It hurt her heart that he wouldn't join in.

Give him time, she reminded herself.

Now that she had Mrs. Carter and Mrs. Rodriguez to herself, she decided it would be a good time to talk about the Swensen girls and make a request for donated clothing. *Please, God, may they be generous and not angry with me.*

"Mrs. Carter, Mrs. Rodriguez, I'd like to talk to you about a family I met while Mr. Gordon and I were searching for his nephew."

Mrs. Carter stopped her unpacking. "Certainly, my dear Miss Stanton. But first, remember, I requested you to call me Pamela."

"I'm about to change from Rodriguez to Thompson anyway." Samantha wiggled her nose. "After all we went through a few weeks ago to save the boys, I think first names are appropriate."

A warm glow of friendship lit within Harriet. She smiled at the two women. "Pamela, Samantha, I met a family last week by the name of Swensen. They have a cabin on Watchtower Mountain. Do you know them, Pamela? He's Swedish. She's American. They have six daughters. The oldest, Inga, is about Christine and Sara's age, and they stair-step down to a toddler. They also have one Lizzy's age."

"I've never heard of them," Pamela said. "But how lovely that there's a girl Lizzy's age. Why don't they go to church or school?"

"They're very poor," Harriet said. "Proud. The girls are barefoot, wearing dresses that are threadbare and too small. The father doesn't want them to go to school looking like that. I assume the same is true for church."

Pamela looked at Samantha, "Would they take hand-me-downs?"

Harriet gave them a triumphant smile. "I was able to convince Mrs. Swensen that she'd be doing me a favor if she would."

Samantha laughed. "That must have taken some talking on your part, Harriet."

"I convinced her that having more girls in the classroom would be a civilizing influence on the boys."

Pamela pulled out a newspaper-wrapped bundle, unrolled the paper, to expose a cut-glass crystal vase. "Good thinking." She handed the vase to Harriet.

Harriet wiped the glass, careful not to cut herself on the sharp rim. "That's not all. I told her that Lizzy was too frail to roughhouse with the boisterous boys her age and needed a girl to play quietly with."

"That's very clever." Pamela pulled out a smaller bundle, this time wrapped in a towel. "Almost true, too. I'd *love* Lizzy to have a girlfriend her age. Even though the older children dote on her, and the boys her age are kind, it's not the same as having an equal." She unrolled the cloth, exclaimed, and held up a china shepherdess in a pink gown. "I remember this. Elizabeth's mother used to keep it on the mantel in the parlor. I wonder why she ended up in this box?"

Harriet leaned forward to study the figurine. "She's pretty."

"There should be a matching shepherd in here somewhere. Elizabeth will be so pleased when she sees this. Genia, that sister-in-law of hers, certainly divested the house of everything that belonged to her husband's parents, and everything Elizabeth had added to the decor. Except, Elizabeth tells me, the heirloom Hamilton silver." She indicated the polished tea and coffee sets, sitting on the table. "These were the newer pieces. Well, Elizabeth and Nick benefit from Genia's bad taste."

Harriet set the cleaned vase on the table. "Would you ladies mind donating some clothes and shoes to the Swensens?"

"Sara has plenty of dresses packed away that are in good shape. She barely wore some of them. There's already enough for Lizzy when she gets bigger. Then there are all the garments that Lizzy has outgrown."

Samantha picked up the vase and placed it in the cupboard that already held several others. "Christine has plenty of outgrown clothes too."

"We can't overwhelm them," Harriet warned. "A good dress and a work dress for each with some room to grow. One pair of shoes, with a second bigger pair for the oldest girl so when they're too small, she can hand them down, but still have something to wear. Some stockings and undergarments."

"How about we meet in town on Monday and ride there together," Pamela suggested. "We can bring the girls. I think even Lizzy could manage her pony on the mountain trail. We can go through the clothes and choose what you think might fit each child."

Samantha reached for the shepherdess. "We'd better bring some food. Otherwise we'll probably overwhelm the poor woman. I'll ask Mrs. Toffels to make some cookies."

"Annie can make fried chicken and roasted potatoes. A jar of her pickles will be a nice addition, too."

Harriet thought of the contents of the store. "I'll bring a canister of tea, some loaves of bread, and a crock of butter."

"Sounds like we're all set." Samantha wiped off the shepherdess before setting it down and taking a cut glass bowl that Pamela handed her.

"Thank you, ladies." Harriet gave them a gleeful smile. "I desperately want these girls in my classroom, and I appreciate you both making it possible."

Pamela tucked some escaping strands of hair behind her ear. "It will be an adventure."

Harriet glanced out the window to check on David. He hadn't moved from under the tree and still had a pensive look on his face. She sighed, wishing she could solve his problems as easily as those of the Swensen girls.

Samantha followed Harriet's gaze. She set the bowl on the table, and wiped her hands on the apron covering her blue calico dress. "Come on," she said to Harriet. "I know just the thing for David. Or, should I say, just the *boy*."

Harriet couldn't help but smile at the mischief in Samantha's blue eyes. "Good idea. They're about the same age."

"They'll be oil and water."

"You're right. Just what he needs."

Outside, Samantha moved closer to the group of children. The sun glinted on her red hair. She shaded her eyes with her hand and called to her son. "Daniel!" It took a couple of tries before Daniel Rodriguez heard her and detached himself from the others. Samantha gripped his shoulder to focus his attention on her. In spite of the gentle restraint, Daniel rocked back and forth, obviously eager to return to the game.

Daniel didn't look at all like his mother except for his blue eyes and the slight auburn tint to his brown hair. He took after his Argentine father, with golden skinned high cheekbones and a narrow nose. When he was distressed or excited his eyebrows tended to wing upward.

Harriet smiled at him. "Daniel, I want you to meet someone." She indicated David. "David is about your age. But...." she hesitated, unsure what to say about her charge. "He's had a hard life. Right now he's not talking to anyone. But he could sure use a friend."

Daniel's eyes lit with glee, and his eyebrows winged up. "Like me, Mama. When we first moved here." He bounced under her hand, about to take off and shoot over to David.

Samantha tightened her grip. "Yes, like you, son."

Harriet knew that despite Daniel's outgoing nature, he was easily hurt. "David might not seem friendly at first," she warned him, ruffling his silky brown hair.

Samantha cupped his chin and raised his face so he'd look into her eyes. "You'll need to be patient with David. Can you do that?"

"I can talk for both of us."

"That you can." Samantha gave Daniel a hug, which he wiggled out of. His mother released him, and he beelined for David.

The two women watched. Harriet held her breath.

Daniel bounced to a stop in front of David and immediately started talking.

David looked startled, and his eyes widened. But he didn't appear scared, and the lost look had vanished.

Daniel plopped himself down next to David and started a one-sided conversation, seemingly unconcerned that his new companion remained uncommunicative.

Sudden tears glistened in Samantha's eyes. "When we lived in Argentina on the *hacienda*, Daniel didn't have friends. His cousins were unkind. When we moved to Montana, he took well to his adopted brothers, but they're older, and it's still an adjustment. Now…to see him go right up to David and pitch himself into a friendship…He's grown a lot since we came here."

"He has indeed."

Samantha hooked her arm through Harriet's. "Come on. Let's leave them to it."

Side-by-side they walked back to the house. Startled by the sense of companionship she felt, Harriet allowed herself to relax. If only she could board at the Thompsons'! But it was too far away from the school in the winter. Still, she felt as though David wasn't the only one making a much-needed friend today.

~

David sat on the hay bale next to Daniel, enjoying the sound of the fiddle and the swirl of the dancers. Daniel chattered away, about his brothers, his horses, Argentina, school, and whatever else caught his attention. David mostly didn't listen, but he liked the sound of the boy's words that rose and fell with only the faintest hint of an accent.

He kept his eye on his uncle, tall and black-haired like the monster Pa had said he was. Just watching him made a shiver of fear go through his belly. David had walked almost on tiptoe around the man, his body tensed to run just in case. So far the big man hadn't given any sign of badness, had been pretty good to him. David tapped his feet, just so he could feel his new boots. The novelty hadn't yet worn off, although he wore an extra pair of socks to protect his feet.

But David knew he had to be prepared. His pa had nice moments too. David scratched his chin. At least he used to.

"Look!" Daniel yelled, pointing to where a man lifted a woman into the air. He spun her until her brown skirt swirled out, and she shrieked with laughter.

David almost laughed, too. He could feel a little bubble of glee inside him, but the feeling died rather than popping out.

Routinely, he tensed and looked behind and around him, then relaxed when there was no sight of his pa. Funny, how he could still worry about that. He caught sight of the pretty schoolteacher sitting by herself on a hay bale. Her eyes looked sad.

David knew sad.

I wish I could live with her.

~

Harriet sat on one of the straw bales that circled the make-shift dance floor. Overhead, Chinese lanterns tied to the trees swung on lines that crossed over the area. They glowed, not unlike the plump moon in the sky that cast milky light over the scene. The crowd spilled out of the house. In the dark, it was hard to tell the porch was still missing and other parts not completed. It looked like a beautiful, moonlit Queen Anne home.

Around her, people milled around talking or sat on straw bales watching the vigorous dancing. A skinny fiddler with elongated arms and legs, whom Harriet didn't know, pranced about the middle of the "floor" like a spider, setting couples to twirling around his web.

Several bales over, David remained side-by-side with Daniel, seeming to enjoy the music. The two boys were complete opposites in their attentiveness. Daniel couldn't sit still. He talked, carved words with his hands, and bounced in his seat, showing his enjoyment of the scene. David sat like a stone next to him. But in the torchlight, Harriet could see the expression on his face had relaxed from its customary tightness.

Harriet smiled, thinking ahead to the next school year. She'd be trying to still fidgety Daniel so he wouldn't distract the others and coax quiet David to recite his homework. Hopefully, by then, the boy would be talking. She welcomed the challenge.

Ant stood talking with a group of men, towering over them with his great height. From the occasional shouts of laughter, they were having a good time. But she could see he didn't forget his nephew. He'd angled himself so he had a straight view of the boy.

Harriet sighed, wistful, wishing she could dance, but her ankle wasn't healed enough to bounce on. Yet as the evening went on, Harriet realized that she wasn't enjoying herself as much as she expected to. While she felt comfortable in the presence of men she knew well—Reverend Norton, John Carter, Mr. Cobb, Wyatt Thompson, and some other fathers of her students, she cringed inside when a stranger approached her, feeling fearful that he might hurt her.

No matter how much she scolded herself, the reaction didn't go away. So she forced herself to be polite and friendly. And she must have succeeded in acting like herself because no one gave her any strange glances. She still had plenty of company, bashful or brash cowboys, some of the men from town. Ranchers. *But not the one I want.*

Nick sashayed by with Elizabeth in his arms. She laughed and held on, her delight plain to see. Harriet turned away from the sight of them.

Miss Tillie Cavin plopped herself down next to Harriet, fanning herself with her hand, panting to recover her breath. "I declare, I haven't sat out one dance!" she said in a complacent, although breathless tone. "It's too bad, Miss Stanton, that you can't dance tonight." She giggled, which shook the curls around her forehead.

Those curls must have taken her an hour with the hot iron.

Miss Cavin giggled again. "You sitting out frees up more men for the rest of us."

With her gaunt body, bony face, and empty head, only the dearth of women compared to men made Tillie Cavin a belle of the ball. Harriet regretted the uncharitable thought as soon as she thought it. Miss Cavin, although silly and empty headed, had a good heart and was always willing to help out those in need. One of these days, a man who could appreciate those qualities would snap her up.

"Oh there's that Mr. Gordon. I declare. He frightens me, him so big and dark. Looks like a bandit or a rustler or a robber, although he's clean and dresses fine. Kept me awake *all* night the first time I saw him. If *he'd* ask me to dance," she tossed her head, bouncing her curls, "I'd say no. Who knows what he'd do to a girl!"

"Miss Cavin, don't be ridiculous. I've spent quite a lot of time with Mr. Gordon, and he's been a perfect gentleman." *Except for those kisses.* The thought made her cheeks heat, and she hoped the darkness covered her blush. "I've found him to be quite kind. Heroic even."

Tillie wrinkled her nose.

"When I first saw him, he frightened me, too. But when I became acquainted with him, I learned to feel comfortable around him. I'm sure you will too."

The woman shuddered. "I don't know, Miss Stanton. Who knows what he'd do to a gal?"

A surge of anger shot through Harriet. She opened her mouth to utter a stinging rejoinder, but a grizzled cowboy appeared in front of them and offered Tillie his gnarled hand. She squealed, put her hand in his, and jumped up.

Annoyed, Harriet stood up, wanting to get away from everyone to cool her temper. As her feet took her away from the scene, she realized she was heading in the direction of the house Nick and Elizabeth had lived in this past year. Harriet decided to keep going. She wanted to go see the house that Nick had built and dream a little in the moonlight. She left the dancing and walked through the trees on the edge of the lake, feeling a breeze cool her face. She needed to escape the sight of Nick and Elizabeth dancing.

Harriet approached from the side along the path that probably led to the kitchen door. She halted at the last oak, making sure no one was around. Moonlight gleamed on the whitewashed boards of the house and on the yellow roses planted on the split rail fence surrounding the yard.

Her heartbeat fluttered, and sadness and longing twisted in her stomach. She couldn't believe Elizabeth had discarded the home that Harriet would have given anything to own. Tears filled her eyes and blurred the outlines of the house. She leaned against the oak until the wave of sorrow passed.

The sound of approaching voices drifted through the trees.

Harriet shrank closer to the tree, so no one would see her.

On the path opposite her, Nick and Elizabeth walked hand in hand. They passed Harriet's tree and kept going until they stopped in front of the house, not ten feet away from her.

Elizabeth leaned into Nick. "I didn't realize how reluctant I'd be to leave."

He put an arm around her. "You mean we could have just stayed here," Nick teased. "Not built that monstrosity on the hill."

"Nick! It's not a monstrosity. You should stop calling it that, or everyone will think I forced you to build it."

"I could have sworn you stood over me and the rest of the builders with a bullwhip."

"That, as you well know, was because Eugenia was standing over me with the whip. Who knows what she would have done with everything if she had to wait one week longer to redecorate my brother's house from top to bottom. We should thank God having the baby slowed her down."

Nick gave her a smile that was so tender it brought tears to Harriet's eyes.

"I thank God for your sister-in-law every day, Elizabeth."

"Silly man." Elizabeth laid her head on his shoulder.

"If she hadn't married your brother, you'd never have come to Montana."

"And we never would have married." She lifted her head. "I'm so glad the mansion is almost finished, and we've finally moved in. Yet... I've spent the happiest year of my life in this house. You built it with your own hands... with some help." She laughed. "Small and fast so we could get married right away, instead of waiting for the big house to finish."

Elizabeth pointed toward an unlit window. "I learned to cook in that kitchen."

"And I learned to eat what you cooked, no matter how burned or strange tastin'."

Elizabeth elbowed him.

"Hey," he pretended to dodge.

"I'm trying to be serious." Elizabeth placed a hand on her stomach. "Our child was conceived in the bedroom." She reached up to wipe away a tear.

Nick hugged her to him. "Now who's being silly?" He kissed the top of her head.

Harriet shut her eyes so she wouldn't have to see any more. But she couldn't drown out the sound of their kissing.

"Do you think anyone would notice if we said goodbye to our house in the bedroom," Nick said in a suggestive tone.

Elizabeth gave a shaky laugh. "I think we'd be missed."

"Then, we'll christen the new house once everyone leaves."

AAGGG! Harriet would have slammed her hands over her ears, but she didn't dare move. If they caught sight of her.... The very thought made her blush with shame.

She opened her eyes.

Elizabeth wiggled free from Nick's embrace. She took his hand, and, with the other waved at the house. "Goodbye, little house. Thank you for being such a lovely home for us. I hope everyone who lives in you will be as happy as we are!"

"Not possible."

She laughed. "*Almost* as happy as we are."

"Now, wife," Nick bent toward her stomach, "and child." He straightened. "It's time to return to our party. We've worked a long time for this, and we need to enjoy the fruits of our labors. I want to dance with my wife some more."

Elizabeth wrapped both her arms around Nick and gave him a kiss. He returned the kiss with fervor.

Harriet squeezed her eyes shut and rested her forehead against the tree. *Will they never leave!*

Finally, the two stopped, and she heard the crunch of footsteps walking away. She pressed a hand to her stomach, trying to quell the nausea churning there. What had started out as a nostalgic and sad little journey had turned sordid and shameful. She'd eavesdropped on the couple's private moments, and all that had done was drive a knife deeper into her heart.

≈

Standing in the group of men, talking crops and politics, Ant felt a sense of kinship...of belonging. They'd worked together today, he and these men, building camaraderie.

Ant watched Harriet leave the crowd watching the dancers and sidle off toward the lake. A quick glance around showed him that no one else had noticed. He checked on David, who seemed as relaxed as Ant had ever seen him, next to another boy his own age. Ant had watched them together for the last hour or so, and, although the other boy did all the talking, a fast friendship seemed to be forming between the two.

I might have made the right decision to stay here.

Conscious of needing a reprieve from uncle duties, Ant eased out of the group of men. He sauntered over to the trestle tables, still loaded with some, although not much, uneaten food and pretended to search for something else to eat. Then, as if he'd changed his mind, he headed in the direction Harriet had taken. He cut through some trees to head her off, hoping for some private time with her in the moonlight by the lake, hidden by the trees from prying eyes. The cheerful violin music trailed after him, and he found himself almost matching his footsteps to the beat.

He rounded some trees and found he'd become privy to some intimacy between a man and his wife, although thank goodness, he couldn't hear what they said to each other. But he could clearly see Harriet's face, and the pain he saw there gave credence to a rumor that had been hinted to him a time or two.

Harriet is in love with Nick Sanders.

Ant felt as if he'd been punched in the gut, and wasn't sure why. Yes, he'd felt attracted to the woman, given her some casual kisses, and might have come to feel more. Maybe did feel more. He didn't know. All he knew was that a place long frozen in his heart had begun to thaw, and look where it got him—an attraction to a woman who loved another— even if he was already taken. Ant had experienced enough grief in his life without looking for more.

He'd been warned and could pull back while there was still time to emerge from this situation without further pain.

Maybe I should leave this town, but I promised the Almighty I'd stay. I'm bound by that.

Ant walked back to the dancers, thinking to collect David and head on home to Widow Murphy's. The music of the violin swirled around him, but the scene that had previously sounded so festive now felt flat. The feeling he'd had earlier—the sense of belonging—had vanished with this realization of Harriet's attraction for another.

An older man with a craggy face framed by a bushy gray beard and thinning hair came up to him. To his recollection, he hadn't yet met the man.

The man stopped in front of him and extended his hand. "Abe Maguire."

"Ant Gordon." They shook.

The man tucked his thumbs in his suspenders over his potbelly and rocked on his heels. "Hear tell you're gonna stay here."

"Hear tell?" He'd only told the minister. Ant didn't like the idea of all and sundry knowing his business.

"Talked to the preacher earlier. Told him I was heading out to live with my daughter. Selling my house."

That caught Ant's attention. "Tell me about it."

The man jerked his head in the direction of town. "Half mile on the other side of town. Nice farm."

Ant shook his head. "I'm not a farmer."

Able snorted. "No more land to farm. Sold it off to Harrison, my neighbor. He didn't want the house, though. Has a good one of his own and only one girl. Don't need another."

"How big?"

"'Bout the size of Doc Cameron's. Three bedrooms. Wife and I had one. Boys one and the girls another."

"Don't any of your children want the house?"

"Scattered around. Except for my daughter. And she has a bigger house."

"How old is your place?"

"Built it for my bride back in '59. Kept it up good 'til the last few years when my wife was doing poorly. Solid though. Logs. Built it to last." He looked away. "Never thought I'd walk away from it. Wife died last year. Ain't the same."

Ant had a feeling the man's grief ran deep. *Must not be easy to leave a place where you belong. Even if it's lonesome there.* Uncomfortable, he shifted, then he, too, looked away. He brought his gaze back to Maguire. "I'm sorry for your loss." The pain on the man's face made Ant offer up a bit more. "Know what it's like to lose a good woman."

The older man couldn't meet Ant's eyes. He just swallowed and scuffed a booted foot across the dirt.

Ant checked on David and saw his nephew raise his hand to point at something. The boy next to him rocked back and forth with laughter. Even in his silence, his nephew was communicating...making a friend.

Suddenly Ant knew. They were staying. David's small victory cinched it. "I'll ride out tomorrow and take a look."

The man shook his head. "Tomorra's Sunday. It's church, then spendin' the day at my daughter's. Ride out Monday, can ya?"

Ant nodded.

Abe gave him directions and walked away, heading for the buggies and wagons parked at the side of the house.

Ant gazed after him, wondering about the depths of grief that came from a lifetime of loving a wife. He'd only had Isabella for six months, and her death still hurt. He thought back to Harriet...the look on her face as she spied on Nick and Elizabeth. *Yes, it's better to keep my heart to myself.*

CHAPTER FOURTEEN

Sunday morning, Ant discovered getting David ready for church wasn't as easy as any other morning. For one thing, even though the boy didn't speak a word, his body protested loud and clear that he didn't want to go to the service.

Truth be, Ant couldn't blame him. He didn't want to either. Irritation made him snappish. At one point, Ant spoke sharply to David for him to hurry up, then immediately regretted it when the boy cringed away from him, a wild look in his eyes.

With a sigh, Ant apologized, making sure he gentled his voice. He picked up a comb and positioned the boy to stand with his back to Ant. In spite of his frustration, he worked the comb gently from the ends up, careful not to yank on the snarls.

David stood acquiescent under his ministrations. Only the rigid set of his shoulders betrayed his discomfort.

Should have found time to get him a haircut. Should have gotten one myself.

Ant dipped the comb in the pitcher of water on the washbasin, and then used it to comb the strands back from David's face, tucking them behind his ears. Then he picked up a long-handled hand mirror, crouched down to David's level and showed him what he looked like. "You tidy up well."

David placed his hand over Ant's, angling the mirror away from him toward his uncle.

Ant could see his own face in the mirror. "Darned if we don't look alike, Davy boy." Especially with their hair styled the same way. Goosebumps broke out over his arms, and he rose to his full height, resisting the temptation to brush his hand over David's head in affection. Wouldn't want to mess up his handiwork. "Ready as we'll ever get, huh?" he said in a drawn-out drawl. "How 'bout some food?"

Ant ushered David into the kitchen. Thankfully there wasn't any sign of Mrs. Murphy, but she'd left out a plate of rolls on the table and scrambled eggs in the cast iron frying pan. They tucked into the food with a good appetite, then washed their hands and headed out the door.

In spite of David's dawdling, they arrived at the church before most of the congregation. A few people smiled and said hello to both him and David. Ant returned the greetings.

David, of course, said nothing, walking stiffly, poker-faced.

A few yards away, Widow Murphy stood talking to Mrs. Cobb. He debated walking over to say a polite good morning. Then they put their heads together, ugly bonnets almost touching, and wearing mirror disapproving expressions. Ant decided he didn't much care to do the polite thing today. When they glanced at him, Ant had to shake off an uneasy feeling. He was an intrepid foreign correspondent. What could those women say that would have any effect on him?

The Carters waved. They approached, but another woman stopped Pamela. The girls waited with her. Ant stood listening to Carter talk about cattle and the price of feed, while their smallest girl, who leaned against her mother's leg, studied David with solemn blue eyes. Just watching the two children, equally reserved, made Ant suppress a grin.

Mrs. Carter beckoned to her husband. "Time to go inside, my dear."

They turned as a group and headed into the church.

Inside, plain glass windows let in plenty of light that reflected off the white wood walls. A table in front, covered in a snowy cloth, held candlesticks. Pink roses in a vase stood next to a cross.

Ant placed his hand on David's shoulder to guide him up the side aisle. The pews had started to fill with people dressed in their church-going best. Ahead, Harriet sat next to the Cobbs, near the center. He'd have known her anywhere, even though she hadn't turned her head to look at him. She wore a gray dress and the straw hat he'd given her.

David also spotted Harriet and swerved into the pew, then slid next to her.

Harriet's smile at David lit up her pretty face, causing a tickly feeling in the vicinity of Ant's heart. Half pleased that David had acted on his own, half-dismayed that he'd chosen the schoolmarm to sit next to, Ant followed his nephew into the pew. He nodded a greeting to the Cobbs and Harriet and took his seat.

Harriet patted David's knee. "It's good to see you here, David." She looked over at him. "You, too, Ant." She reached up to finger the ribbons of her hat, tied in a bow under her chin.

Ant's insides warmed, knowing that his gift had brought her pleasure. He didn't know what to say to her, so he settled on a smile.

Music began to play, a piano and violin duet. Ant recognized the hymn as "Amazing Grace." It was Elizabeth Sanders playing the piano. Her husband stood next to her, violin tucked under his chin, sharing her music.

The lilting notes filled the plain little church with the presence of God until the interior seemed more majestic than all the cathedrals in Europe. Ant closed his eyes for a minute and allowed the beauty of the music to wash over him, settling peace on his skin that seemed to seep into his body and expand his heart. He followed the familiar words in his head, but realized the "sweet sound" the hymn described meant more to him now than at any other time in his life. He and David had both been lost. Until this moment, Ant hadn't realized how much. Now that he'd found his nephew, maybe somehow he'd find his way back, too.

To what?

To love. The answer seemed to whisper on the sound of music.

In the hush of appreciation that followed the close of the song, Ant opened his eyes and glanced over at Harriet, hoping to see a similar connection on her countenance. But she was focused on Nick Sanders, and the sight of her expression slapped away his good feelings. Hopefulness tumbled into a pit of despair, and he had to hold in a groan.

What the hell is wrong with me? It's unlike me to have such flights of fancy—high or low.

He'd spent the years since Isabella's death suppressing all his emotions. Then Emily's murder had ripped him apart, and he'd painstakingly pieced himself back together, more determined than ever to keep his emotions in hand.

But a small schoolmarm with a sweet smile and kind eyes had found a way underneath his armor.

~

David sat next to Daniel Rodriguez in the back of a wagon piled with children dressed in their Sunday best, bouncing along the faint dirt road on the way to Daniel's mother's ranch. Hay filled the plank bed, cushioning the jolts. Laughter and conversation flowed around him; the bond between the children was obvious to a stranger like him. Although everyone was kind, he couldn't help feeling awkward—like the outsider he was.

After church, Daniel's mother had asked Uncle Ant if he could come home with Daniel for a visit. David hadn't been sure whether to stay with his uncle or go with his new friends. His uncle had decided for him. Still, David planned to hang back and not be any bother, a hard-learned habit.

The older boys—he'd worked out their names— Little Feather, Tim, and Jack, swapped stories of their adventures last night at the dance. He kept staring at the twins, liking the merriment he saw on their thin, freckled faces. He'd never seen two people look so similar, and he couldn't tell them apart, although Daniel seemed to have no trouble. Nor did pretty Christine Thompson, whom he avoided looking at because being close to a girl made him uncomfortable. Daniel had no trouble with her either. Maybe because she was soon going to be his sister. He wondered what it would be like to have a sister.

Little Feather sat the closest to David on his other side. The Indian boy wore his hair in a long tail. To David's disappointment he wasn't wearing beaded leather, but a blue striped shirt, neatly tucked into his pants. The Indian didn't say much, just watched with solemn black eyes, and mostly let the others do the talking. But David noticed that when he did say something, everyone else listened.

The only good Indian is a dead Indian. His pa's words, spoken in his angry voice, crashed into his mind. David had heard them often enough. Good thing his pa wasn't here. He'd have had a fit about David associating with an Indian. Would have beaten him black and blue and bloody, too. Then shot Little Feather. Probably would have missed though. When he drank, his pa was a bad shot, and since he drank all the time, that meant a lot of wasted bullets and an empty larder.

The thought of food made his stomach growl.

Daniel grinned at him. "Almost home. Before we left, Maria was making a big batch of stew and rolls. And Mrs. Toffels brought pies." He twisted around, half-kneeling. "Mrs. Toffels," he hollered to the plump woman sitting beside Daniel's mother, who sat next Christine's pa, who was driving. "What kind of pies did you make?"

Daniel's ma turned around. "Daniel!" she said in a reproving tone. "There's no need to yell or talk to Mrs. Toffels' back. Ask her when we arrive at the ranch."

Not at all abashed, Daniel turned and dropped back onto the straw. "Bet it's dried apple and cinnamon."

David's stomach growled again.

Daniel elbowed him, not hard, but friendly like. "I'm going to take you to see the Falabellas before we eat. I want you to meet Chico."

David had heard all about the miniature horses the night of the dance, when the two had sat on a straw bale and talked. Or rather, Daniel had talked out loud, and David had talked in his mind. Seemed to work just fine. Daniel could sure pack a lot of words into a conversation.

His new friend chattered all the way. He rattled off the names and descriptions of each horse, and, by the time the wagon had arrived at the ranch, David was sure he'd be able to pick out each Falabella from David's description.

Daniel pointed to a twisted rock formation. "Hey, we're here." He rose to his knees and scooted around to face forward.

David followed suit, hanging on to the back of the bench seat for balance. Daniel's white frame house with a porch across the front wasn't big and grand like the house they'd been to last night. But it was...he searched for the word...homey.

A big barn, a small corral with the twins' goats—Daniel had told him all about their showdown a few weeks ago with old biddy Murphy—and the big corral with the little horses made a pleasant sight. The wagon drew closer, and he could see the tiny horses up close, some with foals frisking at their sides. In spite of all Daniel's descriptions, astonishment rose in David. An exclamation of surprise had almost burst out of his throat, but stuck against the lump that had frozen his tongue long ago. But he couldn't help the wiggle of excitement at the sight of the horses, echoed by Daniel's bouncing around as he pointed out each one and named them.

As soon as the wagon rolled to a stop and Mr. Thompson helped out the womenfolk, the man walked over to let down the back of the wagon. The boys jumped out.

"Come on," Daniel yelled, pelting toward the corral, then scrambling over the fence and dropping to the ground.

David followed him.

The horses crowded around Daniel. He patted their heads and repeated their names to David.

Anxious to meet them all, David touched heads and shoulders, brushed his hand over backs and withers. He couldn't decide which Falabella he liked best.

"We haven't named the foals, cuz Ma says we can't keep them. She's selling them. Carters bought one." He ticked off the names on his fingers. "Doc Cameron. Christine's pa, which is good cuz with him marrying my mama, we'll still have her. Only one left." He patted a tiny gray foal with a black mane. "This one. Ain't he—" Daniel glanced around with a guilty expression. "Mama says I'm not allowed to say ain't. *Isn't* he a beauty? Well, not beauty because he's a *boy.* But...."

David stopped listening. He ran his hand over the tiny foal's back. Then, disregarding his good clothes, he knelt in the dirt of the corral and put his arms around the Falabella. The little fella butted his head against David's shoulder, and he tumbled into love. As the feeling swelled in his chest, tears welled in his eyes. He tucked his face into the foal's neck so no one would see, inhaling the scent of horse.

You belong to me. Or maybe I belong to you. David couldn't find the words to express the connection, and even if he did, they wouldn't come out of his mouth. But the little fella understood him; he just knew it.

CHAPTER FIFTEEN

The next morning, mounted on Brown Boy, Harriet turned to look down the trail, checking the train of women and girls riding single file behind her. First on their ponies came the eldest girls, Sara Carter and Christine Thompson, both nine. They called out to each other from time to time, pointing out a bird or a squirrel. Several times, Samantha Rodriguez, riding behind them, had to remind the two to stop talking, face forward, and pay attention to the trail.

Lizzy rode next, followed by Pamela Carter, who watched her youngest daughter with a sharper gaze than the kestrel winging overhead. The little girl stayed characteristically silent. But she gazed at her surroundings with big expressive eyes.

Everyone wore divided riding skirts, even Lizzy, and rode astride. Blanket rolls behind the saddles contained the donated clothing, and everyone's saddlebags overflowed with shoes and food.

Satisfied that everyone seemed well, Harriet shifted around, enjoying the beauty about her. Sunlight dappled through the pines. They skirted a small alpine meadow and startled a white-tailed doe and her fawn. The two deer bounded across the grass and disappeared into the trees on the other side.

The trail rounded past a forked stump that Harriet remembered from the previous visit. *Not long now.* Apprehension churned in her stomach. *What if we offend the Swensens? What if they reject our overtures? What if they don't allow the girls to go to school?*

She forced herself to turn away from the pessimistic thoughts, but this time her mind jumped to last night's unseen encounter with Nick and Elizabeth. At the time, she'd been overcome with shame and fear of being caught inadvertently spying on the couple and hadn't really had a chance to ponder how she'd felt about what she'd seen.

Harriet visualized Nick and Elizabeth's embrace... remembered the loving way they'd spoken to each other. She tensed, waiting for the familiar pang to pierce her stomach, the pain that would squeeze her heart. It took a couple of breaths before she realized her stomach didn't hurt. Nor did her heart.

Her chest expanded. She felt so light, it almost made her dizzy. She wanted to shout, "I'm free!" But that would make her look crazy, so all she did was whisper the words to herself, over and over. Harriet wished she had someone to confide in—to share her feelings of relief. But no one knew her secret, so no one could know of her release.

But I do.

Happiness bubbled up within her. Now if only things work out with the Swensens...Finally they rode into the Swensens' clearing. One of the middle-sized girls was in the yard, saw them, and ran into the house, calling for her mother. Harriet noticed the shed had even more animal pelts hanging from the eaves. With a qualm, she wondered if the sight would upset sensitive Lizzy. *Maybe she won't notice.*

The scene was almost a repeat of the first time, with the girls pouring out of the house followed by Mrs. Swensen, carrying the toddler. This time, however, Inga shouted, "Miss Stanton!" The girl leaped down the stairs and trotted over to Harriet. The other girls echoed their sister, jumping up and down and calling out Harriet's name.

But when Christine and Sara pulled up next to her, Inga's blue eyes grew big. She looked up at Harriet, then back at the girls, then past them to the women and Lizzy. "Oh, oh, oh!" She dance-stepped in place in excitement. "Who are you?" She looked back and forth at the two older girls.

Christine pushed her hat back off her face. "I'm Christine Thompson, and that's Sara Carter."

Sara took up the introductions, pointing to each person. "That's my mama and Christine's almost-mama and my sister Lizzy."

By this time, Mrs. Swensen had followed Inga to them, and the other girls peeked behind her.

Harriet gave them a reassuring smile. "Mrs. Swensen, I've returned as promised. She gestured at Pamela, giving a more formal introduction than the girls'. "I'd like you to meet Mrs. John Carter——."

"Pamela," Mrs. Carter interjected.

"Pamela. I told you about her daughter Lizzy." Harriet waved toward Samantha. "Mrs. Rodriguez, who I'm sure will want you to call her Samantha. Samantha is marrying Christine's father."

Christine urged her horse forward a step. "She's going to be my mama. And I'm going to have *four* brothers."

"Oh, my," Mrs. Swensen said weakly. She rolled her hands in her apron. "I'm Anna."

Pamela sent the woman a charming smile. "Please forgive us for dropping in on you this way. However, Miss Stanton told us about your daughters, and I was so eager to have Lizzy make a friend." She gave her daughter an anxious glance. "If you don't mind, I'd like to get Lizzy off her horse and into the shade. This is the farthest she's ever ridden."

The request galvanized Mrs. Swensen into action. "Of course, come onto the porch." With her free hand, she flapped her apron at one of her daughters in a shoo-ing motion. "Krista, fetch a bucket of cold water from the stream."

"Yes, Mama." The girl about Lizzy's age ran to the house.

Harriet dismounted, grateful that her ankle barely gave her a twinge when she landed on it. She took off the rolled blanket, tied with a leather strap. The rest of them followed suit.

Mrs. Swensen handed the toddler to the second oldest daughter. "Elsabe, hold the baby. Inga, help the girls with the horses."

Inga nodded, and then took Harriet's reins from her. Pamela handed hers over, and Samantha gave hers to Christine.

Samantha leaned close to Christine. "Bring all the saddlebags with you when you come to the house."

"Yes, Mama." She led the horses away.

For a moment, Samantha watched the child. The sun glinted off her red hair, and her face looked luminous.

She glanced at Harriet and gave her a happy smile. "It's been years since I dreamed of having a daughter."

Harriet couldn't help a feeling of envy—not that she begrudged Samantha her new life, but that she too wanted love...children.

As Samantha gestured toward Christine, the sapphire and diamonds in her ring sparkled. "She's the reason for my joy. If she hadn't fallen off her horse into the stream near my house...gotten sick, her father and I never would have...." Her voice caught on the last word.

Harriet took Samantha's hand, giving her a tug to head her toward the house. "Oh, it would have happened all right. Just taken longer, that's all."

Anna waved for the women to go to the porch.

Pamela, holding Lizzy's hand, stepped onto the porch. She moved to one side so Samantha and Harriet could join her. The smell of cooking meat drifted through the open door.

Anna vanished into the house. She reappeared minus her apron. She glanced over her shoulder at the house, then back, looking uncomfortable. "I was cooking up a batch of squirrel and beans if you'd like some." She bit her lip. Obviously, there wouldn't be enough food for visitors.

Once again, Pamela eased the tension. "Squirrel and beans sounds lovely. We knew you wouldn't be prepared for such a large party dropping in on you, so we brought food and drinks to share with you. If we could just wash up first...."

Anna indicated a chipped basin sitting on the bench near the rail. A rusted coffee can, a bar of soap, and a grubby towel were next to it. "There's fresh water in the can. Let me get you a clean towel."

The older girls walked up to the house, each carrying a saddlebag that they handed over to the women.

Pamela took two from Sara. "Wash up, girls."

Once everyone was clean and dried, they went inside.

Harriet blinked, adjusting her eyes to the gloomy interior. On one end of the cabin, a big bed pushed against the wall, covered in a patchwork quilt. Next to it was a neat pile of bedding the girls must use as pallets.

The kitchen consisted of a round three-burner stove and some crates nailed to the wall on either side of a window. A homemade pie safe with a punched tin door stood underneath one the crates. Beans boiled in a pot, and long strips of squirrel meat sizzling in a frying pan gave out a delicious aroma that made Harriet's stomach growl. She clenched her middle, hoping no one had heard.

A long table took up the center of the room, stretching almost all the way across, leaving a narrow space on either side. Tucked underneath both sides, plank benches looked as if they could hold the entire family plus a few. One carved and polished high-backed chair at the head of the table contrasted with the rough-hewn table and benches—a piece of furniture handed down from family or bought in more prosperous times.

Anna pulled out the chair, and then looked back and forth at the women, obviously uncertain whom she should invite to sit in it.

Pamela tactfully solved the problem for her. "Miss Stanton, with your injured ankle, you should take the chair. She turned to Anna. "We've brought tea, if you would boil water."

The woman's worn face creased in a smile. "Tea will be a real treat."

Harriet seated herself and made shooing motions at the girls to slide to the middle of the benches.

One child, who looked about three, lingered. With one arm, Harriet drew her close. "What's your name, my dear?"

The child reached out to finger a tiny rose sprinkled in the pattern of Harriet's green shirtwaist. Even though the fabric was old, it was in far better shape than the grayed-out dresses Mrs. Swensen and the girls wore.

"You like flowers, don't you, sweetheart?" Harriet touched a gentle finger under the child's chin and raising it so she could see the girl's eyes. Like her sisters, this little one had big blue eyes in a thin face, long gold eyelashes and brows, her blond hair pulled back in tight braids, and skinny limbs.

"That's Marta," her mother said. "She doesn't talk much. Understands everything, though."

"Marta, nice to meet you. Next year when you come to school, I'll be your teacher." The child gave her a slight smile and ducked her head.

Krista ran into the cabin, lugging a bucket. She plopped it down on the table in front of Lizzy. "Here you are."

The adults laughed.

Pamela said, "Thank you, Krista."

"Bring the glasses and cups, child," Anna said, gathering up three china plates, one with a chip on the side, and setting each in front of the women. The visiting children had tin plates, and the Swensen family made do with wooden platters. Instead of silverware, crude wooden forks were the utensils. Anna placed one sharp knife in the center of the table, meant to be shared by all.

Pamela and Samantha started pulling food out of the saddlebags and unwrapping the napkin-and paper-wrapped parcels. They used the wrappings as serving platters.

Around the table, the eyes of the Swensen girls grew bigger, bodies shifting with suppressed eagerness. But, obviously-well mannered, they didn't reach for anything.

Mrs. Swensen moved around the tables, carrying the pot and ladling a dab of beans on each plate. Then she returned with the squirrel, setting what must be a quarter of the animal on each plate.

Pamela pursed her lips. "If you don't mind my fingers, hand me your plates, and I'll pass out the chicken and potatoes." She reached for Harriet's plate.

Harriet handed it to Pamela. "And I'll do the pickles. Perhaps, Mrs. Swensen, you could pour the tea?"

The woman nodded. "If you don't mind, I'll make a plate for my husband for when he returns. He's always hungry after a hunt." Receiving agreement, she filled a wooden platter, covered it with a napkin, and set it aside.

Once everyone had a full plate, Anna looked around the table. "We have a prayer we say before our meals. It's in Swedish, though, but sometimes, we say it in English." She looked around the table at her daughters. "English today, girls."

"Lovely," Pamela said, folding her hands and bowing her head.

Everyone followed suit, and the girls, led by their mother, recited a short verse:

"In Jesus' name, to the table we go.

Bless God the food we get."

Their voices swelled on the last word as if eager to get the praying over with and the eating started.

Although Harriet was hungry, she ate lightly, wanting to leave as much food as possible for the Swensens, and she noticed Pamela and Samantha did the same. She received far more enjoyment in watching the children tuck into their food than she would have in filling herself up.

After they'd finished eating, all the girls cleared the table. The women opened the blanketrolls and saddlebags, pulling out the dresses and shoes and spreading the garments out on the table. They lined the shoes on one of the benches and dumped the socks and undergarments on the bed. Harriet picked up one dress and held it against Inga's front. "I wasn't quite sure of sizes, so we brought enough to sort through."

The women began to pick up the dresses and hold them up to the girl nearest them. If they looked too big or small, they were passed on to another child.

Elsabe clapped her hands. "It's like Christmas in the summer."

Inga elbowed her. "It's *better* than Christmas."

Elsabe made a face at her. "Yes. At Christmas, you're the only one who sometimes gets a new dress. I have to wear your old one."

Anna shook her head at the two. "Each daughter's clothing gets passed down to the next," she explained to the visitors. "So only Inga's ever had anything new. Not really new, either. I make her clothes out of my old dresses." She jiggled the toddler on her hip. "Maria's practically threadbare."

Pamela looked over at Lizzy, standing next to Krista and solemnly watching her. "Sara either ruins them, or avoids dresses as much as possible. I'll send the two girls out looking perfect, and Lizzy will return the same way. But Sara's

192

clothes will be torn and dirty. Most of the time on the ranch, she runs around in her brother's cast off clothing. It's easier that way."

Soon all the Swensen girls clutched their dresses to their skinny chests, their blue eyes shining. Each wore a pair of stockings and shoes, which they had put on as soon as the correct size and some room to grow had been determined. In addition, Inga had two larger dresses, giving her clothes for when she outgrew the new ones. This way her old ones could always be handed down, shifting the outgrown clothes to the next sister, so each had a plain dress and a special one.

Anna reached out a hand to Harriet and another to Pamela, and included Samantha with her look. "I can't thank you enough."

Harriet squeezed Anna's hand, glowing with pleasure. "Then I'll see your girls when school starts?"

"You will, indeed," said Anna fervently. "And hopefully at church on some Sundays."

The women gathered the blankets and saddlebags, and walked outside to the horses. Everyone called out their good-byes and mounted up.

They rode down the mountain, Harriet in the lead. She relaxed in her saddle, thinking about the events of the day. With Anna's promise that the older girls would attend school while the weather remained clear, Harriet knew she'd accomplished her dream for the Swensens.

She couldn't help spinning a few fantasies about what the Swensen girls could do with their future educations someday. Maybe become teachers or merchants. Harriet thought of an article she'd read about medical schools admitting women. Maybe nurses, or even doctors. All because she'd found a way to get them to school.

I can hardly wait to tell Ant.

~

Ant reined Shadow in and studied the log house situated on the edge of the prairie, where fields of golden wheat fluttered in the breeze. While he didn't particularly want to live in a log house, at least it wasn't a soddy. Anyway, he didn't have much choice unless he wanted to buy some land and build his own—something he didn't have time for if he wanted to get David settled right away.

As log homes went, this one wasn't bad. The logs were square-timbered, the chinking smooth, with a stone foundation, steep-pitched shake roof, and double-hung glass windows in the front. More prosperous looking than he expected for a house on the edge of the prairie.

Ant liked that Abe had added a broad front porch across the length of the house. Two rockers sat there, and he wondered how Abe felt about sitting alone in the evenings without his wife. Did he imagine her in the other rocker? Did he talk to her like the conversations Ant had with Isabella in the first years after she'd died?

He turned to look at the view of prairie on one side and mountains on the other. *Definitely worth looking at.*

What would it be like to plant myself here? The reality of his decision to remain in Sweetwater Springs made him uneasy.

He glanced around, seeing a barn that he mostly wouldn't need, although he'd have to get David his own pony. To the side, a half circle of cottonwoods shaded hitching posts, a trough for the horses, and a stone well. A large garden straggled to the right of the house. *What the heck do I know about gardening?* Rows of fruit trees marched across the back of the garden. A small grove of birch shivered in the breeze to the left of the house. He could make out a root cellar, what looked to be a smoke-house, a rickety privy, and the hen house. And dirt. Lots of dirt.

A weight settled around his shoulders. A feeling of being overwhelmed made him long to flee back to his familiar life. Ant had to resist turning Shadow toward the East and riding away. His nephew too effectively rooted him here.

Could David be happy in this place?

Could I?

Abe Maguire opened the door. A dog dashed out, some kind of brown hound, followed by two fat puppies. The momma dog galloped toward him, barking all the way. The puppies waddled after her, adding their yaps to the cacophony.

Ant placed a calming hand on Shadow's neck.

Abe stomped onto the porch and called the dogs to him, and they reluctantly obeyed. He squinted up at Ant. "You sure look like a giant up on that horse."

Ant grinned at him. "So I've been told." He dismounted.

"You didn't bring that boy of yours?"

"No, he went home with Daniel Rodriguez after church yesterday. The boys have formed a fast friendship, and Daniel begged for him to come for an overnight visit."

"Your boy's in good hands then. That pretty widda done miracles with those Cassidy twins."

"So I've heard."

"Thompson snapped her right up." Abe paused to consider. "Well not right up, but soon enough."

"Right. Well, I'll just see to my horse, if I may."

The man nodded and hooked his thumbs in his suspenders.

Ant led Shadow to the trough and pumped in some water. After the horse drank, he tied him to the post, grateful that the trees provided some shade.

Back at the house, he instinctively glanced up at the porch overhang before he stepped onto the planking. To his surprise, there was plenty of headroom.

Abe saw the look. "You'll find my ceilings a good height, too. My Emmeline was a tall gal, and she wanted a place where her family would feel comfortable. Plus, she thought we might have a few big uns ourselves. And we did." He chortled.

That took care of one major problem. He'd been in many a place where his head brushed the ceiling, and some where he couldn't stand upright at all. He had no fancy to live in such a cramped place.

Abe continued his rambling. "Had one tall un like his ma's family. One like me." He patted his potbelly. "And a gal in between." His face sobered. "And the two who didn't make it."

Ant took off his hat. "I'm sorry." Two words that couldn't begin to dent what must have been the tremendous pain of losing a child, not once, but twice.

"We were luckier than most, but not as lucky as some."

Ant remained silent.

"It was a long time ago." Abe waved to a distant circle of cottonwoods. "That's the boundary of the property. My

Emmeline and the young uns are buried there. I aim to join 'em someday. Don't want to lay by myself in the ground behind the parsonage."

"If I live here, I'll pay them my respects."

Tears sheened in the old man's eyes. "Sure would appreciate that." He swallowed and gave a decisive nod. "I'll be by now and then to visit them. You see a wagon parked there, you just pay me no mind."

"Will do."

"Be hard to leave a place that I started from scratch when I came here with my bride." Abe scratched his beard. "Empty prairie it was then, 'cept for the trees by the river. Well, it's really a stream, but after the snowmelt it becomes a river. My wife, she loved trees. Planted more by the river and a lot around the house. He pointed to some spruce by the outhouse. "Drove to the mountains one day to dig those up when they were this high." He spanned his hands six inches. "A surprise for my Emmeline. Made her real happy it did. Wanted them planted by the outhouse. Pine fragrance, you know."

"Ah, yes. Pine fragrance." Ant echoed, taking a moment to understand that Abe's wife had hoped the trees would mask some of the privy odor.

Abe's expression brightened. "But I got me a passel of grandchildren. Does a body good to be around them. That's why I'm pulling up stakes." He made a come-in motion with his arm. "Let me show you the place."

Although Ant had to duck to get under the doorway, that was normal for him. He straightened to his full height and glanced up, admiring the plank pine roof that was still a good foot from his head at its lowest point. That settled, Ant surveyed the room. This would be the parlor, with a settee and two comfortable looking wooden chairs with worn leather cushions, one of them even big enough for him to sit in and stretch out his legs. A few portraits hung on the log walls, and some pictures that looked as if they'd been taken from magazines and framed.

A bookcase on one wall contained several volumes, and a whatnot in the corner held some decorative items. He liked the room. A man could sit in that chair and relax, read, think. . . .

He checked out the kitchen, which looked like a kitchen should. Stove, cupboards, dry sink, pie safe, and table and chairs. His heart sank a little about the lack of water in the house. But he'd lived rough before. So had David. They'd make do. Maybe could add a pump later.

The three bedrooms were a nice surprise. One held the big marriage bed. A second small room had bunk beds. The third only had one bed. All had windows that looked on the mountains or prairie. Everything should suit. He wished he felt more excited about the idea and less overwhelmed by the new responsibilities he faced.

Back in the front room, Ant tilted his head toward the big chair. "That come with the house?"

Abe looked at the chair in question, thought about it, then slowly nodded twice. "That chair, most other things. Can't take it all to my daughter's. They've built a room for me, furnished it too, except for a bed. Have to take that." He waved at the whatnot. "I'll take the do-dads. There's always room for do-dads. Can leave the rest."

"How about dishes and pots and pans?"

"Seems to me my daughter has all she needs. Her husband comes from a fancy Eastern family. Rich. He's a good man for all that. When they got married, his relatives sent out enough to stock a store. Far as I can tell, they haven't stopped. You should see what Christmas is like in that house! She's got far nicer dishes than her ma ever had. More of 'em, too."

Ant smiled at the image that came to his mind. Before his mother remarried, he'd been raised with similarly lavish Christmases. This year he'd have to give David one. "How about if you check with her first. I don't want to cause any hard feelings. Then I'll buy what you want to leave." *First thing is finding someone to make a big bed. Even Montgomery Ward doesn't carry them long enough.*

"Sounds like you're fixin' to take the place."

"I am."

The men got down to haggling, and in the end, Ant owned a home and two surrounding acres—lock, stock, and almost barrel, along with one of the puppies and some livestock. What the heck he'd do with a cow, pigs, and chickens...? Maybe put David in charge of them. Animals should tie the boy to his new home.

But what is going to tie me here?

He thought of the big chair... of sitting there and reading a book by lamplight, while David did his homework. An unexpected thrill of excitement surprised him. He'd been a wanderer all his adult life. Except for that time with Isabella, he'd never thought to settle down. But maybe... just maybe, the idea of having a home to call his own could have unexpected attractions.

Although I'm still not sure about the pigs.

CHAPTER SIXTEEN

Ant had some heavy thinking to do on the way back to Widow Murphy's. After talking to the men last night, he'd learned that there were still some parcels of land available on the main street. There was also a small store, almost a shack, abandoned by the previous owner, which he could move into. The men he'd talked to agreed that if he wanted to use that store for a few months while he built a newspaper office there wouldn't be anyone to pay rent to.

Should he go for broke? Sink his money into building an attractive brick office, with room to grow, and buying the latest printing equipment—the linotype. Or should he stay in the pokey building and buy some secondhand equipment—preserve some of his capital?

Permanence. The very thought made his stomach churn. It was bad enough buying a house and a little land, but to sink his fortune into a newspaper meant he would be so committed to living in Sweetwater Springs there'd be no turning back.

And what to do with David while he set up an office and worked long hours to establish a newspaper? He could bring the boy with him, but then what? Later there'd be chores David could perform, sweeping, running errands, etc.

But he'd have to learn to talk first. And the boy needed to learn to read, write, and cipher so he wouldn't be too behind when school started.

Ant slumped in the saddle, feeling weary.

On the outskirts of town, he straightened. Seeing the mercantile in the distance, he headed Shadow in that direction. It wasn't until the horse stopped in front of the store that Ant realized why he'd ridden here.

Harriet. Ant wanted to talk to her, receive her wise counsel. He swung down from the horse and looped the reins over the hitching post.

Inside the store, Ant paused, grateful to be out of the sun. He inhaled the briny smell of pickles from the crock near the door and decided to buy one. He picked up the serving fork resting on top of the wooden lid. Then he lifted the lid of the crock to see pickles of various sizes packed in their briny liquid. He stabbed a large one and lifted it out, shaking it to get rid of the drips, and then dropped the pickle on a sheet of waxed paper. He folded the paper around it. Then he took the parcel to the counter to pay for it.

Cobb sat on a stool behind the counter, his normal taciturn self. In the hopes that Cobb would reveal where Harriet was without him having to ask, Ant made small talk over paying for the pickles.

"You missed a fine shindig Saturday night."

Cobb's red nose twitched.

"Good food, dancing, and conversing."

The man scowled.

"I even saw your wife take a turn about the floor. Mighty light on her feet," he commented.

Cobb's face relaxed. "Met her at a dance," he volunteered. "I couldn't put two feet in a dance step without falling over myself. Made her laugh."

Ant tried to keep a straight face at the picture his mind conjured up. He wondered what had happened to turn the light-footed woman who had laughed at a bumbling dancer into the dour, critical woman she was now. He thought of Emily and Isabella. Maybe the Cobbs also had hidden pain.

For a moment he felt some sympathy for the couple. Then he thought of how they treated Harriet and the feeling vanished. He knew plenty of people suffering afflictions and hardship, who managed to remain kind and respectful to others, or at least polite.

"Miss Stanton didn't dance, with her sore ankle and all." Ant tried to keep his tone casual. "How is she doing today?"

"Well enough to go traipsing up the mountain to that Swensen family."

"Alone?" Ant felt a stab of alarm at the thought.

"Na. Mrs. Carter and Mrs. Rodriguez and their girls went along."

That's right. Samantha Rodriguez had mentioned that she'd be away from the ranch part of the day, and the boys would be under the auspices of her housekeeper, which had been fine with him.

So much for talking to Harriet right away.

Ant nodded good-bye to the shopkeeper, and once outside, thought about what needed to be done next. He settled on buying a pony for David. Unlooping Shadow's reins from the hitching post, he didn't bother to mount up. Instead, he led the horse down the street to the livery stable, munching on the pickle and enjoying the tart taste while he walked.

Once inside the stable, Ant blinked in the dimmer light and saw Mack sitting on a hay bale mending a harness. At the end of the barn, Pepe mucked out a stall.

Mack looked up from his mending and gave him a nod. He studied Shadow, and apparently finding everything to his liking, bent to his task.

David's old mule put his head over the stall door and brayed a greeting, and Ant rubbed the gray muzzle. Already the animal looked better. Whatever salve Mack had used on the sores had started to heal them, and the ribs, while still sticking out, weren't so prominent. Even the dull coat was brushed and the tail, what there was of it, combed out.

Ant led Shadow to the stall and was glad to see Pepe had already cleared out the soiled straw and added fresh feed and water. He unsaddled Shadow, took off the bridle, and began to brush him down.

The horse drank noisily, chomped on some hay. Once Ant finished with one side of Shadow, he started on the other. From where he stood, through the open stall door, he had a good view of Mack, and they were close enough to talk.

"I need to buy a pony for David."

Mack looked up from his mending and cackled. "I've seen that young un of yours. He's too big for a pony. Scrawny tike. Reckon that's from his Pa starving him. But once you feed him, he'll shoot up like a weed." He looked Ant up and down. "Might not grow as tall as a pine tree, but big enough. That boy'll need himself a horse."

Ant blinked a few times, adjusting his thinking. His memory of David on his pony was so strong, he didn't realize it was two years out of date. He thought back to seeing the boy stand next to Daniel Rodriguez and realized his nephew was tall for his age. And still probably behind in his growth like Mack said.

He rubbed his chin. "A horse then. You have one that's suitable?"

Mack slowly shook his head. "Not at the moment. You need to talk to Sanders. The horses he raises are top of the line. Well broke, but with spirit."

Ant sighed, adding a trip to the Sanders' ranch to the list of things he needed to accomplish.

Mack held the harness up to a shaft of light, as if checking the stitching. "Sanders will probably be in town today or tomorrow. With that new place and the barrage of things his wife's family sends out, there's usually some letter to send off or parcels and boxes to pick up from the depot. I'll let him know you're lookin' for him."

"Much obliged," Ant said, feeling relieved not to have to make the trip to the ranch today.

Mack returned to his mending.

Outside, Ant heard the approach of riders and happy girlish voices. Harriet called something to one of them. He couldn't make out the words. With a traitorous lift of his heart, he set the brush down; he was practically finished anyway, and left the stall, closing the door behind him.

Outside, he saw a pack of ladies and girls, which on closer inspection proved to be three of each. He walked over to Harriet.

Mrs. Carter and Mrs. Rodriguez called greetings to him, which he returned.

Harriet gave him a smile that lit up her whole face and made something flutter in his stomach. She moved her leg, starting to dismount.

Ant went up to her and placed his hands around her waist, lifting her off the horse, and gently lowering her to the ground.

Cheeks pink, she thanked him.

"Your ankle all right?"

"Well enough."

"I'm going out to the Rodriguez ranch to pick up David. I'll rent a buggy from Mack Taylor. Will you come with me? There's something I'd like to talk to you about."

Samantha Rodriguez had dismounted, and stood within earshot, holding onto the reins of her horse. "Do come, Harriet. You haven't been to my ranch since that horrible day when the boys were in the caves, and the foals are adorable."

Alarm prickled up Ant's spine. He thought it had been safe to leave David with Daniel. "Caves?" He visualized losing David in a cave system. He must have looked alarmed because both women smiled.

Harriet laid a reassuring hand on his arm. "It's a long story, and those were extenuating circumstances. I'm confident the boys won't go anywhere near the caves."

Samantha nodded. "Let's refresh ourselves at the Cobbs' and water the horses. That will give you time, Mr. Gordon, to rent the buggy and harness the horses. Then we'll be off."

Behind them, Mack cleared his throat.

Ant turned to look at him.

Mack's attention was directed toward the ladies. He swallowed, obviously uncomfortable. "I have a favor...." His voice trailed off, and he seemed to struggle for words. "My daughter's coming out to live with me."

Pamela briefly touched the man's arm. "Why Mack! I didn't know you had a daughter."

"Her ma died when she was five. I didn't know what to do with a girl child on my own." He looked away and rubbed his hand up and down his gray-bearded cheek. "Powerful pain to lose your wife. And my Constance looked just like her ma."

Ant's gut clenched. *Twice in one day!* He couldn't look at Mack, remembering all too well the agony of loving a woman, of losing her....

"I came out here." Mack jerked his head toward the stable. "Established the livery."

Mrs. Rodriguez drew the blond girl to her side and kept a protective arm around her. "Did you ever see your daughter again?"

The man shook his head. "Write her at Christmas and her birthday, though. She writes back."

The oldest Carter girl, who looked like her mother except with blue eyes, piped up. "How old is she?" Her tone indicated that she hoped for another friend her age.

"Twenty."

The girl's face fell.

"Had a fella, or so I thought. But nothing must of come of it. Anyway...she'll be a fish out of water here. Used to big city life. Won't know nobody, not even her own pa."

Pamela gave the livery owner a warm smile that lent beauty to her plump, plain face. "We'll take care of that."

Harriet laid a reassuring hand on Mack's arm. "We'll give her a warm welcome, Mr. Taylor."

His shoulders relaxed.

"When do you expect her?"

"Not sure. She's got her aunt's affairs to settle. Probably before winter."

The women exchanged glances. Ant could feel unspoken female undercurrents that a mere male wouldn't understand. They were probably making plans.

Mack thanked everyone and turned back to the barn, leading Brown Boy. He looked ten pounds lighter.

Glad to leave the ladies to their plans, Ant fell into step beside the man so he could make arrangements for the buggy. But he knew he only had a few minutes of a reprieve before he'd be diving into feminine conversation again.

~

One by one, the women and girls used the privy in the back of the mercantile, and then went inside the kitchen to wash up. Although no one said anything, Harriet sensed everyone was glad the Cobbs were at work in the store. She offered them all a drink of water from the dipper by the pump, and then everyone trooped out again.

A horse was already harnessed to the faded black buggy.

Everyone but Harriet mounted their horses. The Carters waved good-bye and set out in the opposite direction.

Ant helped Harriet up into the black leather seat and handed her the reins to hold. Then he went around to the other side. When he climbed inside, his presence filled the buggy, even though he didn't take up as much actual space as the Cobbs did when Harriet rode with them. He took the reins from her and flicked them to start the horses.

The buggy wheeled forward. The fringe hanging across the canopy of the buggy danced with the motion of the vehicle.

Samantha and Christine headed their horses along a faint track that was wide enough for the buggy. Ant followed them, but far enough behind to let the dust kicked up by their horses hooves settle to the ground.

Ant handled the reins with ease, and Harriet relaxed. During the first part of their journey, she recounted the trip to the Swensens. He was an attentive audience, listening intently, giving her quick side-glances, and nodding or grinning at the tale.

When she finished, he gave her a thoughtful glance. "Not that I had any doubt you'd find a way to finagle those girls into school... but you managed without causing a blow to Mrs. Swensen's pride. Took a delicate, yet controlling hand on the reins. Well done, Harriet."

She blushed at his praise.

"I have no doubt, with the education you provide your female students, they're going to do fine in their lives. Make good wives. Or—"

"Doctors!"

He gave her his crooked grin, his eyebrow pulling up in the upside down *V*. "I was getting there," he drawled. "Actually, I was going to say politicians. Your girls will probably become part of the suffrage movement when they grow up."

"As well they should," Harriet bristled.

Ant laughed. "That wasn't a criticism. I'm all for a woman's right to vote."

"You are?"

"Yes. My sister Emily had gotten involved in the suffrage movement the year before she died." He paused, losing his cheerful demeanor. "I think that's what ultimately led to her murder. Lewis wasn't pleased with her growing spirit of

independence. When he couldn't beat it out of her, he..."
Ant's voice tightened.

Harriet placed her hand on his leg for just a few seconds.
"I'm so sorry about your sister, Ant."

He exhaled, put the reins in one hand, then reached
over and squeezed her hand. "I wanted to talk to you about
David." He took the reins back in both hands.

"I'm surprised you let him go stay with Daniel."

"I'm surprised he wanted to, although it was Daniel who
got his mother to do the asking. It was the most eager I'd
seen David. I didn't have the heart to say no."

"I'm sure it will do him good."

"I bought the Maguire place today."

Her heart gave a quick leap. "You did?"

"Abe approached me at the party. Rode out to look it
over today, and we shook hands on it."

Excitement bubbled in Harriet. "I'm *so* glad. David's
going to be my student!"

"That's one of the reasons I'm choosing to stay here.
David already has people in this town who care for him.
That's important to me."

"Staying in Sweetwater Springs will be good for him.
He's certainly made a new friend."

"One who doesn't need him to talk."

Harriet laughed. "Daniel talks enough for both of them."

Ant's expression sobered. "If I'm going to establish a
newspaper..."

Harriet clapped her hands together. "You are?
Wonderful!"

"And a printing business for leaflets and advertisements.
I'm thinking I'll build a newspaper office, but in the meantime,

I'll move into the store on Second Avenue. I'll order a printing press and supplies, and have them shipped out."

"Where will you build the new office?"

"I'm thinking Main Street. There's that plot of land next to the mercantile."

"To the right or the left?"

"Haven't decided."

"Are you excited?"

He squinted into the distance. "Maybe a bit. I'm shouldering a big financial burden, which is…disconcerting. Then there's David. I don't know what to do with him. Come autumn, he'll be in school. But until then…"

"Why don't you drop him off at the mercantile. I could start tutoring him while you work." Even as she said the words, she realized that the Cobbs would never allow her to tutor David in their home. "Or maybe at the schoolhouse."

"Harriet, I know you're not happy living with the Cobbs. Would you consider working for me as David's governess? I could use a housekeeper, too. If you can cook, that is. I'll pay you well. There's a bedroom you could have. Just 'til school starts." He named a sum that had her head spinning. "After that you could continue to live there to see to David after school. Do a little cooking and housekeeping."

Harriet's thoughts jumbled all around in her mind. *I'd be free of the Cobbs.* The money would go a long way to getting her a home of her own, plus she wanted to live with Ant and David and help the boy grow out of the shell he'd locked himself into. Possibilities danced through her mind. *This could hurt my reputation.* She shrugged that idea away. Ant was a gentleman, and she'd be *working* for him. *It wasn't as though we'd be living in sin!*

Harriet thought of David and how much she had come to love the boy. She did *not* want to leave his care in another woman's less loving hands. "I'll do it!" The words jumped out before she could modulate them, and her heart soared.

CHAPTER SEVENTEEN

When they pulled up to the ranch house, Ant could see the boys in the corral with the midget horses. The last time he'd been by, looking for Lewis and David, he hadn't had time or attention to spare for the little critters. Today he allowed himself to be charmed by them, glad to see David kneeling by a tiny creature, petting it. Although he was too far away to see the boy's expression, just the fact that he was moving on his own volition, instead of being led around like a puppet was a good sign.

The other boys in the Rodriguez clan saw them and let out whoops that made Ant grin. He looked forward to meeting them.

After he and Harriet had finished discussing their plans for moving, she'd told him the story about Samantha Rodriguez's adoption of two unruly twins and an Indian boy, how the town had turned against them, and Samantha's staunch defense of her boys. Wyatt Thompson had stood by her side, and after everything was satisfactorily resolved, had proposed.

Ant had no trouble in knowing Harriet's opinion of the whole situation. She showed her concern for the boys in her voice and gestures. Admiration for Samantha and anger at the Cobbs, Mrs. Murphy, and Banker Livingston's family came through the narration. Whenever he could take his eyes off the road, he enjoyed watching the battle light flare in her gray eyes at her retelling about the fight to keep the boys from being sent off to an orphanage, then soften as she told the tale of the romance.

The Thompson and Rodriguez families, including the odd assortment of boys and Thompson's daughter, Christine, were all going to be one big happy household come Monday next. A wedding would be held at Wyatt Thompson's house and attended by their special friends.

Maybe David will be talking by then. Ant allowed himself to hope. He set the brake, gave the reins to Harriet, and jumped down.

Wyatt Thompson, followed by another man, came out of the house and walked over to the horses to lift his daughter off her mount. She gave him a hug, handed over the reins to the other man, who must be one of Thompson's hands, and scampered over to join the boys.

Thompson strode over to Samantha, who greeted her betrothed with a smile that made her pretty face glow. He put his hands on her waist, and they exchanged a few words before she dismounted, sliding into his arms.

It was obvious to Ant that if the two had been alone, Thompson would have kissed her. He looked away, uncomfortable with their restrained passion.

Once Thompson released Samantha, she hurried over to Harriet's side. "Wyatt's going to see to the horses. Let's go see if we can pry David away from that colt." She gave Ant a wry glance. "I have to warn you, the Falabellas are hard to part with."

They walked to the gate of the corral. Samantha pushed it open, and then closed it behind them. Daniel ran over to them. "Ma! Ma! David's fallen in love with Pampita's baby."

Samantha gave him an "I told you so" glance over her shoulder.

Ant walked over to where David sat next to the tiny gray foal, engrossed with petting it and ignoring everyone around him. He squatted next to his nephew.

David looked up at him, his face alight with pleasure. He smiled, his brown eyes clear and alert.

Ant took a quick inhale of joy. *This* was the nephew he remembered. "Davy boy," he murmured. He ran his hand over the foal, instead of sweeping David into a bear hug like he longed to. *Slow and steady.* "What have we here?"

David looked as if he might say something, and Ant held his breath, hoping. Then his eyes shadowed.

Although disappointed, Ant could sense David's struggle. *Slow and steady*, he reminded himself again. Rather than push to see if he could help David force the words out, Ant turned his attention to the foal. The colt stood no higher than his knees. It looked at him with wise brown eyes, as if the baby horse knew it was here to help David. Then the look disappeared, and the foal butted his head against Ant's thigh.

Captivated, Ant scratched the foal's head as he would a dog's, then brushed his hand down the black mane, untangling some knotted strands.

All this time, David didn't stop petting the horse.

"What do you think, Davy boy? Think we can see if Miss Samantha might sell this little guy to us?"

David's eyes widened, and he nodded vigorously.

Ant laughed. This time he did let himself touch the boy, rubbing his head with affection. "Let's go ask her."

David dropped a kiss on the horse's forehead and jumped to his feet.

A little creaky from squatting, Ant straightened to his full height. When he looked for Harriet, he saw her watching them, unshed tears making her gray eyes bright. Her lip trembled.

Ant wanted to lean over and kiss her. Instead, he gave her a look that asked if she'd seen David's reaction to the horse.

"I saw him! Oh, Ant, how wonderful!"

Samantha must have also watched them. She reached over and squeezed Harriet's hand, then walked over to stand in front of David. She reached out and brushed a lock of hair out of his eyes. "You're in luck," she told the boy. "That colt is my last unsold foal. But...." Her tone turned serious as she stared into the boy's eyes. "I don't let my foals go to anyone who won't love them and take good care of them. So before I sell him to your uncle, I'll need your solemn promise that the foal will be in good hands."

David wiggled with excitement and gave her an eager nod.

Samantha laughed. "I'm going to want to use him for stud when he's older. Is that all right?" She gave Ant a questioning glance.

He'd give her anything if he could keep the foal for David.

She looked down at David. "He won't be ready to leave his mama for a while. But you can come visit whenever you want. He's about ready to learn to accept a halter and be led around. We'll work on those things when you're here."

Daniel jumped up, pumping his fist in the air. "Yes!" He clapped David on the back then danced around him and the foal.

Daniel gave him a grave smile.

Christine walked over and patted David's shoulder. "We'll both have Falabella foals." She pointed to a brown one. "That one's mine. I named her Anastasia."

Anastasia, eh. Ant made sure not to laugh. He looked down at his nephew. "Guess we're going to have to do some hard thinking to come up with a name for your horse that's as fancy as Anastasia." But even as he teased David, his spirits drooped. He and David wouldn't be able to decide on a name together—no back and forth conversation for them. Not until his nephew was talking again.

How long will that take?

What if David's never able to call his Falabella by name?

Humming under her breath, Harriet almost danced into the Cobbs' kitchen. She inhaled the mouth-watering aroma of fried chicken, and then stopped abruptly when she saw the Cobbs sitting at the table eating supper. An empty place setting was laid out for her.

They looked up, giving her identical glares.

Mrs. Cobb set down her fork. "Where have you been, Miss Stanton?"

Harriet's high spirits deflated. "After riding to the Swensens, Ant and I drove to the Rodriguez ranch to pick up David."

"You've kept us waiting to eat. We didn't know where you were and finally gave up. That's not very thoughtful of you."

Harriet's temper flared, but she struggled to hold onto it. "I'm sorry. I didn't mean to keep you waiting." *I've had to apologize too many times to them. I'm so glad I won't have to any more.*

Mrs. Cobb folded her napkin into a neat square and stood up. She picked up Harriet's plate, walked to the stove, and began to dish up the food.

Harriet washed her hands and sat down.

Mrs. Cobb placed the plate in front of her, then went to the icebox, took out a jug of milk, and poured Harriet a glass. Once she'd served Harriet, Mrs. Cobb took her seat, and they all ate in silence.

Although Harriet was anxious to break her news to the Cobbs, she wanted to enjoy her meal first. The conversation wouldn't be pleasant. She just knew it. *Although maybe they'll be as glad to be rid of me as I am to leave.*

Once she had finished supper, including the molasses cookies Mrs. Cobb had made for dessert, Harriet set down her utensils. "Thank you for dinner, Mrs. Cobb."

The woman nodded, her heavy features still pinched in disapproval.

In for a penny, in for a pound. "I have some news for you. Mr. Gordon has decided to stay in town with his nephew. He's going to open a newspaper and printing office."

Mr. Cobb sat back in his chair, but left both hands gripping the edge of the table. "That's good news, indeed. We'll be able to advertise our specials. Bring more people into the store." He nodded several times, obviously thinking. "Could advertise new merchandise, too."

Mrs. Cobb's tight features smoothed out. She patted her husband's hand, a rare gesture of affection. "You know how much you enjoy reading the paper, Isaiah. Now you'll have a local one as well."

Harriet tossed out her next tidbit. "Mr. Gordon has also bought Abe Maguire's home."

Mr. Cobb rubbed his chin. "The man must have some money. Good thing he's throwing it around our town. He'll need quite a lot from the mercantile."

Glad that the first part of her news had smoothed her path, Harriet figured she'd better share the rest while they were in a good mood. "There's more. Obviously David is going to need extra care and tutoring to help him recover from his ordeal. Mr. Gordon has hired me to be David's governess." She rushed out the hard part. "I'm to live with them. I'll have my own room, so I'll be moving out three days hence." She braced herself for their reaction.

Mrs. Cobb shot upright in her chair. "Miss Stanton! You *cannot* live with an unmarried man without a chaperone. Tell her, Isaiah."

The man's red nose twitched, although he didn't say anything.

"Governesses do so all the time," Harriet said calmly, even though she could feel her stomach tighten.

"In big houses with other female servants."

"Not always."

"You'll be ruined."

"Mrs. Cobb! I'm not going to live in sin with Mr. Gordon. I will be his *employee* working with his nephew."

"Your reputation will be ruined. You won't be allowed to teach school."

That threat was a blow that shook Harriet's confidence in her decision. Could that really be true? *No.*

As Mrs. Cobb harangued her, Harriet allowed the words to slide around her. She waited for Mrs. Cobb to take a breath so she could flee to her room. All the time, she clung to the fact that she *knew* a governess was a respectable occupation. Surely the town leaders would agree.

~

The next afternoon, Ant walked up the brick pathway to the imposing three-story brick mansion, the nicest home he'd seen in the town, his steps dragging. Cobb, with a disapproving voice and look of malicious glee, had brought him the news that the civic leaders wanted to meet with Ant to discuss Miss Stanton. Ant had almost refused before realizing that he didn't want to cause Harriet any trouble. He'd better see what the men wanted. *But I don't have to like it.*

Before he could knock on the carved door, surrounded by stained glass windows, it was opened by a woman in a lavender gown, whom he hadn't met before. She waved him in. "I'm Edith Grayson, Caleb's sister." She gave him an appraising look. "His *widowed* sister."

Now that she mentioned it, Ant could see the relationship. Both siblings stood tall and dark. Edith's beauty reminded him of Isabella—similar long-lashed, big brown eyes and brown hair, although Bella's had been sable. Edith had a kissable mouth and curvy figure. His interest quickened, mostly because she was beautiful and the kind of woman he was attracted to. But he remembered Harriet's story about Edith's actions against Samantha Rodriguez's twins, and the woman lost much of her appeal.

With a jolt of awareness, Ant realized in the past week he hadn't given a thought to his former love, when before this week, he hadn't gone a day without thinking of her since she'd died. Maybe after all these years he'd finally been freed of Bella's ghost. If he could go one week without remembering—without nightmares—maybe she'd stop haunting him forever.

Ant introduced himself to the widow and was rewarded with a flirtatious smile, which did little to attract him.

She held out a hand for his hat and hung it on a hat rack in the foyer.

Ant ran his palm over his head, smoothing his hair. He followed Edith down the hall, barely noticing the black and white tiled floor, sweeping stairway, and carved woodwork, in his focus on her backside, swaying under the small bustle of her dress. She had a nice backside, although not as nice as Harriet's.

She gestured with a graceful, white hand to the open doorway. "The others are in there."

"Thank you, Mrs. Grayson," he said gravely. He walked into the room with an odd feeling of going to his fate.

Reverend Norton greeted him from the comfort of a blue wing chair. Rancher Wyatt Thompson and Caleb Livingston, both tall men, although shorter than half a head to Ant, stood near the fireplace. They nodded a greeting. Merchant Cobb grunted from where he was seated on a settee.

Ant had previously met Livingston when he'd gone to the bank to arrange for a transfer of his assets and to discuss his plans with the man. At the time, they had been all business, but now, seeing the banker in his domestic realm, Ant wondered why Livingston remained unmarried. Remarkable given his dark good looks and his wealth.

A woman, wearing the black uniform and white apron of a servant, with her gray hair pulled back tightly, brought in a tray of coffee steaming from cups. The aroma was a welcome scent. All the men took one. Cobb added cream and sugar, while the rest drank theirs black. They held the saucers, blew on the brew in their cups, and took careful sips, the mood tense.

Ant looked around, noticing the high ceilings, the tall brick fireplace with an elaborately carved mantel, and polished woodwork that gleamed from the sunlight streaming through the lace-framed windows. He couldn't help contrasting the room with the "parlor" of the log house he'd be living in from now on. The comparison wasn't favorable, and his spirits settled lower. He tried to shrug away the thoughts. He'd never been a man who cared much where he lived—provided the ceilings were high enough.

Ant sipped his coffee, sizing up the other men, planning his strategy.

Cobb's bulbous nose twitched. "Who else is coming? I have to get back to the store."

Reverend Norton gave him a reproving glance. "We're waiting for Carter and Sanders. Doc Cameron's been called out to a birthing. But he gave me his opinion already."

Livingston scowled. "Since when did Sanders become a town leader?"

Thompson raised his eyebrows. "You mean besides the fact that he married the wealthiest, most beautiful woman—next to my bride-to-be, of course—ever to step foot in this town?"

Cobb cackled. "Stole her right out from under your nose, Livingston."

The banker shot him a glance of dislike.

So the Boston beauty, Elizabeth Sanders, was the reason Livingston was still a bachelor. Ant wondered if the two men hated one another and whether the banker had any interest in Harriet. It could hurt his chances of getting a governess for David.

At that moment John Carter entered the room, followed by the man in question, Nick Sanders.

They all nodded hello before Livingston waved toward a doorway, pointedly changing the subject. "I thought it might be easier for us all to sit in the dining room. Mrs. Graves has made cookies and there's lemonade for anyone who wants something cold to drink."

As they walked across the room, Carter ambled next to the banker. "You still have much ice, Livingston? We ran out Sunday. Used the last of it to make ice cream. After Lizzie's brush with influenza, I had the men cut more blocks last winter. Consequently, we used more ice and ran out at about the same time as before."

The banker shrugged. "I don't know. I leave that kind of thing to Mrs. Graves."

Carter turned to Ant. "How's that nephew of yours?"

"Adjusting. Slow going."

Carter clapped a brief sympathetic hand on his shoulder, but didn't say anything. The gesture was unexpectedly warming, and Ant hoped the rancher would aid his cause.

A large table, of a size Ant hadn't seen since he'd left New York, dominated the room. A portrait of a couple in old-fashioned clothes hung above the ornate fireplace. The man had the chiseled Livingston features. *Father? No, the clothes were too old-fashioned.* "Your grandfather?" Ant asked the banker.

"Yes, he founded the family business in Boston."

A big blue-and-white platter of sugar cookies sitting on the table drew his attention. Ant hadn't had sugar cookies in ages, but his stomach felt too tight to eat. "Those cookies look good. Maybe I could take one home for David?"

Reverend Norton leaned over and pushed the plate closer to Ant. "Go ahead. The boy's too skinny. Probably has a sweet tooth."

Nick swiped a cookie. "Doesn't everybody?"

A rumble of laughter went around the room.

Livingston went to take the chair at the head of the table. Carter and Norton took a seat on either side of him. Thompson sat next to the minister, and Cobb slouched beside him. Sanders dropped into the chair next to Carter, leaving Ant to slide into the seat at his right, setting down his empty coffee cup and saucer.

Ant took some time to assess the men, all of whom he'd previously before. *Never had to face a moral committee before. Don't like that I do now.* If he hadn't already bought the house and paid the architect to start work on the office building, he'd take David and leave.

Livingston picked up the pitcher of lemonade and poured a glass for himself. "Do you know why you're here?" he asked Ant, his tone pompous. He handed the pitcher to

Reverend Norton, then took two cookies and set them on a plate in front of him.

"You summoned me." Ant allowed some of his resentment to edge his voice. To cool his temper, he picked up the pitcher, tipped a flow of lemonade into a glass, and took a long draught of the sweet concoction. He nodded approval to his host.

Wyatt Thompson poured himself some lemonade, "First of all, Gordon, we're meeting here because of *who* you asked to be a governess to David," he said, his gray eyes steady. "If you'd chosen another woman, it would be none of our business."

Reverend Norton cleared his throat.

With an apologetic glance at the minister, Thompson continued, "Except for the good preacher here. But because Miss Stanton is the schoolteacher and paid by the town, some people—" he gave Cobb a pointed look "—feel they have to bring up the issue."

Carter segued in. "And others of us are concerned about Miss Stanton's well-being. She's a valued member of our community, and we care about her." He took a sip of his coffee.

Ant sent a glare at the men assembled around the table. "This conversation does no service to Miss Stanton's strength of character, which I've seen plenty of in my few days here. You, who've known her longer, should know her better."

The men exchanged glances, but for the life of him, Ant couldn't figure out what the looks meant. A hum of energy filled the room, making him uneasy. *What's going on here?*

Thompson nodded in agreement to Ant's statement. "Personally, I think this meeting is a waste of time. I'd rather be spending time with my beautiful bride-to-be. This is all a tempest in a teapot. I trust Miss Stanton's good sense.

224

And—" he slanted a glance at Sanders "—Miss Stanton's partiality for another is well-known."

The younger man's face reddened.

Why did Ant's stomach knot at Thompson's words? The man was only confirming what Ant had already learned.

Carter ran a hand over his head of thinning sandy hair. "No one took Livingston, here, to task for living alone with his housekeeper in the years before his sister moved in."

Livingston coughed and set down his glass.

Carter's blue eyes twinkled. He blithely continued on. "Not that Mrs. Graves looks anything like our Miss Stanton, but the point is the same. No chaperone."

"She's older," Livingston said in a strangled voice. "A widow. Not at all the same thing."

Reverend Norton smoothed his white beard. "You could always marry her," he said to Ant with an angelic smile.

Ant choked on the bite of the cookie he'd just taken. He could feel the pressure of the men's heavy gazes. He didn't know what to say. The silence lengthened.

Thompson came to his rescue. He shook his head. "Then we'd lose our schoolmarm. Samantha's boys have had enough difficulty adjusting to school. They love Miss Stanton, and she's done an excellent job with them."

Carter looked thoughtful. "Even the troublemakers tend to mind her, which is interesting with her being a bit of a woman."

Marriage! Ant's head spun. "Now, hold on."

John Carter looked thoughtful. "Nothing says that we couldn't have a married lady teacher. Male teachers are often married." He tipped his head toward Ant. "Providing that Gordon allows her."

Ant made a gabbling noise, which the other men ignored.

The conversation carried on without him. Finally, Sanders, who hadn't yet spoken, seemed to take pity on Ant. "You'll have to forgive us, Gordon. Except for our banker here, you're corralled with a herd of happily married..." He lifted his chin at Thompson. "Or almost married, men."

All the men except Livingston laughed.

The banker scowled at the younger man, then turned the frown on Ant. "If you sully Miss Stanton's good name, are you prepared to marry her?"

"Good idea," said Thompson, who took a bite of a cookie.

Livingston scowled at Ant. "The truth is it's not Miss Stanton's character that's an issue here. It's yours."

Cobb grimaced at him. "We don't know you from Adam. There's been nothing but trouble since you came. Murder and..."

Ant could feel anger heating up his neck.

Carter shot the shopkeeper a sharp glance that shut the man up. He turned his attention back to Ant. "We want to know that you'll marry Miss Stanton if need be."

"*If* I sully Miss Stanton's good name, which I *don't* intend to do, I'll marry her."

"Sometimes the best of intentions aren't good enough," Reverend Norton said in a tone of gentle reproof.

Ant didn't care if Norton was a man of the cloth. His patience unraveled. "I said I'd marry her if need be," he snapped. "But for now, let's leave the subject alone." He stood. "I think I've made myself clear." He swiped a cookie from the platter. "Good night, gentlemen!"

CHAPTER EIGHTEEN

After talking to the Cobbs, Harriet stormed off to the schoolhouse, a book tucked under one arm, anger giving fuel to her stride. *How dare the Cobbs meddle in my business, calling a meeting of the town leaders to talk to Ant without consulting me!* She held her head high, conscious of her stomach churning and flags of embarrassed color in her cheeks. She barely acknowledged anyone walking past her.

Once at the schoolhouse, she unlocked and flung open the door, stepped inside the hushed, hot room, then shut the door behind her. The sun streamed through the windows, providing welcomed light. Even though school was out for the summer, she'd left the shutters to the windows open because she often came here for peace and quiet.

Harriet walked up the aisle and set her book down on the table she used for a desk. Then she wove her way through the rows of long plank benches with corresponding narrow tables in front of them, to the windows on each side of the building. She flung open the sashes to let some air into the stifling room. A slight breeze wafted in. Not enough to cool her cheeks. But at least with the huge old oak shading one side of the building the temperature in the schoolhouse was more pleasant than at the Cobbs'.

In winter—she shuddered at the memory—the room would be freezing, except for the area near the stove in the right front of the room. Harriet made sure to rotate her pupils, so each had some time near the stove and some away. Yet, even close to the stove, it wasn't uncommon to have one side of your body warm and another chilled. She'd heard some teachers only allowed their favorites to sit next to the stove, or they punished students by forcing them to sit in the coldest part of the room all day. Other weak-willed teachers allowed the oldest students, the bullies, or most popular ones, to decide who sat near the stove, another practice she didn't condone.

Harriet sighed and stepped away from the window. Just thinking about winter seemed to cool her somewhat.

Unable to sit just yet, she strolled around her domain. Harriet knew she was lucky in the teaching tools the more prosperous citizens of Sweetwater Springs had provided. Her school had a slate chalkboard in the front of the room, with a map of the United States hanging on one side and one of the world on the other. She twirled the suspension globe donated by the Carters, glad that she didn't have to use an apple and a ball as she'd done at her previous school.

A shelf held *Harper's Young Ladies, Chatterbox, McGuffy's Readers,* and *Youth's Companion,* several books of poetry, dictionaries and almanacs, a Bible, and some well-read novels by Louisa May Alcott, Jane Austen, and Jules Verne, and a copy of *Elsie Dinsmore.* Hopefully soon, Ant's newspapers would also have shelf space.

Another shelf held a pile of extra slates for those students whose families couldn't afford one per child, along with a box of chalk. Each student was supposed to bring his or her own, but an appeal to Pamela Carter had resulted in extras to loan out. She made a mental note to request more. She doubted the Swensen girls would be able to provide their own.

Stopping at her desk, she straightened the ruler and pencils propped in a tin can. She fingered the horsewhip, inherited from the former schoolmaster that she kept on the side of her desk, not that she'd ever had to use it, thank goodness. Nevertheless, the whip was a deterrent to potentially disobedient students.

Harriet sat down in her chair, opened *The Count of Monte Cristo*, and began to read. But even in the solitude of the schoolhouse, she had a hard time concentrating on the book. The delights of a new story and the freedom to read in peace couldn't stop her from worrying about the outcome of the meeting at Banker Livingston's. *I've never taken so long to finish a new book before.*

She'd barely read a chapter when the sound of hoofbeats and wheels made her get up from her desk and run to the window. She saw Ant pull up in front of the schoolhouse driving Mack Taylor's rented buggy. Although she was tempted to fling open the door and run outside, she knew it would be better for Ant to come inside, away from prying eyes.

Harriet returned to her desk, placed a piece of paper in the book to mark her place, and closed it. Carrying it with her, she hurried to the door just as Ant came in. His tall frame filled the entranceway.

All of a sudden, her stays seemed too tight, and she struggled to breathe.

When he saw her, he grinned, his smile big and white, and canted a tad to the right. "I've been released on my own recognizance, but it was a close call."

"What did they say?"

"Only good things about you, my dear lady," he drawled. "They obviously value their schoolteacher as they ought."

For the first time since she'd heard about the meeting, Harriet took a deep breath. "Then they're going to allow me to be David's governess?"

His eyebrow pulled even higher. "It's not their place to disallow you from working an extra job as long as it doesn't interfere with your duties as a teacher. Not that they agree with me. It wasn't your duties that were in question, just your virtue."

Heat flooded Harriet's cheeks, and she put her hands on her face. "They didn't?"

He winked at her. "I assured them that your virtue was safe with me."

"Oh, Ant. I don't even know what to say."

He sobered. "Don't worry, Harriet. They were just being protective of you. They gave us their blessing." He looked as if he was going to say more, but stopped.

"What?"

He shook his head. "Nothing. You are now free to teach school in Sweetwater Springs *and* be David's governess."

She clapped her hands. "I'm *so* thankful."

He walked over to her desk, picked up her new bonnet, and held it out to her. "David's waiting in the buggy. Do you want to drive with us to see your new home?"

She grabbed her bonnet and set it on her head. "Oh, yes!"

～

David sat in the buggy between his uncle and Miss Stanton. Once Uncle Ant had gotten the Falabella for him, David had started to trust him and stopped cringing away from the big man whenever he got close...mostly. Instead he had a warm feeling inside his body and knew he hadn't felt this happy in a long time.

The big man still scared him. Not because of anything he did or said. Uncle Ant wasn't mean—drunk or not—like his pa. The way the man loomed over him was enough to sometimes send creepy crawlies scuttling through David's stomach. But he no longer wanted to run away.

Most times, he held back the good feeling. He still felt like he had to look over his shoulder for his pa. He knew Pa was dead. But it didn't feel that way. He kept expecting that heavy hand to land on his shoulder, the beginning of bad things. He shrugged his shoulders as if shaking off the memory.

Miss Stanton looked at him. "Are you all right, David?"

He gave her a quick nod, staring at the brown horse pulling the buggy.

Tomorrow Uncle Ant said they were going to drive out to the Sanders' ranch and buy a horse for him. He wiggled in his seat, just thinking about having two horses of his own, although from old habit, he was careful not to touch his uncle or Miss Stanton. He started daydreaming about riding his own horse, galloping it down the road. Would it be black or brown? Maybe an Appaloosa like he'd seen Mr. Sanders riding.

The track they followed curved around a hill, and a house came in sight. Not tall like Widda Murphy's and the mercantile building, but long, with a great, shady porch. David had never lived in a home with a porch.

Across the yard was a big barn with weathered gray wood. The barn interested him more than the house because his horses and Ole Blue would live there, and he wanted them to be snug in winter.

When Uncle Ant pulled up to the house and helped them down, David pointed to the barn.

Uncle Ant laughed and ruffled David's hair. "Go ahead and explore, Davy boy. We'll be in the house. Give my regards to the pigs." Then as David took off running, he called, "There's a surprise for you in the barn."

David increased his speed, liking the feel of the flat land, so different from the mountain he'd gotten used to. *Much easier to run.*

He reached the broad barn door and pushed it aside. Light filtered in through the opening. In the front was a big open area, probably, he recalled from seeing other barns, for the wagon. Up above was a loft with hay spilling over the edge. A ladder was propped against it.

David ran down the aisle peeking into the six empty stalls, the floors swept clean of straw. He imagined his horse and the Falabella in them and could hardly wait until the horses were real not just in his imagination.

Ole Blue will like it here. For a moment he faltered, feeling guilty about the mule. Ole Blue had been David's only refuge. That mule loved him. *Said something when a mule cared about a boy more than his own pa.* His throat tightened at the familiar pain.

Ole Blue had been the only one David had talked to. Sometimes while feeding or brushing him, David would whisper in his ear. *Secrets.* The mule's ear would twitch, and he'd toss his head like he understood. He'd felt frustrated and sad how Pa mistreated Ole Blue.

But he's going to be all right. Uncle Ant said so.

Reassured, David kept going.

In the last stall, curled up on a bundle of straw, a fat brown puppy with a black masked face plunged to its feet and waddled over to him, plumy tail wagging. Joy washed over him, and David scooped the puppy into his arms, where it wiggled in ecstasy and licked his face. He giggled before turning it over to see. Boy or girl? *Girl. I'll have to think of a good name.*

David played with the puppy for a few minutes and then carried her with him while he explored the rest of the barn. One last stall held a brown cow with big soft eyes. He wanted to go into the stall and get acquainted, but the puppy squirmed in his arms, and he wasn't sure what might happen if he introduced the two.

There was another open area, then a back door. He pushed it open and saw some pigs wallowing in mud. The hot breeze carried pig stench his way, and he wrinkled his nose at the odor. He wanted to go closer to them, but the hayloft lured him back inside. He waved at the pigs. *Uncle Ant sends his regards.*

He scrambled up the ladder, one arm holding the puppy, then set her down and bounced into the soft hay. With a giggle, he spread his arms and let himself fall backward onto the springy hay. The puppy galloped over and licked his face. *Yes, this is good.*

~

Harriet loved the house on sight. Although her dream home had planks instead of squared off logs, this one, although bigger, was close enough to her imaging to make her heart quicken. She put her hand over her chest to still the rapid beating. "I love the porch." Harriet could imagine herself sitting in one of the two rockers and reading.

Ant had told her that the house had been well cared for until Abe's wife died. And she could see the truth of that statement. Weeds poked through the hard-packed dirt between the house and the barn. The roses needed to be deadheaded and more weeds had overgrown the garden—what there was of it. Abe probably hadn't planted new vegetables this year, and only ones that had seeded themselves or came back year after year had straggled through the ground. She hoped Abe at least had watered the garden and that she could save some of the plants.

Her gaze continued around. "Look," she pointed. "There's an orchard. There'll be apples in the autumn. I can make applesauce and pies."

"So you bake?"

"My mother wouldn't allow either of her daughters to forego the fine art of domesticity. Although Mrs. Cobb never lets me do anything, so my skills are rusty."

"I'm sure lucky in my selection of governess and housekeeper."

"What would you have done if I couldn't cook?"

"Muddled through. You should see what I can cook over a campfire."

"What?"

"Beans, beans, and more beans."

Harriet laughed and looked at the house again, imagining it with a picket fence with roses growing on it. "I want a house just like this someday."

She didn't realize she'd said the words out loud until Ant gave her a curious glance.

"My father died when I was three. My mother and sister and I moved from relative to relative, never a place to call our own." Harriet lifted her chin. "But I will have my own place. As soon as I save up enough money."

"Why don't you claim a homestead?"

"I've thought of it. I know other women who have." She gave him a wry smile. "But I don't think I have the fortitude to spend long months alone on the prairie. I'd rather have a house in town. Near people."

He gestured to the house. "Shall we go inside?"

"Of course."

He took her elbow and escorted her to the porch.

Harriet shivered at his touch. *Why does he have this effect on me?*

"Abe told me his wife wanted high ceilings. She was a tall woman apparently."

"Tall and big-boned. She towered above her husband. I always thought them a comical sight. He adored her, though. That was obvious." *And touching.* Harriet looked up, comparing the top of Ant's head to the roof. "You must bump your head a lot."

"That I do." He took off his hat and ran his hand through his dark hair. "Ole knothead. That's me." He reached a long arm out to open the door for her.

Harriet took eager steps inside.

"Abe left me most of the furnishings. I'm having a bed made for me. Nothing fancy, but the carpenter promised to have it ready and delivered tomorrow."

Harriet looked around. The main room was spacious—for a log cabin, with chinking between the logs. A settee and a big chair grouped in front of the stone fireplace were the only furniture.

A doorway led to a kitchen with a table. A simple wood hutch on one side held rose-patterned dishes. Harriet walked over and picked one up, admiring the pattern. "Did he leave these for you?"

"And more. Said his daughter already had plenty. I wrestled him for a few extras. Still didn't cost me nearly what it would have if I'd had to buy new."

Harriet glanced out the window over the dry sink, approving of the view of the mountains. Then she admired the heart pattern punched through the tin doors of the yellow pie safe that stood next to the sink. She peeked inside, imaging the empty shelves filled with baked goods. She walked over and touched the stove, which was desperately in need of cleaning and blacking.

Ant sat on the edge of the table watching her.

Heat rose in Harriet's cheeks. She walked over to the far wall and poked her head through an open doorway. Instead of the lean-to she expected, she saw a square pantry. The logs, set at precise right angles, created a space a housewife with a far bigger home would envy. Plenty of shelves for food and supplies lined the walls. On one side a wooden tub was tucked under the lowest self, and a broom leaned against a corner. She imagined how the pantry would look filled with cans, jars, and crocks, and bags of beans and rice. "The Cobbs will be pleased about the big order you're going to have to place with them." *That's good because nothing else about this move pleases them.*

Ant leaned over her, his height making it easy to see into the pantry. "Didn't even know this was there." He backed away from her.

Harriet rolled her eyes. *Just like a man.* She turned toward him. "You didn't make a thorough investigation of the house?"

Amusement glinted in his eyes, although he kept his face deadpan. "No, my lady."

"Did you look through the outbuildings? Henhouse? Smokehouse? Root cellar? Icehouse?"

He held up both hands in a placating motion. "I'm a newspaper reporter. What do I know about henhouses and root cellars?" he said, laughter in his voice.

"Well, *I'm* a schoolteacher, and I know about them."

"I'm a *roving* reporter, not one who has a regular beat in town." His expression changed. From the look on his face, he obviously was remembering that he no longer roamed Europe in search of news stories.

Not wanting to lose the feeling of happiness and camaraderie between them, Harriet grabbed his hand and tugged him toward the doorway. "Come on. I want to see the rest of the house, and," she teased, "the barn, henhouse, smokehouse, root cellar, icehouse, privy, and pig pen."

Ant groaned. His huge hand enveloped hers, and then he obediently followed.

When they reached the doorway, Harriet knew she needed to drop his hand. Their connection, the playfulness between them felt too good. *I'm his employee,* she reminded herself, and slid her fingers out of his, feeling a sense of loss when he pulled his hand back.

Living under the same roof might be harder than I thought.

CHAPTER NINETEEN

Ant drove David in the buggy over the final hill lead-ing toward the Sanders place. At the top, he couldn't help but pause the horses to admire the beauty of the scene before them. In the valley, a small lake sparkled in the sun. A long pasture fenced with barbed wire on the opposite side of the lake provided room for horses to graze.

A more distant field held cattle, although Ant understood that Sanders mostly focused on horses. He didn't have a spread big enough for cattle, and, with a wealthy wife, the man didn't have the need to run a herd. By all accounts Nick Sanders was a wizard with horses and could afford to specialize.

Near the lake, a grove of trees sheltered a small house. Ant looked away, not wanting to remember the last time he'd seen that house...his discovery of Harriet's feelings for Nick Sanders. Instead, he glanced at the Queen Anne on the hill, reigning over the valley.

Even in the few days since he'd last been here, Ant could see the workmen had made more progress on the house. They'd finished the front porch that wrapped around two sides, but not painted it yet. Ant figured he could knock on the front door instead of going around to the kitchen, as the guests had at the party.

The sound of hammers rang through the air. On the other side of the Queen Anne was a tent town for the workers who still swarmed the place to get more of the house completed by winter. He'd have to speak with whomever was in charge about building his office.

But not today. Ant glanced down at David, seeing the eager expression on his nephew's face as he watched the horses. *Today is a time for David.*

Ant didn't have long to ponder which door of the house to use because Nick Sanders walked out of the barn. He swerved to avoid some chickens pecking at the ground and glanced over at the visitors. He pushed his black hat back, grinned, and gave a friendly wave.

Ant pulled up beside him. "Sanders. Came to see if you have a horse I can buy for my nephew."

"My friends call me Nick."

Ant had to rein in his instinctive growl at the idea of being friends with the object of Harriet's affections. But in spite of some lingering hostility, Ant couldn't help but like the man.

"Also going to need a horse to pull a buggy. We're renting Mack's buggy so often it would be cheaper to buy."

"You mean that big black of yours won't demean himself to pull a buggy?"

"Not Shadow. If I value my life, I won't even try."

Nick laughed and reached up a hand to help David jump down.

To Ant's surprise, the boy accepted, although he let go when his feet touched the ground. Then David allowed Nick to drop a casual hand on his shoulder without flinching as he did with his uncle.

Nick pointed at a corral. "Why don't you go look at those horses, David, while I talk to your uncle."

Ant stared after David as he ran toward the corral. The boy had always shied away from being touched, yet he'd just let a virtual stranger help him down and place a hand on his shoulder. Ant stored that fact away to mull over.

One of the cowhands ambled out of the barn, walking in the bowlegged stride of a man who practically lived on horseback. Nick summoned him over with a jerk of his head.

As he drew close, Ant could see the cowboy was old with a tanned, seamed face.

Nick asked the hand to see to Ant's horse. The man smiled and nodded at Ant, showing stumps of teeth in pink gums.

Ant set the brake, gave the man the reins, and stepped down.

They started toward the corral. Then Nick slowed his steps and shot him a quick upward glance. "From what I've heard, your boy's looking better."

"Still doesn't talk though."

"Well," Nick's voice slowed to a drawl. "I wasn't ever much for talking either. You know if he's ridden much?"

"He was quite experienced for a city boy. Had lessons. I took him riding a few times. Good seat. Light hands on the reins. Since then...." Ant shrugged. "They had an old mule. Bag of bones. Doesn't look like it could carry a sack of beans, much less a man."

Nick's eyes narrowed, giving a menacing cast to his pleasant features. "Saw the mule at the livery yesterday. Recognized it. Saw David's pa once. Rode into town on that mule. Thought it would collapse, but it kept right on plodding along. Stronger than it looks. Was tempted to take a whip to the man for starving an animal that way."

"I wish you had," Ant muttered.

Nick grinned. "Snuck the mule some feed while the man was in the saloon."

Ant stopped and stared. "You fed a stranger's mount?"

"Woulda bought the poor thing. Planned to approach the man. But that was when we had all that ruckus about Samantha Rodriguez's twins and the fires. Reverend Norton came up to me to tell me about the town meetin' and the poor critter went plumb out of my mind. Then later, when I remembered, I figured I'd meet up with the owner again. But I never did." He gave Ant a quick apologetic glance. "David wasn't with him, though."

"Harriet—Miss Stanton told me about what happened with the twins."

Nick's eyes twinkled. "Goin' to be interesting, you and Miss Stanton living together."

Ant didn't want to talk about Harriet with the man she loved. "You have a horse that would suit David?"

Nick flowed with the conversational switch. "Let's mount him on a gentle old mare. See how he does."

For the next few hours, Nick worked with David, first with the placid old mare, then, when satisfied with his riding skills, with a more spirited animal.

All the while Ant leaned against the rails of the corral and watched.

Nick's assessment of David impressed Ant. The man didn't just stand back and watch how David rode, he stepped in to teach, giving directions in a calm voice, and using brief touches to guide the boy.

David took everything in, responding with a promptness that spoke well of his understanding and eagerness to ride. Ant watched his nephew so closely that he didn't realize anyone had approached, until with a swish of skirt and the scent of perfume, Elizabeth Sanders leaned into the rail next to him. She smiled in greeting, but didn't say anything, joining Ant's focus on man and boy.

Nick had David canter to the other end of the corral and strode after him, calling out a command.

"Your husband has a way with him," Ant murmured.

Elizabeth turned to Ant and gave him a luminous smile.

He had to blink to break the attraction that would naturally occur to a man in the presence of a beautiful woman who smiled at him so openly. He inhaled, breathing in the smell of horse and manure and dirt, combined with Elizabeth Sanders' perfume. Even dressed in simple clothing and wearing a straw hat, the woman exuded elegance.

"Nick's wonderful with horses and children. The first day I was here in Montana, I watched him work with Lizzy Carter. The Carter children adore him."

"I can see why. David's relaxed around him, and you don't know how much that means to me."

Her expression sobered. "I've heard your nephew's not speaking a word. Widow Murphy's cutting tongue has spread the gossip."

Ant had to refrain from another growl. He was turning into a bear today.

Mrs. Sanders didn't seem to notice. "But David looks perfectly normal to me."

"He doesn't talk."

"He doesn't talk *yet*."

"What if he never does?" *Why am I telling this woman about my fear?*

Mrs. Sanders placed her hand on his arm. "There are plenty of men out here who don't say much. My husband was one of them, although with me, he managed to work his way around that…eventually. Nick's changed quite a bit. So even if he doesn't talk, David will be able to read and write, gesture. He'll get by."

David walked the horse over to them, Nick striding by his side.

"He's been so frightened of everything…everyone… even me."

Elizabeth waved toward David. "Yet to see him there, except for being so thin, you'd never know something was wrong. He's a regular boy on a horse."

David reined in the mare.

Nick patted the boy's knee, then the horse's withers. "David's doing well. I have several horses that should suit him. But I have one I think will be the best. A well-mannered gelding that has enough spirit to please a boy."

Sanders tapped David's knee. "Wait here. I'm going to saddle a horse up for you." He turned and headed toward the barn, climbing over the railing instead of going through the gate.

Ant glanced at Mrs. Sanders for more information.

She just looked amused and shook her head.

In a few minutes, Nick appeared, leading two horses, a pinto gelding and a brown filly. When he came closer, Ant could see a patch of white hair on the mare's forehead, shaped like a star.

The brown horse nickered at Elizabeth, who ran a hand down the filly's nose.

"I saddled her for you, Elizabeth, because when I walked past her stall, she made it clear to me it was time to go outside."

The woman smiled at the horse. "I don't have a treat for you right now, Star."

Nick handed her Star's reins, then looked up at David. "Dismount, and I'll put that saddle on the pinto."

The boy obeyed.

Nick opened the gate and led Chester the pinto into the corral. He made quick work of changing the saddle, then motioned for David to come forward and mount.

Once on the horse, Nick motioned David to walk the horse around the corral. Again, he studied the rider and gave instructions.

David became more relaxed in the saddle. The joyful look on his face brought a lump to Ant's throat.

"They look good together," Elizabeth murmured.

After about half an hour, Nick motioned for David to come to the fence and dismount. He took the reins and led the pinto out of the corral and over to them. David trotted by his side.

Elizabeth laughed. "You're going to turn into quite a cowboy, David."

The boy grinned at her and petted the filly's nose.

"This is Star," Nick said. "I brought her out to show her off. She's a special horse——."

"Magical," Elizabeth interrupted.

Nick laughed. "A magical horse," he echoed. "Star was just a day old when haughty Miss Elizabeth Hamilton, newly arrived from Boston, visited dam and foal and went down on her knees in the stall and gave the filly a hug. I knew right then, I was in big trouble."

David looked up and gave him a curious look.

Nick ruffled the boy's hair. "I fell in love, David."

The boy made a face.

Nick flicked the tip of David's nose. "You just wait until it happens to you."

"And I...," Mrs. Sanders picked up the story, "fell in love too." She paused for emphasis. "With a foal."

Ant laughed, and even David crooked a smile.

She petted Star's nose. "I realized that living in Montana might have some redeeming features after all."

Nick grinned at her. "You mean me?"

She playfully lifted her nose in the air. "I meant the foal."

"The Carters gave us the filly as a wedding present." Nick looked down at David. "Your uncle can bring you here as often as you want, and I'll work with you to develop your riding skills."

A generous offer from a man who must have a lot better things to do with his time.

Elizabeth touched David's shoulder. "As I said, he's going to turn into a cowboy, Mr. Gordon."

"Call me Ant."

Elizabeth giggled.

Ant gave her a sheepish look. "A university nickname. Now, about the pinto..."

David's face was turned to his. The pleading in the boy's brown eyes took Ant back years. Emily had given him those looks before, and Ant had been equally unable to resist his young sister.

Ant stuck his hand out to Sanders. "You have yourself a deal."

David clapped his hands together and gave a little bounce, which was all the thank you Ant needed.

He'd only bought a horse, but Ant realized that what he'd really just received was a gift of friendship from an extraordinary couple. He'd met a lot of people in his life. With his career, he'd mostly focused on the bad ones, and thus he had developed a cynical outlook on life.

Maybe it's time to turn my attention to the givers.

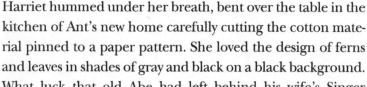

Harriet hummed under her breath, bent over the table in the kitchen of Ant's new home carefully cutting the cotton material pinned to a paper pattern. She loved the design of ferns and leaves in shades of gray and black on a black background. What luck that old Abe had left behind his wife's Singer sewing machine! Although she wasn't the best dressmaker, she could sew a skirt to go with the white bodice she'd picked out at the mercantile with the credit that Ant had gifted her.

Harriet loved the leg-of-mutton sleeves—the first she'd ever had on a dress—and the lace at the cuffs, as well as a froth spilling at the neck. Then she'd splurged on material to make a skirt with the back flared in the latest style to wear to Samantha's wedding.

It had been a long time since Harriet had made herself anything new. Not since she'd come to Sweetwater Springs. Even if she'd wanted to use some of her house money, Mrs. Cobb wouldn't have let her commandeer the kitchen for a sewing project.

She gave a wiggle of happiness, enjoying having the kitchen of Ant's house to herself. David was asleep in his room, and Ant sat in the big chair in the parlor reading.

Their first day in the new place had gone perfectly. Ant had dropped off Harriet and her possessions and left her with David, while he went back into town on business.

David had sat on her bed while she unpacked, watching everything with curious brown eyes. She kept up a stream of one-way conversation, although sometimes he nodded or shook his head in the appropriate places, so she knew he'd listened.

She and David had explored the house together, peering into every nook and cranny. Harriet took an almost proprietary delight in each new discovery. After they'd exhausted all the possibilities inside, the two had roamed around the property familiarizing themselves with each building. Then they'd wandered down to the stream, where David taught her how to skip rocks. Somehow he managed to convey what he wanted without using any words at all.

Harriet finished cutting out one piece of fabric and started on another one. A line of a poem came into her mind, and she started playing with it. By the time she'd completed the pattern, she had several lines.

I need to write them down.

Eager to find a paper and pencil, but not wanting to leave a mess in the kitchen, Harriet unpinned the paper from the material, sticking the pins into her little velvet cushion. Then she rolled the skirt into a neat bundle. Gathering up everything and taking the oil lamp, she walked into the other room. Ant didn't look up from his reading.

In her bedroom, she allowed herself a sigh of satisfaction at seeing the colorful crazy quilt made by her mother draped over the bed. Setting the dress pieces and the rest of her sewing things in a box in the corner, she found her poetry journey and pencil.

Harriet carried them into the main room, sat down on the settee, pulled the oil lamp closer so she could see, and began to write. When she'd jotted the words down, she played with them, scratching out a couple and substituting new ones.

Ant looked up from his book. "Working on your new column?" he said, a teasing light in his eyes.

Harriet pulled herself out of her reverie. "A poem."

Ant's expression shuttered. He gave her a short nod, and then turned back to his book.

Harriet's pencil hovered over the page as she tried to figure out what had just happened. Although he hadn't said anything, Ant seemed to radiate disapproval about her writing. *No, not about the writing.* When he thought she was working on a column, he was approving.

About my poetry.

Well some people didn't like poetry or judged it frivolous. But she hadn't thought Ant would be in that group and couldn't help feeling hurt about his dismissal of something she found so pleasurable.

It doesn't matter what he thinks. Harriet tried to finish the line she'd been working on when she was interrupted. But she did care, and Ant's disapproval had dammed up her creative flow.

Being around him doesn't bode well for my future poetry efforts.

～

Ant walked up the steps of the whitewashed brick bank that had a barred window on either side of the entrance, turned the handle of the door with *Livingston's Boston Bank* painted in black letters across it, and stepped through. He took off his hat, closed the door behind him, and hung it on a rack, from which dangled a shapeless brown hat and a black bowler.

An elderly, balding clerk, perched behind a wooden counter looked up from writing something, his faded blue eyes widening as his gaze kept traveling upward to Ant's face. "May I help you?"

"I'm here to see Mr. Livingston."

"May I tell him who's calling?"

"Anthony Gordon."

The clerk laid down his pen, rose, and went to an inner door, where he tapped three times and went inside, closing it behind him. He reappeared almost immediately and said, "Mr. Livingston will see you, sir."

Ant stepped into the office and closed the door behind him. A gilded cage holding three finches caught his attention. *Wouldn't have thought Livingston was the type to have birds.*

Livingston, sitting behind a desk spread with papers, rose and walked around to shake his hand. "Mr. Gordon, how can I help you?" He gestured for Ant to take a seat on the wooden chair in front of his desk, then walked back behind it and sat down.

Ant admired a seascape hanging behind the banker before bringing his attention back to Livingston. "Wanted to talk to you about putting up an office building."

"Heard you were going to start a newspaper."

"Been thinking I might want to expand a bit. Build something big enough for the paper and have some space to rent to others. Wanted to know if you think that would be a viable concern."

Livingston tapped his index finger on a stack of papers. "I'm planning on building a hotel. Guests shouldn't have to stay at Widow Murphy's. She's enough to drive them out of town."

"So I've experienced," Ant said in a wry tone.

The banker gave him a faint smile of acknowledgment. "I want people to stay—do business here. We need to expand the town."

"Also be good for families driving in from farms and ranches that are more than a day's drive from town. They can stay overnight."

Livingston nodded in approval. "Exactly."

"How fast can a building go up around here?"

"Depends on how much money you want to throw at it."

"I have money, but the venture will probably come close to tapping me out. What do you think of such an investment?"

"Are you looking for a loan?"

"No. Just advice."

The banker sat back in his chair and steepled his fingers, obviously thinking. Silence stretched out. "Sweetwater Springs is a growing town. I think you'd be able to attract tenants. And…there might be a way we could combine forces to our mutual benefit."

Ant's interest quickened. "What do you have in mind?"

"If we build at the same time, we can use the same architect, workers, masons. Place bigger orders for wood and stone and other materials and get cheaper prices."

Ant straightened in his chair. "We could have a uniformity of design that would enhance the look of the town."

"Exactly what I was thinking."

"Don't know if you've been to South Dakota, Minnesota, or Iowa, Livingston, but they have a stone in that area that's mighty attractive. Sioux quartzite, a pinky brown stone they're using as building façades. Different from brick. Fits a Western look, yet still looks elegant."

Livingston frowned in thought and then slowly nodded several times. "I believe I've seen what you're talking about. Didn't pay those buildings too much attention at the time, but now that you mention it, that stone would work just fine. Provided it's not too expensive."

"It's practically local. Should be cheaper than importing limestone and marble, not that I'd intended marble, anyway."

"I'd love to build a marble bank, but it's just not practical here. I do hope to expand the bank someday, though, when this country's out of a recession." Livingston reached into a drawer of his desk and pulled out a folded paper. He spread the map of the town out across the desk and turned it so Ant could see.

Ant studied the drawing, picking out the mercantile, church, schoolhouse, bank, saloons, and some other businesses. The grid spread far beyond the main street to encompass the whole area. It would take a lot more settlers to fill the spaces.

Caleb pointed one finger at a spot near the railroad, next to the mercantile. "Here's where I'm considering building the hotel. Make it easy for people heading west to stop for the evening, instead of staying on the train all the way through. The train noise will be a nuisance, though."

Ant tapped the other side of the railroad. "You haven't built up this side of the town?"

"Not yet." Livingston slid his finger to the other side of the mercantile. "Here's an empty lot. You could claim it. It's next to a saloon, which should provide you with easy access to news."

Ant looked up at the banker, not sure if he'd made a joke. Since Livingston didn't crack a smile, Ant decided he hadn't.

"Unfortunately, the mercantile is brick, and I don't see the Cobbs as willing to change the façade."

"Maybe we can talk to Mack about adding a façade to the livery," Ant joked, wanting to see if the banker had a sense of humor. *Always easier to do business with a man who can laugh.* "That might cause the Cobbs to make some changes."

Livingston actually cracked a smile.

Ant relaxed a bit. "If we're going to dream, how about turning the church into a cathedral and giving the Nortons a bigger parsonage. Miss Stanton would probably love a two-story schoolhouse, and Red Charlie could use a fancy blacksmith shop."

"You are a dreamer, Mr. Gordon."

"More of a joker."

Livingston drummed the fingers of his right hand on his desk, seemed to come to a decision, and stilled his hand. "I already have an appointment with the architect who designed the Sanders' house for two days from now. Do you want to join us? Give you a chance to meet the man. We can talk about our ideas."

Ant stood. "I'll take you up on that."

The two men shook hands. As Ant put his hat on and walked down the steps to the street, he wondered if he'd gotten himself in over his head. *This venture could be a gold mine, could be a sinkhole. Hopefully, it will average out somewhere in the middle.*

～

Harriet and David wandered from the house to the stream, where a large, flat boulder made the perfect place to sit. But today they didn't linger, instead traipsing along the banks. Cottonwood, beech, and adder trees shaded their passage, and the gurgling of the water accompanied their nature lesson.

David stepped into a shaft of sunlight that bathed him in a golden glow and gave an amber cast to his eyes. Already, he'd put on weight. His angled face had filled out some, and his body had changed, losing the painful thinness he'd first had, although he still looked far too slender. Leaning against a tree, a pensive expression on his face, he reached up and fingered a leaf.

"You look like a dryad. Or you would if you were browner... or greener."

He gave her a puzzled look.

"Dryads are fairies who live in trees. They need to stay close to their tree, and if it dies, so do they." Harriet thought for a moment, wrinkling her forehead. She hastily smoothed out her expression. "Actually, I don't think there are male dryads. At least not in any of the stories I've read. However, there must be." Her voice turned playful. "And maybe you are one. But you need leaves in your hair." She plucked some from the tree and poked them through his hair.

He grinned and gave the tree a hug.

"We'll need to do some research. We'll ask your Uncle Ant to order us some books that have dryads in them."

David released the tree, and they continued downstream. Harriet pointed out birds, plants, and insects. She stopped to touch the yellow center of a pink wood rose. "See David, the petals of the wood rose are flat, not like the roses in the garden."

He followed the line of her finger with his, touching a delicate petal. With a change of mood, he skipped ahead through the stand of trees.

Harriet followed. "Look." She waved at a pool, formed by a low dam, and shaded by majestic cottonwoods. "The perfect place to go wading. What do you think? Do you want to take off your stockings and boots?"

David nodded, his eyes alight.

Harriet sat on a rock and watched.

The boy scrambled out of his boots and socks, rolled up his pant legs. He didn't even check the temperature of the water, just waded in. He explored the pool, moving rocks to make a higher dam. The more he played, the wetter his clothes became. But Harriet, enjoying the sight of him just being a normal lad, didn't say anything. *He'll dry off quickly enough in the sun.*

After about an hour, Harriet called for David to come out of the water and dry off.

He looked disappointed but obeyed, climbing out of the water and throwing himself on the grassy ground near her.

"David, are you ready to talk to me?"

He tilted his head, obviously thinking, and then shrugged. He dropped his head down on his arms.

Although disappointed, Harriet didn't pursue the topic. *He'll speak when he's ready.* But she couldn't help wondering when that would be.

~

Ant rode through the gathering dusk that purpled the sky and cast blue shadows around him. The smell of night-blooming flowers drifted on the breeze, although, deep in thought, he barely noticed.

Ant went over his list, mentally ticking off everything he'd set out to do in the week since he'd bought the house. Furniture for the house ordered and delivered. Tick. A new buggy ordered. Should be here next week. Tick. A mare or gelding to pull the buggy and for Harriet to ride. Tick. A linotype machine ordered. Tick. The building he'd temporarily use for an office cleaned and renovated. Tick. Rough draft plans drawn up for the office, building materials ordered, and money transferred. Tick. Discussions with all the local business owners about placing advertisements in the paper, subscribing, or the design and production of advertising leaflets. Tick.

Now he had time until the equipment actually arrived that he could spend with David and Harriet. At that thought, he slowed Shadow down. He might have bit off more than he could chew when he'd hired Harriet. Her presence was all around his home, and he couldn't escape his awareness of her. The scent of her lingered in the air of the house. Her voice soothed him as she read to David at night. He loved to see her pride as she presided at the foot of the table full of food she'd cooked.

The attraction he'd had for Harriet from the beginning had grown into what Ant had reluctantly realized was love. Living with her was more satisfying and torturous than he'd thought it would be. So he stayed away from the house. Neglected his nephew.

He had a good excuse, in that he was busy settling in, getting the business up and running. But he could have come home sooner most nights.

Now, he realized as he neared his property and saw the lights beckoning from the windows, *I've run out of excuses.*

CHAPTER TWENTY

Harriet drove with Ant in the buggy, David between them, to the Thompson ranch for Wyatt and Samantha's wedding. The summer weather had gifted the couple with a perfect day—hot, but not too hot, and no trace of humidity. A brilliant blue sky arched over them and a slight breeze set the leaves in the trees quivering.

As they approached the big white house owned by Wyatt Thompson, Harriet couldn't help but contrast her feelings about this wedding compared to Nick and Elizabeth's last autumn. Back then, she'd been dreading the event, even hoping it wouldn't take place. Just remembering how she'd felt that day made her cringe with shame.

She squared her shoulders. *But not today.* She steadied the plate, holding a spice cake she'd baked on her lap. Harriet could only feel happy for Samantha and Wyatt, and even more so for their children, especially the misfit boys, who now were going to have both a father and a mother. Harriet was determined keep her composure throughout the day.

Ant drove the buggy over to the other group of vehicles. Before he'd even applied the brake, Daniel Rodriguez pelted over to them.

"David! You're finally here!" He skidded to a stop at the side of the buggy and gave several jumps of excitement. "Hello, Miss Stanton. My mama's getting married today."

"I know, Daniel. You look happy about that."

"'Lo, Mr. Gordon!" Daniel gave a bounce and waved at Ant. Another hop had him facing her. "I *am*, Miss Stanton. I am going to have a new pa. I won't forget my papa, but Mama said Papa wouldn't mind if I call Mr. Thompson Pa. And Jack and Tim and Little Feather are going to have a new pa, too."

Gratitude welled up in Harriet for the horrid events of a few weeks ago leading to this special day. "You're all going to be a complete family." She handed the cake to Ant and gathered her skirts to climb down.

Quicksilver Daniel stilled his body for a few seconds, straightening his shoulders and raising an imperious hand to help her—the perfect miniature cavalier.

Harriet had to suppress her amusement. While Daniel didn't often slow down enough to show it, the boy had been raised in Argentina with strict gentlemanly standards. Harriet enjoyed the rare moments when he appeared the Spanish grandee.

Ant gave her back the cake and took charge of the horse.

After Harriet had warned David and Daniel not to get dirty, she mounted the steps leading to the front door of the house. Harriet walked through the double doors, inset with stained glass panels, moved a few steps to the second set of doors that would keep out the winter cold and into the entryway. She followed voices into the parlor and found Elizabeth, Pamela, and Mrs. Norton putting the finishing touches on the several bouquets of flowers.

The women exchanged greetings.

"Look, Harriet." Elizabeth, clad in a seafoam green gown with only the tiniest sign of her pregnancy showing, patted the top of an upright piano in the corner. "Wyatt had the piano tuned, so I'll be able to play the 'Wedding March.'"

"Wonderful."

Mary Norton crossed the room to her and held out her hands for the cake. "Let me take that to the kitchen, Miss Stanton."

Harriet relinquished the plate.

Reverend Norton, who wore his old frock coat despite the heat, stood looking out the window. He turned and exchanged a conspiratorial glance with Elizabeth.

Before Harriet could ponder what that look meant, the minister turned and greeted her.

"My dear Miss Stanton, I was just observing David Gordon with the other boys. A remarkable transformation you've achieved."

"Thank you, Reverend Norton. However, just as much credit is due to his uncle." *Except for this last week, when he seemed to have disappeared from David's life.*

"Is David talking yet?"

She thought back to their time by the river. "There's been a few times when I thought he would. But so far, no."

"Well, we're praying for him."

"Thank you, Reverend Norton."

Pamela handed Harriet a bouquet of white roses, the stems tied with a light blue satin ribbon. "Harriet, why don't you take these upstairs to Samantha. She's in the first room on the right."

Harriet accepted the flowers and inhaled their sweet scent. Then she went upstairs to knock on the door.

Samantha opened it, peeked out, and, when she realized it was Harriet, opened the door wide. "Harriet, come in. I've been banished to this room, and I'm about to expire of excitement and boredom."

Harriet walked in and the new bodice and skirt she'd been so proud of seemed drab next to Samantha's dress. Her skirt seemed too dark.

Samantha's gown was an ice blue silk, so pale it was almost white, trimmed with satin ribbons a deeper blue. The color brightened Samantha's cornflower eyes and brought out the milkiness of her skin. The lace-trimmed sleeves puffed even bigger than Harriet's. Her auburn hair showed through the gossamer lace of the veil draped over her head and trailing down her back. She looked ethereal, like a fairy princess.

"Oh, *Samantha*," Harriet's words came out in a sigh. "When Wyatt catches sight of you, he just might drop to his knees and kiss the hem of your dress."

Samantha laughed. "Not Wyatt. He didn't even go down on one knee when he proposed."

"Faint then," Harriet teased. "Topple over like a tree."

Samantha's eyes danced. She gave a tiny shake of her head, so as not to disturb her veil.

Harriet tapped one finger to her chin, pretending to think. "Sweep you off your feet and carry you away."

"Now *that* he might do. But not before we're married. He's been quite…eager.…"

Harriet finished Samantha's sentence. "He's quite eager for tonight, when he has you alone."

Peach color tinged Samantha's cheeks. "I'm quite eager, too. I'm glad I've been married before, so I know what to expect." She grimaced. "I'm sorry, Harriet. I shouldn't be having this conversation with you."

"Because I'm a spinster." Harriet's words sounded more bitter than she'd intended.

Samantha looked distressed "Oh, Harriet, I didn't mean to hurt you."

"You didn't. I'm usually happy with my state. It's just that this week, with the changes…" *Living in a new home with a man who makes me feel more uncomfortable each day.…*

"Are things not going smoothly with David?"

"David's a love. He'll talk soon. I just know it."

Samantha fingered the necklace she wore, drawing Harriet's attention to it.

"Is this new?" Grabbing for a change of subject, Harriet leaned forward to study the pendent hanging from a white gold chain. Five little stars, with a diamond in the center of each one, dangled from a crescent moon covered with seed pearls. "I've never seen anything like it."

Samantha's blush deepened. "Wyatt gave it to me last night. He had it commissioned from a designer in St. Louis. Each star represents one of the children."

"How romantic!"

Samantha took Harriet's hand and led her to the side of the four-poster bed. "The no-nonsense man I first met has become quite sentimental." She let go of Harriet's hand, spread her skirts and sat down.

Harriet had to take a small hop to land on the bed next to Samantha. She sank into the featherbed. "Love has a way of doing that." Even as Harriet said the words, she felt an ache in her heart. For the first time since she'd come to Sweetwater Springs and tumbled into love with a shy young cowboy that ache had nothing to do with Nick.

Instead she wondered if a man would ever love her like Wyatt loved Samantha and Nick loved Elizabeth. A man she could love just as deeply in return. *Someone like Ant.* She pushed the thoughts away. *Today is Samantha's day.*

Samantha toyed with the edge of her veil. "We had a talk with the boys this week about their names. Wyatt wanted them to know he'd be proud to have them take his name, but he didn't want them to forget their fathers. Although I don't think Jack and Tim care much about their father. But Daniel and my late husband were very close. So we decided to add Wyatt's last name to the boys'. So my son will be Daniel Rodriguez-Thompson, and the twins, Cassidy-Thompson."

"What about Little Feather?"

Tears sprang to Samantha's eyes.

Concerned, Harriet pulled her handkerchief out of her sleeve and dabbed under her friend's eyes. "Now, Samantha. No crying before your wedding. It's bad luck. Besides, what would Wyatt think if he saw you with red eyes? He might wonder if you're having second thoughts about marrying him."

Samantha sniffed. "They're good tears."

"Tell me."

"Wyatt and Little Feather also talked about his first name. Wyatt suggested he might be outgrowing his name and wondered if he wanted to choose another, meaning an Indian name. Little Feather turned to me and asked what my father's name was. I told him, George. So he said that's the name he wanted."

"Oh, no!" Harriet couldn't help but giggle. "I don't see Little Feather as a George."

"Neither do I."

"It's a good, solid name, though," Harriet declared.

"Little Feather was so serious that Wyatt and I had to try hard not to laugh."

"So we're calling him George?"

The mischievous look was back on Samantha's face. "I told him that my maiden name was Hunter and suggested that as a first name instead."

Harriet gave her a slow nod. "Hunter. That fits him better. Plus, he can have an Indian version if he wants."

"That's what we thought." Samantha sighed and looked pensive. "It's only been a few months, but my boys are already growing up."

Harriet leaned over and gave Samantha a hug, careful not to wrinkle her dress. "That's because you're feeding them. Boys have a way of growing when you do that."

Samantha beamed with pride. "They certainly have big appetites. And the twins have already grown out of the pants I first bought for them."

"Well then, I guess you need to have a baby." She touched Samantha's necklace. "Add another star. Maybe more."

Samantha stared into Harriet's eyes. "Oh, I *do* hope so."

"Maybe a little girl to help Christine balance all those boys of yours."

Samantha clasped her hands together. "I'd love another daughter."

"I expect you and Wyatt to keep my school populated for years to come." Harriet stood up. "I'd better get downstairs because it's almost time, my dear Samantha, for you to become Mrs. Wyatt Thompson."

Harriet leaned forward, pressing her cheek to Samantha's. "Be happy, my dear friend." Her voice caught. Before the sentimental tears started, she escaped the room.

Once in the hallway, Harriet paused to pull herself together. *Another wedding. This time one I'm happy about.*

~

Ant stood in the corner of the group of people crowding the parlor. The parlor had been emptied of furniture except for the piano in the corner, leaving space for the guests to stand.

Everyone talked and laughed, obviously good friends. He knew them all, except for Mrs. Cameron, whose pregnancy didn't show. The redheaded doctor's wife had introduced herself to him in a lovely Scottish brogue even thicker than her husband's.

Interesting that the Cobbs and the Livingstons hadn't been invited. They must only have people here they like. Not guests who are invited for expediency or to add to their social status.

Ant felt like an outsider, and he had to resist the impulse to stride out of the room. To keep himself anchored, he studied the painting of a blond woman hanging over a carved mahogany mantel. Two crystal vases of pink roses decorated each end of the mantel, matching the bouquet the woman in the portrait held.

He guessed, from the resemblance to Thompson's daughter, that the woman must be his first wife, and he wondered how Samantha felt about that portrait hanging in the parlor. Probably fine. She impressed him as a levelheaded, confident woman, although with that red hair, she might have a temper.

He glanced out the lace-curtained windows. Outside, he could see various Thompson, Carter, and Rodriguez children playing tag. And David, he was glad to see, was in their midst, running and laughing like the rest of the children. A welcome change.

A stout, older woman bustled over to the group of children, calling out and waving her arms. It took a while before the children stopped their game to listen to her. She gestured to the house, and the children headed inside.

A minute later, they trooped into the room. The volume increased, and each child found his or her parents. David slipped through the crowd toward him and was greeted by several people. Ant was glad to see the boy give a slight nod in response to the greetings. *Politeness is winning over reserve.*

Ant dropped a casual arm across David's shoulders, mirroring John Carter who was in front of them next to his son, Mark. David looked over at the Carters, then up at Ant, and stilled, instead of cringing away. *Another victory.*

John Carter smiled at the two of them. "My daughter, Lizzy, turns five in two weeks. Wednesday." He gestured to a little girl holding onto her mother's hand. She had long brown curls framing a delicate face and wore a cobalt lace dress that made her eyes look bright blue. "We'd like to invite you two to her birthday party."

Ant looked down at David to see his reaction. Did the boy remember birthday parties? He'd only been in New York for one of David's birthdays. Emily hadn't thrown a party because Lewis didn't want a bunch of children underfoot. He'd started drinking around then, becoming meaner. But there'd still been a quiet celebration with presents and cake. In the evening, after the boy had gone to bed, Lewis had gotten drunk, and Ant had left early.

Ant brought his thoughts back to the present. Lewis was dead. It was time his nephew had a chance to enjoy the pleasures of childhood. "You like cake and ice cream, don't you, David?"

The boy gave such a rapid nod that both men laughed.

John looked at Ant. "Last year after her birthday, Lizzy became ill, and we almost lost her." He rubbed a hand across his forehead, obviously remembering the dark time. "We have much to celebrate."

"We'd be delighted to attend, wouldn't we, Davy boy?"

The boy smiled.

Ant took that as a yes.

The older woman he'd seen outside bustled in, making shooing motions. "Everyone clear an aisle for the bride. Mrs. Sanders, please take your place at the piano. Reverend Norton, are you ready?"

John Carter leaned close to Ant. "Mrs. Toffels, Thompson's housekeeper. Makes the best apple pies."

"Good to know."

"Not, of course, as good as my wife's saskatoon pies. You wait and see."

"I'll look forward to it." Ant stepped back, taking David with him to clear the center of the room.

The housekeeper left, probably to escort the bride downstairs.

Everyone formed on two sides of a ragged aisle, leading to Wyatt Thompson, who waited in front of Reverend Norton, dressed in a black suit and vest with a gray shirt. His daughter next to him wore a white lace dress and matching white bows on the end of her blond braids.

Harriet peeked around the door, then wandered in, smiling and greeting everyone. She ended up next to Mrs. Cameron, opposite the room from him and David. She leaned over to whisper in the doctor's wife's ear, and the two women exchanged an excited smile. While they spoke, Harriet fiddled with the gold broach pinned at the neck of her dress.

Elizabeth began to play Mendelssohn's "Wedding March." The strains of the music filled the room, setting an anticipatory buzz through those assembled.

Mrs. Toffels opened the door, and Samantha stepped though—a Titian-haired vision in a pale blue gown that did marvelous things for her figure. Her eyes sparkled brighter than blue topazes. When she smiled at her bridegroom, she glowed, looking even more beautiful.

Ant had a moment of envying Thompson his wedding night before his gaze slid to Harriet, whose big gray eyes looked misty. His kitten didn't have the more classic beauty of Elizabeth and Samantha, the two most beautiful women he'd seen in Sweetwater Springs, but to him she had an appeal, a sweetness, that did something to his jaded heart.

Samantha's boys stepped to her other side. As Daniel took his place next to his mother, he gave a slight bounce before obviously forcing himself to stand still. Probably a

Herculean task—every time Ant had seen the boy, he'd been in motion as if he had wasps in his britches.

The twins followed Daniel—he couldn't tell them apart—and an Indian boy he'd never seen but assumed from Harriet's tale must be Little Feather. The boys all wore identical black suits that matched the groom's, although their shirts were white.

Thompson looked like a mule had kicked him. Either that, or he'd died and gone to heaven. Maybe both. The few times Ant had met the man, he'd usually seemed reserved. Now, the pride on his face, the joy in his gray eyes, showed a different side of him.

Ant remembered a few times with Isabella when he'd felt so full of happiness and sexual energy that it must have been apparent to everyone in the vicinity. For the first time, Isabella's memory didn't bring him pain...not even the slightest twinge. *I wonder if I'll ever have a chance to look at Harriet with that feeling in my heart?*

As Reverend Norton united Samantha and Wyatt in matrimony, Ant found himself feeling gratitude that went deep into his bones. He glanced down at his nephew, then around at the people who'd recently become friends, finally accepting that he had indeed entered another stage in his life. And for the first time, Ant left resentment behind and focused on a feeling of enthusiasm for the future.

~

Ant drove the buggy home from the wedding at a slow pace through Sweetwater Springs. The heat of the day had cooled to a comfortable temperature. Overhead, the stars twinkled in the black velvet sky. The moon, while not as full as the night of the Sanders' shindig, cast a glow faint enough to see the road. They drove through the silent town, the houses and businesses dark for the night. The only light showed in the windows of the saloons, although he wondered at the lit lantern hanging on a hook outside the livery door.

Beside him David slept with his cheek on Harriet's shoulder, and she'd laid her cheek on top of the boy's head. Worn out, the two of them. The children had played outside until dark and then managed to entertain themselves in the house.

After a wedding supper that had the table practically groaning under the weight of several candelabra, dishes, silver serving pieces and place settings, and food enough to feed them all for a week, Samantha and Wyatt had taken themselves off, barely containing their obvious eagerness to be alone. They planned to stay at her place for a few days by themselves, while the boys remained at the Thompson ranch with Mrs. Toffels. Apparently they'd already settled into their bedrooms, or so Daniel informed Ant the one time his path had crossed the boy's.

The rest of the company had relaxed around the huge table, chatting with companionable ease. The more Ant came to know these people, the more comfortable he felt with them. *Yes, I've picked a good place for a home.*

He flicked the reins and gave Harriet and David a tender glance. He was conscious of a connection to this place, unknown a few weeks ago. A little drowsy and content, Ant realized he didn't want the drive to end. Maybe once they reached home, he should keep going and circle around a few times. He almost laughed at the whimsy. Everyone belonged in bed. Including him.

When they pulled alongside the livery, Mack stepped out of the shadows, wearing a gunbelt, his hand hovering over his Colt. He glanced at the two sleeping next to Ant, and then motioned him to stop.

Apprehension displaced his contentment. Ant pulled up, set the brake, and when he saw Harriet and David didn't awaken, stepped down.

Mack led him out of earshot. "Thought you should know, someone stole that mule of your boy's."

A sick feeling kicked Ant's gut. "When?"

"Sometime in the last few hours."

"You see anyone?"

Mack shook his head. "Addison's hands drove their cattle in to ship back East on the train. The men stayed to let loose at Nelson's Saloon. Those workers building Sanders' house came into town tonight, too. Had them a time at Hardy's Saloon. Ain't like a usual night. Place was bursting at the seams with men I didn't know."

Ant glanced over at Harriet. "Let's not say anything to Miss Stanton. I don't want to worry her tonight. But you spread the word to look for Lewis March." Ant thought back to the glimpse he'd had of his brother-in-law before his fall off the cliff. "He's tall, 'bout six foot. Big frame, but not a lot of meat on him, except for his belly. Thinning brown hair, thick features. Might be limping."

Mack stroked his chin. "Might not be him. Any one of those men could have taken that mule."

"Why not steal a horse?"

Mack gave him a sardonic glance. "Bigger risk. We string up horse thieves. A mule thief…might just run him out of town, but his neck stays straight."

"Tomorrow, I'll drive out to the Sanders and Addison ranches. Check things out."

"I'll pass the word around town."

"If it's not Lewis March who took the mule…maybe a boy playing a prank. Someone who needed a quick ride somewhere…. Spread the word that there'll be no consequences as long as the mule's returned." But even as Ant said the words and made plans with Mack, he had a bad feeling in his gut that he couldn't ignore.

"I don't want to leave Miss Stanton and David alone tomorrow while I'm hunting for March."

"How 'bout I send Pepe after you tonight? Armed."

"You don't need him here to keep watch?"

Mack whistled. The sharp sound pierced the silence of the night.

"Ant?" Harriet sounded sleepy and unafraid.

"Be right there, Harriet." He raised his voice so she'd hear him. "I'm talking to Mack."

"Alright." She didn't say anything more.

A large hound stalked toward them.

Mack placed a hand on the creature's head. "I'll sleep in a stall. Rex, here, will stand guard. I can spare Pepe."

"You know my place—the Maguire place?"

"I know where ya are." Mack said in an irritated tone.

And if you do, so does Lewis.

CHAPTER TWENTY-ONE

A nt ran up to Isabella's house, tearing open the door and bursting into the parlor. He threaded his way through the furniture. Opening the dining room door, he saw the shambles an artillery shell had made of the room. "Isabella!"

Dropping to his knees, he crawled under the table to the far door, ignoring the dust catching in his throat and the pinch of pain as a glass shard sliced his palm.

The kitchen door was blocked. Ant jammed his shoulder against the door and squeezed inside.

Isabella lay trapped beneath a large beam. Dust covered her body and powdered her dark curls to gray.

Ant scrambled over debris to get to her, but the more he tried to reach her, the farther away she seemed. He reached out a hand to grab the hem of her skirt. The cloth anchored him, and he was able to pull himself to her. Yet when he finally knelt by her side, he saw the schoolteacher pinned under the heavy wood. Fear stabbed him.

"Harriet!" He knelt by her side.

Her eyes were glazed in pain, and she mouthed his name.

"Kitten, I'm going to get you out of here. Just hold on."

He struggled to move the beam, but the more he tried, the heavier it became.

Harriet whimpered.

The tiny sound pierced his heart.

Don't die, Kitten. "Stay with me, Harriet."

A trickle of blood ran from her mouth.

No! Despair and rage gathered within him. With superhuman strength, he raised the beam. It became as light as dandelion fluff drifting in the breeze. The beam floated across the room until it landed on a pile of rubble.

Ant knew he was too late; the life light faded from Harriet's eyes. He gathered her into his arms and held her against his chest, rocking her back and forth.

Ant knew the minute Harriet's soul left her body. Something snapped inside him. He clutched her tighter to him. A howl of anguish tore up from his gut and out of his throat.

The sound woke him. Ant lay still for a few minutes, staring at the darkness and willing the tension to leave his body. He tried to slow his heartbeat from a gallop to a trot, then to a steady walk. The nightmare had felt so real. As real as the ones he'd had of Isabella's death. As much as he hated them, he knew those past nightmares were based on what had really happened. *But not this one.* He breathed an unformed prayer of thankfulness that Harriet was alive and well, sleeping in the next room.

He kicked off the covers and stood up, padding on bare feet to Harriet's bedroom, where he silently opened the door. Harriet had left the curtains open, and a pale shaft of moonlight played over her. She slept curled on her side like the kitten he called her, one long braid draped over the cover.

At the sight of her sleeping safely, something tight in his chest eased. He wanted to look some more, breathe in her presence, but he didn't want her to wake and see him looming in her doorway. He'd probably frighten her straight back to the Cobbs. He needed her here where he could protect her.

Experiencing Harriet's death in the dream had ripped the heart out of him. Odd, considering how since Isabella's and Emily's deaths, Ant hadn't thought he had a heart—except for David.

He shut the door and went to the next room to check on his nephew, who slept with his back against the wall. Still not that little boy sprawl he used to have. *Will he ever feel safe while he sleeps?*

I'm going to keep him safe.

He shut David's door.

You can't be with him every minute, a voice in his head chided.

Ant walked across the front room to check that the door was barred and the latchstring pulled inside. He flopped into his chair, sliding down until his head rested on the back. His eyes burned from tiredness, and his whole body ached. But he doubted he'd be able to get back to sleep. He'd tossed and turned most of the night before dropping into sleep and the nightmare had seized him. He had no desire to go back to bed and give it another chance at him.

He'd stay put and think through what he needed to do.

At first light, I'll track down Lewis and kill him.

Then he would figure out what to do about the petite schoolmarm who'd mystically woven herself into his dreams.

∽

Extra ammunition in a saddlebag, Colt at his hip, rifle in its scabbard, Ant rode Shadow over the hill to the Sanders ranch. This time he didn't pause to admire the early morning beauty. In spite of the lack of sleep and an on-the-edge feeling that had propelled him out the door before Harriet and David had woken up, he had a sense of calmness. He'd left two letters for Harriet. One, telling her he'd gone to town early, which he'd left on the kitchen table. The other he'd placed on his bed, leaving the door to his room closed. She wouldn't see it until there was a need. In it, he'd made out a will, asking her to bring up David if anything happened to him.

Nick Sanders stood at the corral, engrossed in a conversation with John Carter. John wore a gun belt with a Colt at each hip and carried a rifle.

Good. I can talk to both of them at once.

The men turned toward him showing serious faces. Ant had an idea he knew the subject of their conversation.

He rode up to them and dismounted, tossing Shadow's reins around the middle rung of the corral.

Nick nodded at him. "Glad you're here, Ant. John was just telling me about the theft of the mule, and that you think it could be the boy's father?"

John took off his hat and ran his hand through his hair. "Could be a regular horse thief."

The two men exchanged glances. "Either way," Nick said. "It's not good for the town."

John put his hat back on his head. "Left two of my hands guarding my family. Sent the rest out searching the property.

Nick jerked his head toward the house. "Let me warn Elizabeth. Get my guns. Set someone to guard the house, then we can head over to the workers' camp. I'll have someone see to your horse." He headed toward the house at a trot.

John reached up to stroke Shadow's nose. "Times like this make me wish I'd put more effort into a search for a new sheriff. But we're generally a peaceable place, and, after Rand left, there wasn't a sense of urgency. Had other things on my mind." His thin face looked drawn.

Ant gave him a curious look.

"Lizzy's illness took all the starch out of me for a while. When you almost lose a child, it's hard to think of anything else. Then the focus was on helping Nick build his house and marry Elizabeth. Wasn't until winter slipped by and we had the trouble with the boys setting fires that I realized this town needed a sheriff. But I don't want just anybody. Some lawmen are as bad as the lawbreakers."

Ant had to agree with him. "A corrupt sheriff could control the town. You'd want a man of character to wear the badge."

"That's essential! Sent some letters out to folks in other towns seeing if they could recommend any candidates. So did Reverend Norton and Banker Livingston. Should hear back soon."

"But not soon enough."

"No."

Nick hurried over to them, a revolver in a holster at each hip, a rifle in his hands. "Elizabeth has her revolver. Left Jed in the kitchen for extra protection." He set his free hand on the handle of his Colt. "Let's go check out the camp."

Ant fell into step on one side of him, John Carter on the other. The camp sat level with the house, although about a hundred yards away. Higher ground than them. If Lewis was on the lookout, he'd clearly be able to see trouble coming his way. Ant's skin itched, and he wanted to stride forward with his gun in his hand. But he knew most, if not all of the men were honest laborers. Didn't need to scare them out of their boots.

But Lewis could pick us off easily. Ant quickened his step, wanting to put himself ahead of the men. He figured Lewis would aim for him first, anyway. Not that he'd draw on the three of them with a camp full of men around him. But he could see them coming and slink off by himself to do the dirty deed.

Ant halted. "If anything happens to me, I've left a will for Harriet asking her to bring David up. Will either of you help her?"

Nick looked as if he was about to deny the possibility of Ant's death, then changed his mind. "They could live with us. We've got the room, and I guess my baby would like an older brother."

"Or with us," John said, his tone serious. "Mark would like a brother, too."

"That's settled, then." To avoid twisting himself in knots with his imaginings, Ant strode around the tents.

The tent town straggled in an uneven circle around a campfire. The smell of coffee and frying salt pork drifted over to him. About fifteen bearded men sat on the ground or stood with tin plates in hand shoveling food into their mouths. They wore shirts in varying states of cleanliness, tucked into their pants, with suspenders to hold them up. Others moved slowly and avoided food, obviously having indulged too much at the saloon last night.

Before Ant moved into their line of vision, he took a quick glance around. *No Lewis.* But he could be in a tent or around somewhere. Ant didn't relax his watchfulness.

John and Nick caught up with him.

One man, more clean than the others, with neat side-whiskers and no beard, detached himself from the group and came to meet them. He shot a nervous glance at their guns and rubbed his hands together. "Is there a problem, Mr. Sanders?"

Nick glance at Ant. "Harrison, here, is the foreman of the crew."

"We're looking for a man named Lewis March."

The foreman shook his head. "No man of that name's on my crew."

"You take on any new men in the last two weeks?" Ant asked

"No, sir. My men have been with me for a long time. Hard workers. Know their jobs." He waved toward the house. "As you can see."

Ant nodded in acknowledgment. "Could someone be hiding out here without you knowing?"

He gave a slow shake of his head. "Don't think so. But come over to the fire and I'll ask."

They moved closer to the men, who stopped eating.

"Do we have a new man hanging around here?" Harrison asked.

Ant gave them a quick description.

A slight wiry man with big hands stood up and gave a couple of slaps to his legs to dust off his pants. "Ya, boss. Sounds like Fred Smith. A group of us found him down-river a few weeks ago. Battered and bruised with a broken leg. Sid—" he pointed to a stoop-shouldered man "—set the leg with some splints and leather strips, and we brought him back here. He's been in Sid's tent ever since."

Ant wanted to grab the man and shake him until his head fell off. They'd saved the murderer instead of letting him perish.

The boss turned red. "You didn't think to tell me, Groening?"

Groening looked down. "He promised us money for keeping quiet. Said he'd be coming into some soon. Didn't say how, though. Said while he waited, he just wanted some peace and quiet to heal. Nothing wrong with that."

The boss shook a finger at him. "It is if you're feeding him our grub. You're as good as stealing from Mr. Sanders."

Groening gave a quick shake of his head. "No, sir. About ten of us gave him a little of our portion. Made enough for a grown man."

"Ten of you knew and didn't tell me?" Harrison gave the men a long, hard look. "We'll talk about this later."

"Where is he?" Ant growled, deliberately taking advantage of the fearful effect he had on people who didn't know him.

Groening shifted away. A nervous expression crossed his face. "Smith was feeling well enough, Boss. Could walk with a stick. We took him with us to town. Had us a rip-roaring time at one of the saloons. Said he was going to the other saloon. Never saw him again. Didn't remember much 'til now, either. Too damn drunk, the lot of us."

Ant stepped closer to the man. "He's a dangerous murderer."

"Who'd he murder?" Sid said in a disbelieving tone.

"My sister," Ant snapped. "If he returns, capture him."

"Uh, that might be a problem," Groening wouldn't meet their eyes.

Nick snapped out, "Why is that?"

Groening scuffed his feet in the dirt, puffs of dust rose on the morning sunbeams. "Noticed I had an empty holster this morning. Think Smith might have taken my gun?"

Damned fool. Of course he took the gun. And no telling who'd see the business end of the weapon pointed right at them. Made Ant's blood run cold just thinking of it.

~

Sitting at the table in the kitchen, his slate in front of him, David wrote the letters of his name. Miss Stanton had printed *David Gordon* across the top of the slate, and he had traced the letters, and then started writing on his own. At first, his lines wobbled and he'd rub them out and try again, but soon his fingers caught on, as if dimly remembering performing this same task many times before.

Miss Stanton stood at the sink, drying dishes she'd washed earlier, looking out the window. She wore a long white apron over the gray dress that David liked because it made her eyes so pretty. She hummed, almost under her breath—a happy sound—that made him feel content.

As soon as his lesson was finished, Miss Stanton promised he could go out to the barn where Pepe worked. Uncle Ant had said in the note Miss Stanton read him that Pepe from the livery was making the barn nicer for the horses and that he'd show David how to groom Chester and muck out his stall.

David sat up straighter. Chester was his responsibility, Uncle Ant had said. A man always took care of his horse before himself, although Miss Stanton must not think like a man because she'd already made him wash his hands, face, and behind his ears, eat breakfast, and do some school work before he could attend to Chester.

He wrinkled his nose. *Didn't have to wash when I lived with Pa. Probably the only good thing about that time.* But he wouldn't trade his new life for anything.

Bending back to his task, David dredged up the letters from his memory and wrote them out. *David March.* He stared at the words for a long moment. Then with a resentful swipe of the rag, he wiped out the hateful name and began again. *David Gordon.* He made each letter as big and precise as he could.

I'm David Gordon now.

CHAPTER TWENTY-TWO

A nt rode Shadow home. His eyes burned from fatigue. He was hot, sweaty, sore, and frustrated. Hunger growled in his stomach and made him lightheaded. John and Nick had insisted on riding out with him to the Addisons' ranch and then to the shack in the mountains. Too eager to finish their search, they hadn't taken provisions, nor rested at the Addisons' ranch. They'd talked to dozens of people—many had already heard the news and been on the watch—but the men had found no sign of Lewis.

Now with the sun heading to the west, Ant had given up the search. *For today.*

His gaze swept the house and barn, yard and outbuildings. All seemed peaceful. Already the place looked more like a home with the weeds gone and flowers bursting into bloom. The puppy bounded across the porch, down the steps and waddled over to him, barking like a miniature fiend, plumy tail thumping. Ant kept a firm hand on Shadow's reins, but he sensed the horse was becoming used to the latest addition to their family.

Pepe stepped out of the barn, body tense, shotgun in hand, then relaxed when he saw who'd ridden up.

Ant felt a surge of relief. He'd done well in his choice of guardians to protect the two he loved. With the vigilance of the Mexican and the puppy, Lewis wouldn't have had a chance to sneak near the house.

But the relief didn't ease his frustration. He still needed to wrap his hands around Lewis' neck and squeeze the life out of him. He needed to make sure the man was dead this time.

He rode to Pepe and dismounted. "All clear?" The pup frisked at his heels, and he crouched for a head rub, which had the dog wiggling in ecstasy.

"*Sí, Señor*," Pepe said. "The boy, he came here to the barn. After we feed Chester, I tied the gelding outside. The boy, he groom the horse where I can watch the house too. Miss Stanton feed the chickens and the pigs and work in the garden. Then she call the boy back inside for more lessons. The dog's been quiet till now."

Ant straightened. "Thank you, Pepe. You've done well."

The young man drew to his full, although short, height. A proud smile crossed his round, dark face. "You want I watch this night again?"

Ant almost dismissed the man, thinking he'd be able to protect the house by himself. But what about the barn? He wouldn't put it past Lewis to steal Chester. Shadow wouldn't let the man near him, but Chester might. And a bullet would take care of Shadow. The thought sickened him.

"I'd be obliged if you'd sleep in the barn tonight. Protect the livestock."

"*Sí, Señor.* I will be here tonight."

"I'll bring some food out for you."

"*Gracias, Señor.*" Pepe indicated a straw bale he'd hauled next to the entrance of the barn. The dusky shadows would hide his watchful figure.

Ant touched his hat in an acknowledgment.

Pepe propped the shotgun against the bale and collected Shadow's reins. "I take care of him, *Señor.* You go inside."

Too tired to argue, Ant thanked the man. He took his rifle, turned, and trudged toward the house, his back to the setting sun, thinking about what to do about Lewis. The pup followed him.

As the search had dragged on today, Ant had realized he'd made a mistake by planting himself in Sweetwater Springs. Now with his fortunes tied to the town, he couldn't just pluck David from his surroundings and escape. He couldn't leave Harriet vulnerable. Lewis might punish her for getting in his way, for taking David, for siding with Ant. He didn't need another woman's death on his conscience.

Harriet will just have to marry me. I'll take her and David to Europe. Lewis won't follow us there. I know she loves another, but he's roped and tied. She'll be safe with me. With so much of my capital invested here, we'll be on tight rations but everyone will be safe. That's what's important.

As his boots clunked on the steps of the cabin, he prepared himself for the argument. *Can't just launch into asking her to marry me. She doesn't know Lewis is still alive. We will have to discuss everything after David's gone to bed.*

Ant took off his hat and rubbed his arm over his face. *How can I be so exhausted, yet so wound up?* He knew the answer. He'd experienced enough dangerous times when pursuing news stories. *But I didn't care about the people around me, only about the story.* Now he cared. Cared deeply.

Ant opened the door and stepped inside. He hung the rifle on the rack next to the door. The pup sniffed his boots before trying to gnaw on the toe of one. He did a fancy shuffle to save the leather, unbuckled his gun belt, and hung it on a hook underneath the rack holding the rifle.

Harriet's voice echoed from the kitchen. The cadence sounded as if she was reading out loud. The words seemed familiar.

With a flash of recognition, Ant realized that he was hearing one of Emily's poems. Anger burst within him, ancient and bitter. Without stopping to think, he strode through the house and into the kitchen.

~

Harriet had discovered a book of poetry on the bookshelf. It stood next to Ant's other books that looked as well-worn as hers. Delighted, she'd paged through the book, stopping here and there to read a poem. She sighed with envy. *These are much better than mine.* She turned the book over, looking for the author. *Emily March. Isn't Emily the name of Ant's sister?*

Harriet had found David in the kitchen, hunched over the table in the dwindling shaft of sunlight from the window, brow furrowed with concentration, writing out his numbers. She held the book out to him. "Do you recognize this?"

He looked up, eyed the book and shook his head.

"The poems are by Emily March."

His eyes widened.

"Your mother?"

He nodded, looking fearful and scrunching down in his chair.

She pulled up a chair next to him and put her arm around his shoulder. "Nothing to be afraid about, David. Let's try reading them and see what happens."

Harriet opened up the book, turning the pages until she came to one with a bookmark. She glanced at it, noting that the poem seemed different from the other work, not of the same caliber. More like a ditty really, about a boy playing with his boat. "David, I think this is for you." She read the verses out loud, enjoying the catchy refrain:

> Sail away down the pond, little boat.
> How I love watching as you float.
> Then you tack round about to me,
> Returning even though you are free.

David sat up straighter, a dawning expression of recognition on his face. His brown eyes, usually so somber, sparked to life. Halfway through, David mouthed the words with her. By the end, he croaked a word aloud.

"David, you talked!" Filled with excitement, Harriet leaned over and hugged him. "You do remember this poem. Oh, David. I'm so pleased. I think your mother wrote this about you, didn't she?"

He nodded.

"Let's do it again. I'll read a line, and you repeat it after me."

Slowly they worked their way through the poem. David's voice sounded low and rusty, his speech hesitant. But they were spoken words, nevertheless. Each one chimed a musical note in her heart.

When they finished, Harriet had to restrain herself from dancing around the room. Instead, she smoothed back his hair. "Well done, David. How does it feel to talk again?"

He gave her a faint smile and a shrug before ducking his head.

Harriet laughed. "Looks as if you're still going to keep most of your words to yourself for a while. I can hardly wait to tell your Uncle Ant. Better yet, you tell him. Imagine how happy he'll be. Think you can do that?" She tapped the open page of the book. "Let's test your memory. I'll read a whole verse, and you repeat it after me."

"Alright," he whispered.

She read the first verse. Her foot tapped to the cadence of the lines.

Rapid footsteps banged across on the wooden floor of the other room. Ant appeared in the doorway of the kitchen, his face like a thundercloud about to shoot lightning bolts at her.

Harriet had never seen him looking that way. Fear tightened her stomach. "Ant, what is it?"

David slid down his chair and scooted under the table.

Ant didn't answer. Instead, he strode over and grabbed the book out of her hands. He stomped to the stove, opened the door, thrust the book inside, and then slammed it shut.

"Ant," she protested, feeling her heart thumping rapidly. "What in the world?"

"What do you think you're doing?" His voice was rough with anger.

Reading? Bewildered, Harriet struggled to grasp what he was so upset about. "You mean something written by his mother?"

"I mean poetry."

"Poetry?" she echoed.

"A man has no business learning that kind of nonsense."

She shoved to her feet, placing her hands on her hips and squaring off to him. "Nonsense! Poetry is one of the highest forms of literature."

"You're going to turn him into a sissy."

David crawled out from under the table, slipped behind his uncle, and continued out the door. *Good. He shouldn't be exposed to this.*

"I've never heard such a ridiculous accusation. Through the ages, men were the ones who wrote poetry. Think of the psalms written by David—a *warrior* king. Knights who wrote chivalrous poems to their lady loves. Nothing *sissy* about them."

Ant opened his mouth to argue, but Harriet rolled right over him, not letting him get a word in edgewise. "Very few women have achieved recognition from their poetry. Emily Dickenson is an exception. Elizabeth Barrett Browning. I haven't seen many of your sister's poems, but those I've read are laudable. You should be proud of her, not acting like a mad man. Storming in here, destroying a precious book, frightening David."

"We'll talk about this later. Right now there's something more important." He slashed his hand through the air, cutting off the topic.

"More important than frightening your nephew, undoing all the work we've done to make him feel safe?"

Ant took off his hat and set it on the table. He ran his fingers through his hair, sighed. "He's not safe, Harriet," he said, sounding tired. "Neither are you. Mack told me last night that someone stole David's mule."

Harriet's mind fumbled to keep up with him.

"I think Lewis might still be alive. And if that's the case, David's in danger...we're all in danger."

Harriet felt as if Ant had yanked the rug out from under her. "You didn't tell me?"

"You were asleep while I was talking to Mack and barely woke up to get yourself into the house. I left Pepe here to keep watch until I returned."

Harriet's anger didn't abate. She wanted to shake the man. "You could have written the information to me in the note you left. I'm not a child, Ant. Yet, you keep treating me like I'm one with your secrecy about Lewis."

"Let me explain."

She ignored him. "You certainly have turned into a despot. My eyes are open to your character."

"Harriet," Ant grabbed her wrists.

She tried to wrench herself away, but might as well fight a mountain.

"If we don't find Lewis, we'll never be safe here. We'll always be looking over our shoulder. We need to leave."

"I'm not going anywhere. I teach here."

"Marry me. You won't have to work. You and David and I will go to Europe. Lewis will never find us there."

"Marry you." She gaped at him. "Anthony Gordon, I wouldn't marry you if you were the last man in Montana!"

"I know you love Sanders, and I'm not asking for an intimate relationship, just—"

You know I love Nick? Harriet jerked her arms back. When he didn't release her wrists, she kicked him in the shins. "Let go of me, you oaf!"

He opened his fingers, stepping back and holding up his hands. "Just hear me out, Harriet."

"How did you know about Nick?" she snapped.

"I saw the way you look at him, Harriet. Like a lovesick puppy."

Humiliation lodged in her stomach, sending waves of heat through her body. Harriet put her hands to her burning cheeks. "You're perceptive," she said in a bitter tone.

"It's common knowledge."

"No. No one knows. I ... I never told...."

"People figured it out anyway."

Dismayed, she whispered, "It can't be."

A look of pity crossed Ant's face, and he stepped forward. "Yes, they know, my dear. I'm not certain about Elizabeth, but Sanders surely does. It was mentioned in his presence at the meeting with the town leaders. He didn't look surprised." Ant gently grasped her shoulders. "Now, will you hear me out?"

Anger twined with the shame. Harriet pushed him away, but he didn't budge. "I have nothing to say to you, Anthony Gordon. Not another word! Do you hear me?" She put all her schoolteacher authority in her voice.

He stepped back and let her pass. "We'll talk later."

"We most certainly shall! But for now, I'm going to find David. Hopefully, you haven't rendered him permanently mute!"

Harriet marched across the room and out the door. On the porch, she could see the sun heading toward the horizon. She scanned the area for David and caught a glimpse of him at the edge of the trees that led to the stream. He was probably headed for the pool they'd discovered yesterday.

She hurried after him. *I'll have to catch him...reassure him he's safe.*

～

Like a locomotive, Harriet steamed out of the house, leaving Ant with all his persuasive words still unsaid. *Might as well try to stop a train.*

Ant followed Harriet to the porch, feeling an odd sense of helplessness. He watched her head to the stream and figured he'd better let her cool down before going after her, although he'd keep her in sight. If he caught up with her while her anger was still in full boil, he'd have a wildcat on his hands. Her head start wouldn't matter. With his longer legs, he'd be able to overtake her soon enough.

He paced back and forth across the porch, careful not to trip over the puppy, who decided to shadow him.

In front of the barn, Pepe rose from the straw bale and took a few steps toward the house.

"Stay there and watch the house and the horses," Ant called to him.

Pepe waved his understanding.

Ant scooped up the puppy, who licked his chin. Petting the dog seemed to help soothe him, yet it took a while for him to calm his smoldering emotions. The intensity and heat of his reaction alerted him that something was wrong—something far greater than a book of poems.

Ant knew he wasn't a man given to hot anger and hasty words. His wrath tended to burn cold and quiet, a characteristic that had served him well in the long hunt for his brother-in-law. This reaction wasn't like him.

Ant began to pace again, all the while keeping an eye on Harriet, who continued her trek to the river, her back ramrod straight. *Why did I get so furious with Harriet?*

I was tired and on edge already. Easily set off. But he'd been exhausted and edgy and in danger many times before without exploding at anyone. *Why Harriet? Why now? Why poetry?*

He'd blown up at Harriet for reading Emily's poems, yet he was the one who'd carried the book in the bottom of his saddlebag for two years. Ant had known of Harriet's love of books and poetry. It was inevitable that she'd find the book and read it.

A long-forgotten recollection surfaced—his stepfather snatching a paper out of his hand, reading it, and then tearing it up, before taking a whip to him. "A man doesn't write poetry," he shouted with each blow. "Only sissies write poems." Ant's back tingled from the memory.

Deliberately forgotten childhood memories flooded his mind. After that experience, Ant had never written another poem, although he hadn't lost his love for writing. He turned to journalism instead, a more manly and rational form of writing. The beatings lessened, but didn't stop.

The man ignored Emily, which probably was a good thing. He'd been known to break a stick over Ant's bottom and legs for the slightest infringement of his rules.

Emily had been so anxious to escape the brute that she'd married a man just like him. Although it had taken several years for the darkness to surface in Lewis, surely there'd been shadows that Emily should have recognized while the man was courting her.

But this isn't about Emily. The chiding voice brought him to his present predicament.

"What have I done?" He'd been unreasonable and cruel, just like his stepfather. He'd turned into a bully like him. Ant groaned. *What an idiot I've been. The man's been dead for ten years, and I was his parrot instead of being myself—a man of reason and moderate passions. Well, except for a certain woman.*

I've hurt the two people I care about most, perhaps damaging my relationship with them beyond repair. All because of a man I hated, yet became. Harriet was right to call me an oaf, and worse.

Still carrying the dog, he leaped off the porch.

I need to fix what I've damaged, explain. Ask for forgiveness.

The pup squirmed, and he squeezed his arms tighter so he wouldn't drop the dog.

Will Harriet understand?

I'll find a way to make her. I just have to reach her before she becomes dead set against me.

He hurried to the barn and handed over the dog to Pepe. "Keep her with you."

Pepe stood, grabbed the dog, and sat back down on the straw bale, stroking the puppy to calm her.

Ant clapped his hand to his hip and realized he'd left his gunbelt in the house. In his eagerness to catch up with Harriet, he almost continued after her. But a ration of common sense made him turn back for his gun. He wasn't about to let his sidewinder of a brother-in-law catch him unarmed.

CHAPTER TWENTY-THREE

Fear propelled David away from the house, past the barn and toward the trees shading the stream. *I can hide there.*

Once he reached the shelter of the trees, he ran upstream, leaping over rocks and dashing around trees until the constriction in his lungs and the ache in his side forced him to a walk. Gasping for air, he searched his surroundings for a hiding place.

Seeing an oak with a hollowed out trunk, he crouched down and used a nearby branch to poke around the interior. When no critter charged out, he crawled inside, drawing his knees up to his chest and wrapping his arms around his legs.

There, he sat panting, mindless. His breath had eased long before David felt his awareness return. He replayed the scene with his uncle and Miss Stanton and started shivering at the enraged look on his uncle's face and the angry sound of his voice.

I left Miss Stanton alone with him.

Shame coursed through him.

Uncle Ant could have beaten her. Killed her. And Miss Stanton was littler than his mother. David pictured her lying in a pool of blood like....

The memory tore aside the curtain of the past, ripping through the gray fog of forgetfulness he'd cloaked around his mother. *He saw his pa, staggering drunk, with a knife in his hand and an evil look on his face. "You think you're leaving me," Pa had yelled at his mother. "You'll never leave."*

David had dodged behind a wingchair in the corner of the parlor, crouching until he was out of sight. He'd peered around the side, watching.

Pa had grabbed his mother. She'd screamed and fought him, trying to break away. But he'd held on tight and slashed the knife across her throat.

Blood spurted from her neck. She made a horrible gurgling noise. Pa let go of her. She dropped to the ground like a red-stained rag doll.

David had wailed at the sight, but he hadn't let the noise out for fear Pa would hear him. But the sound had exploded in his mind.

Then Pa had kicked her in the side, cursed her. Finally, he'd turned and staggered up the stairs.

David had listened for his footsteps to die away. He crept out from behind the chair and tiptoed over to his mother. She lay motionless on the wooden floor, blood pooling around her.

He'd stooped to touch her cheek. The coppery smell of her blood filled his nostrils.

"Mother, Mother," he whispered, trying to get her to turn and look at him. But she'd stared wide-eyed at the ceiling, an empty look in her brown eyes. He began to shake.

David was so engrossed with his mother that he didn't hear his pa come back into the room. A heavy hand dropped on his shoulder, shooting him out of his boots. "You come with me, boy. We're leaving."

Pa jerked David around to face him. With one hand on his shoulder, he shook his finger in David's face, his blue eyes so icy, they froze him in place. "Don't you ever say a word about this to anyone, you hear? You even think about talking, and I'll pull out your tongue and cut it off." He gave David a shake for emphasis that almost knocked him over.

The wail David had held inside for two years boiled out. The sound filled the hollow of the tree, vibrating around him. An invisible cord tight around his chest released, and he screamed and screamed. The noise amplified by the trunk made his ears ring. The tree seemed to wrap its essence around him, comforting him at that same time as it drew out the pain. "Mother, Mother, Mother!"

He sobbed, crying out some of the tears he'd stored up over the pain-filled past. When the sobs eased, leaving him snot-nosed and wet-faced, he sniffed and wiped his sleeve across his face. Although he felt ashamed about blubbering like a baby, he felt better than he had in a long time. *Cleansed* was the word that came to his mind from something Reverend Norton had said in his sermon on Sunday.

David relaxed against the tree, limp and almost dozing. Then he remembered Miss Stanton, left alone with his angry uncle, and jerked awake. He shot up so fast he bumped his head on the top of the hollow.

David scrambled out of the oak and ran downstream. He leaped over a fallen log, dodged around a tangle of willow. Just past the trees, a pair of hands reached out and grabbed him. David yelped.

"Got ya, boy." At the sound of the raspy voice and the familiar stench of whiskey, David went limp like a dead rabbit, the reaction he'd always had to his pa's abuse.

"Thought ya could git away from me, ah?" His pa leered at him. "Well I don't want ya either. But I got some use for ya."

David's terror of his father wiped his fears of Uncle Ant from his mind, and he could only long for his uncle's protection. *Uncle Ant, save me!*

Pa fingered the butt of the gun tucked into his pants. "Then again, I could always kill your interfering uncle, take that pretty little lady of his for a ride, and then kill her too. What do you think about that, boy?"

David could only stare into his pa's cold, reddened eyes in his puffy face, feeling his limbs freeze.

"You'll be good for something, alright." He pointed at Ole Blue, munching on some grass. "Now git on that mule!"

~

Harriet reached a stand of cottonwoods and ran on, searching. The impact of Ant's revelation burned through her body. All this time she'd thought her feelings for Nick had been secret, but to learn they'd been common knowledge.... *Have people been gossiping about me? Laughing at me?* She hurried downstream along the path, her face hot from embarrassment, her stomach tight and sick with shame.

She wished she could stop and sink into the bark of one of the giant cottonwoods, like the dryad she'd fancied David to be, leaving her shame behind. *Inside the tree, no one would find me. I'd be safe. Protected from the world, from the shame I'll feel each time I go into company—wondering what people are thinking.* But Harriet couldn't stop and hide. She had to find David. Reassure him before he retreated back into silence.

The shadows lengthened. She slowed to peer behind trees and under bushes. Yet as Harriet searched, images tumbled through her mind. She remembered remarks and looks she'd ignored, like Samantha's look of pity and understanding when Harriet needed to flee from the news of Elizabeth's pregnancy...Mrs. Cobb's insistence on her attending the Sanders' moving party. *She wanted to punish me.* In retrospect, she could think of dozens of remarks and knowing glances that had hinted of people's knowledge of her infatuation.

Panting, she rested against an elm, scanning ahead. *I'll have to leave this town. Find another place to teach where nobody knows me.*

That decision brought relief. She could start all over with a clean slate. Focusing on the decision, Harriet refused to let herself mourn the loss of Sweetwater Springs...of students and friends...of Ant and David. *Not now. Time for grieving later.*

Now she had to find David. *Where is he?*

Confident she'd find him near the pool, she straightened away from the tree and traipsed downstream, the gurgle of the water over stones guiding her.

Harriet reached the clearing by the pool with a sense of relief. So strong was her expectation of finding David here that she had to blink several times before she realized he wasn't.

"David," she called. "David, where are you?" She peeked behind some trees and parted the branches of some bushes. "David, come out. It's all right. Your uncle won't hurt you."

Once she'd searched the clearing without finding him, Harriet continued downstream. But the farther she moved, the more she became convinced she was going the wrong way. Finally, she decided to follow her intuition and turned, heading upstream.

A sense of urgency made her increase her pace. She passed the place where she'd started and kept on going, scanning the surroundings, her ears pricked for any sound from David. She'd made so much progress with him. He'd just begun to talk. "Please, God. Let him keep talking. Let him be able to make a joyful noise to you," she whispered.

In an answer to her prayer, a distant yelp cut through the air.

David. Her heart leapt into her throat. She spied a large stick on the ground and scooped it up. Then she gathered her skirts with her other hand and began to run. But she hadn't gone far when she had to stop and gasp for breath. The tight corset constrained her from going farther, and Harriet feared she'd pass out. *I knew I should have burned this corset!*

As soon as she caught her breath, Harriet picked up her pace, but didn't break into a run. It wouldn't do David any good for her to keel over before she reached him. She listened for more wails but didn't hear anything. Surely if something was wrong, he'd yell for help?

She rounded a tree and saw David seated on a mule, his body stiff. His father stood next to him, squeezing the boy's leg in a painful grip. He wore a stick tied around one leg. Without stopping to think, Harriet sprinted toward them, brandishing the branch.

Lewis saw her and shot her a predatory grin that would have sent chills down her spine if she wasn't so focused on rescuing David.

"Let him go," she yelled, banged the branch on the man's arm.

Lewis lost his grin and snarled at her. Letting go of David, he reached for his gun.

David came to life, flailing and kicking. One elbow caught Lewis in the ribs while at the same time, the heel of his boot connected with Ole Blue's sides. The mule brayed and laid back his ears, shifting his weight into Lewis, knocking the man off balance onto his bad leg.

I have to keep his hand away from his gun. Harriet whacked Lewis again. While the man was unsettled by the mule and his struggling son, she reached up and yanked David off the mule. Then she kicked Lewis in the knee of his bad leg.

The man let out a string of curses. "You'll pay for that!" He made a grab for the boy, but missed.

David landed in a heap on the ground but jumped to his feet, his eyes bright with unshed tears.

"Run for your uncle," Harriet ordered, not taking her gaze off Lewis.

"But," David croaked.

"Run!"

David took off.

Harriet shoved the end of the stick into Lewis' side.

The man let out an expletive and grabbed the wood, jerking her toward him. He stank of body odor and whiskey. He caught her hair, giving it a nasty pull to bring her face closer to him.

Tears came to her eyes, but Harriet refused to cry out. She fisted her hand and thumped it against his thigh.

He cursed and backhanded her across the face.

Agony knifed through her, and she couldn't breathe. Her knees buckled from pain, but his grip on her hair kept her tied to him. Thousands of needles stabbed into her scalp, making her want to scream. She bit her lip to hold it in.

He relaxed his hold on her hair, but didn't let go.

Harriet collapsed against the mule, inhaling the dusty smell of its hide.

"I have you now, girly. You fight anymore, and you'll get a fist to your face. Break that pretty nose of yours and lay you out. Makes no difference to me whether you're conscious or not. Pleasure is pleasure."

"Ant will kill you," she ground out.

He slapped her face again. Her head snapped to the side. For a moment, the light dimmed. A ringing in her ear deafened her.

"Thanks for the reminder, girly. Guess I don't have time to pleasure myself after all." He reached for his gun. "Too bad for you."

~

Ant hurried to the river, urgency spurring him onward. Reaching the water, he realized he didn't know which way to head. He'd just chosen downstream when he heard the sound of yelling, which settled the question. Turning, Ant drew his gun, moving through the trees as quickly and silently as he could.

David burst out of a stand of willows, panic on his face.

Ant dropped the Colt into the holster and reached out to catch him.

"Uncle Ant," the boy gasped out. "Pa's got Miss Stanton."

"You're talking." Ant gave him a quick hug. "Go get Pepe. Then saddle Chester and ride to town for help." He released him.

David pelted away.

No matter what happens, he'll be safe.

But Harriet!

Although Ant wanted to race to Harriet's aid, he restrained himself, drawing his gun and creeping through the willows. *It won't do to get us both killed.*

Ant couldn't help some sticks crunching under his boots, but the sounds of the struggle covered up his footsteps. He parted the drooping branches to see Lewis backed against the mule, one hand fisted in Harriet's hair, the other on his gun.

Even in the fading light, he could see Harriet's face was bone-white except for a red splotch on one cheek. The coward had hit Harriet—beaten her, as he had beaten Emily.

A lightning flash of anger struck Ant, igniting an animal instinct to defend. He couldn't get a shot in without risking Harriet, so he dropped his gun into the holster and charged, barreling into Lewis before the man knew what hit him. With one hand Ant forced Lewis' gun arm up. He fisted his other hand, driving it into Lewis' stomach.

Lewis growled and released Harriet, who jumped back. But hampered by her skirts, she tripped and landed on her backside.

Lewis retaliated with an uppercut to Ant's side.

Ant grunted, absorbing the pain. He kicked Lewis in his broken leg, hard enough to knock him off his feet, while at the same time grabbing for the gun and bending it out of Lewis' fingers.

A shot went off, the sound made his ears ring. But he wrenched the gun away and had it in his possession. He knocked Lewis on the head with the butt end, just as Lewis elbowed him in the stomach.

Ant doubled over and gasped for breath.

Lewis staggered back a step into the rump of the mule.

With a loud bray the mule kicked. Its hooves connected with Lewis' midsection, sending him flying.

Panting, Ant straightened. He raised the Colt, took careful aim at the man on the ground. Lewis lay sprawled on his back amid the rocks edging the river. He didn't move, his body limp.

Keeping the Colt trained on Lewis, Ant edged closer. But what he saw made him release a deep breath of relief and holster his gun.

Lewis' eyes gazed blankly at the sky, his head at a sharp angle. To be sure, Ant knelt down and felt for a pulse, even though he'd seen enough dead people to know death when he saw it. He stood, turned to Harriet, and took quick steps to help her up.

Harriet, her hair straggling around her face, threw herself at him. He wrapped his arms around her, feeling her tremble.

Safe. He closed his eyes in gratitude. *Thank you, dear Lord! Thank you, thank you!*

They embraced for a moment without speaking. Although Ant wanted to kiss her, he didn't push. He'd woo Harriet. Give her time.

Reluctantly he loosened his arms. "Are you hurt? Can you move?"

Harriet rubbed her head, an expression of pain on her face. "I think my hair is six inches longer."

He smoothed his hand over her head. "Where does it hurt?"

"All over."

Ant messaged her scalp.

She gave a little moan. "That feels good."

He rubbed her head for another minute, feeling some of the tension leave her body. He dropped a kiss on her forehead. "I promise to do more later, but Pepe is going to come charging over here any minute now. And if we don't stop David, he'll lead a posse back from town."

"I can move."

"That's my girl. Don't look at Lewis," he ordered. "You don't want to see him. Pepe will take the mule, then he and I will come back for the body later."

Harriet kept her face turned away from the body.

Ant took her hand. When Harriet didn't pull away, he had to quiet a stir of hope. *Might be that she's just shaken up.* Together they walked downstream.

When they cleared the trees, they saw Pepe running with the shotgun, a determined look on his face. He skidded to a stop. A single glance took in their joined hands and relaxed bodies. "The bad one, he is no more, eh?"

Ant waved his hand in the direction of Lewis' body. "Go see for yourself. We fought, but it was the kick from the mule that tossed Lewis onto the rocks and killed him."

"*Bueno, Señor.*" Pepe rattled off a string of Spanish that included "*hombre malo*" and a few indecipherable words.

"That mule's a hero," Ant said. "Take him in and give him some warm mash and a good grooming."

"*Sí, Señor.*"

Ant glanced down at Harriet. Color had returned to her cheeks and the skin was beginning to bruise on one side of her face. "Ole Blue has earned warm mash for life, don't you think?"

Although a haunted look shadowed her eyes, she gave him a half smile that twisted his heart. *Soon please, God, she'll laugh and be happy.*

~

With shaking hands, David mounted Chester and, inside the barn, kneed him into a trot. As soon as they cleared the open doors, he kicked the horse into a gallop, heading for town.

He heard a shout behind him. "David, wait!"

Uncle Ant's voice.

David glanced back and saw Uncle Ant holding hands with Miss Stanton. He slowed Chester and wheeled the horse around, trotting back to them. He released the reins and slid off into his uncle's arms. Uncle Ant gave him a big hug, holding him in the air, and letting his legs dangle before setting him down.

David wiggled away and launched himself at Miss Stanton, almost bowling her over from his onslaught.

She braced herself, clasping him to her.

"Miss Stanton, I thought he was going to kill you like he did my mother."

She held him close, dropping a kiss on the top of his head. "But he didn't, David love. He didn't. We're safe now."

As David burrowed into Miss Stanton's arms, he felt his uncle place a hand on his shoulder. He turned, looked up at his uncle's face, and saw the pain in his eyes. *Uncle Ant must have killed my pa.* At the thought, the knot in his stomach unwound.

Uncle Ant's words confirmed the knowledge. "Your father's dead now, David. We saw the body. I promise, he'll never hurt you again."

For a moment, David felt a wave of sadness, then he glanced at Miss Stanton and saw the bruise on her face, and his heart hardened. *My pa was a bad man. It's good he's dead.* But he couldn't help the wistful wish, one he'd often had, that he had another man for his pa—a good one.

Uncle Ant crouched until his face was at David's height. "I'm so sorry for what I did with your mother's book. I became a bully. I frightened you...and Miss Stanton. I was wrong. Can you forgive me?" He looked at Miss Stanton. "Can you *both* forgive me?"

Miss Stanton gave him her pretty smile.

Pa never apologized. David nodded, then for good measure, said, "Yes."

Uncle Ant looked relieved. He held out his hand to David.

David stepped away from Miss Stanton and took his uncle's hand. *Maybe I don't have a good pa, but I sure do have a good uncle.* He eased his hand into Miss Stanton's. "Let's go home."

The three of them walked toward the house, David sandwiched between the adults. For the first time, he felt like part of a family and wished they could always be this way.

They separated to go through the front door. David led the way to the kitchen. He walked over to the stove, pried opened the round cast iron cover, and fished out the book. Although it had some streaks of ash on the leather cover, it wasn't ruined.

"Good thing I cleaned out the stove today, and David and I became so engrossed in his mother's book that I hadn't started supper," Miss Stanton said. She walked over to the sink, moving stiffly like she hurt, and picked up the dishcloth. "Here, David, let me wipe that off." She gave the book a careful cleaning and handed it back to him.

David laid the book on the table, pulled out a chair, and sat down. "Let's read it together."

His uncle gave him a crooked grin. "That sounds like a very good idea, Davy boy. A very good idea. But first, Miss Stanton needs to lie down and rest. You and I are going to make her some willow bark tea and scrape together some supper." He grinned at her. "I hope you like beans, my lady."

Although her face didn't change, probably because it pained her to move, her eyes twinkled at his uncle, and she gave a tiny nod.

And in that moment, seeing the connection between the two of them, David knew everything was going to be all right.

CHAPTER TWENTY-FOUR

A few nights later, Ant and Harriet walked outside, hand-in-hand. By unspoken accord, they headed toward the stream. In the days since Lewis' attack, their bruises had turned green and yellow; the killer had been interred in the plot behind the church; and David had taken to talking up a storm.

The faint moonlight cast just enough light to follow the path that the Maguires had trod into the dirt over the years. Under the trees, it was nearly black with just the sound of the rustling leaves and rushing water to tell them where they were.

They spoke of Ant's new building, plans already begun, and Harriet's attempt to make David a new shirt. Commonplace topics, but all the time an awareness of each other's presence shimmered between them.

They stopped at the stream's edge near the flat boulder, where the trees parted and the moon-glow showed on the milky bubbles, dancing over the silky black water. A night breeze, fragrant with earth and greenery, wafted over them.

Ant stared at the water. "I've been an angry man, Harriet. Angry enough to kill. But when all is said and done, I'm glad I didn't have to. I'm not sure what to do about the anger though. I think it's still there."

"Of course it is. Lewis' death doesn't erase your feelings about your sister's murder."

He let out a long, slow breath.

"I suggest you take some paper and a pen and write the story about what happened, including your feelings. I know that works for me. I haven't had anyone to talk to for a long time, so all my feelings have spilled out in my journal. I think it's the only thing that has helped me keep my temper with the Cobbs."

"I'll give it a try. Probably end up writing a book, though."

"Is that so bad? Fuddy duddy professor?"

He grinned at her. "Not any more. I reckon I could stand a dose of fuddy duddy after the excitement of the last weeks. But my anger was about more than Lewis murdering my sister and kidnapping David. It started before... in Europe with a woman named Isabella, whom I loved."

Harriet's heart clenched at his words.

Ant proceeded to tell her the whole story.

The story stirred her compassion. Harriet leaned against him. "Thank you for telling me."

He dropped his arm around her shoulders and squeezed. "I never told anyone before. It actually felt good... good to remember... without the pain."

Harriet looked up at him. "I don't love Nick Sanders."

His body stiffened, and he slowly turned to face her. "What do you mean?"

"I did love him. Or thought I did. He made me feel safe, and I needed that. After my father died, we moved around a lot...stayed in some...rough places. All I wanted was stability and security. But I started to feel differently a few weeks ago. It's only lately that I realized my feelings had changed."

"Different how?"

"I still want stability and security, but not with Nick." She looked up at him, hoping the moon's light showed him the love in her eyes.

"Harriet." Still holding her hand, Ant dropped to one knee. "Will you marry me? Not because of Lewis. He's finally dead and out of our lives. I love you, Harriet. You don't know what a miracle that is. Perhaps, with time, you can come to love me back."

As Harriet absorbed his words, joy flooded her, and she laughed. "Too late."

"What?"

"I already love you."

Ant flashed her that crooked grin and picked her up, twirling her around.

She let out a little scream and held him tight.

"Guess we haven't had a normal courtship, have we?"

She laughed. "We certainly haven't. Do you think we can manage a more comfortable married life?"

"I certainly hope so," he said fervently.

With her arms draped around his neck, Ant carried her over to the boulder and set her feet on the surface, holding her waist until she could stand on her own.

Now she was almost his height. He looked into her eyes. "Guess I'm always going to look for things to set you on so I can kiss you right."

"You can make stools for me all over the house," Harriet murmured, leaning forward to press her lips on his.

≈

A week later, Harriet stood in the Cobbs' kitchen, wearing the first silk dress she'd ever owned. Mrs. Cobb, as happy as Harriet had ever seen her, bent down to straighten the misty-gray folds of her skirt, while Samantha Thompson, clad in the dress she'd worn to her own wedding, placed her veil over Harriet's head, then stepped back to survey Harriet, tears brightening her blue eyes. "You look beautiful, my dear Harriet. This color really brings out your eyes."

Harriet had to blink answering tears away. "Thank you for lending me your veil."

"Enough, Harriet," Samantha said in a firm tone. "You've already thanked me three times. I know it's only been a week and a half for me, but I wish you all the happiness I've found with Wyatt."

Mrs. Cobb straightened, fluffing out Harriet's puffed sleeves. In an unexpected gesture of affection, she took Harriet's hand. "I, too, wish you happy, Miss Stanton. I was hard on you, I know. But it was because I was concerned about you. A woman's good reputation is above jewels."

Harriet exchanged an astonished look with Samantha. She couldn't help glancing out the window to see if any pigs happened to be flying by, but the sky remind clear of porcine creatures with wings.

Mrs. Cobb sniffed, as if holding back emotion. "Soon, I'll be calling you Mrs. Gordon."

Surprised and touched, Harriet squeezed Mrs. Cobb's hand. "Thank you, Mrs. Cobb."

As if putting sentimentality behind her, Mrs. Cobb released Harriet's hand. "Mr. Cobb told me that after Mr. Gordon left the meeting of the town leaders, the men all had a bet that he'd marry you before school started again. That's why they didn't protest more about you living together."

"A bet!" Harriet wasn't sure whether to feel horrified or amused.

Mrs. Cobb sniffed again. "Not really a bet because they were all in accord, so there was no one to bet against. Mr. Cobb swore me to secrecy."

Harriet settled on amusement. A giggle bubbled up in her, and she could see laughter reflected in Samantha's eyes. "This town knows me too well."

Samantha gave her a hug. "Everyone loves you, that's why."

Harriet thought back to Ant's revelation about everyone knowing her feelings for Nick. She gave Samantha a wry smile. "I guess that's not such a bad thing after all."

Mrs. Cobb reached for her hat where it lay on the table and placed it on her head—a new one without a stuffed bird adorning the brim. She tied her bonnet strings. "It's time to go, Miss Stanton. I watched from the window. Almost everybody is already in the church." She sniffed. "Seems like everyone and his brother has turned up. Good thing you didn't marry from a house. Wouldn't have been anyplace big enough."

Samantha handed Harriet a bouquet of roses, the same kind of white ones she'd carried for her wedding.

Harriet sniffed their sweet scent. *I'll have to press one later as a keepsake.*

The three women left the house and strolled down the street. As they crossed to the church, Harriet saw Nick and Elizabeth Sanders standing out in front. Samantha and Mrs. Cobb greeted them and continued inside, leaving Harriet with the couple.

Elizabeth was dressed in a sapphire silk gown that allowed the slight bulge of her pregnancy to show and made her eyes look like gems. Nick had on the suit he'd worn for his own wedding, although today he seemed more comfortable in it. The couple looked content and prosperous, and for the first time, Harriet could whole-heartedly wish them every happiness. The realization made her feel light and free.

Nick took her hand, the first time he'd ever touched her, and gave it a quick squeeze before letting go. "I want you to know, Miss Stanton, how very glad I am that Mr. Gordon has had the good sense to choose you for his wife. I wish you all the best."

"*We* wish you all the best, Harriet," Elizabeth chimed in. "May you have as happy a marriage as we do."

In looking from one to the other, Harriet could see in their eyes that they had known of her feelings for Nick. Today, she didn't feel shame. Instead, she allowed their genuine good will to seep into her body, twining with her joy. "Thank you. That's a wonderful blessing, indeed!"

Elizabeth leaned forward to kiss Harriet's cheek. Then the couple turned and climbed the steps to the church.

Harriet touched her cheek, marveling at how much things had changed. She fiddled with the gold pin at her neck. *Elizabeth and I are going to be friends. Who would have thought?*

Harriet brought her bouquet to her nose for one last fortifying sniff. *The last time I entered this church for a wedding, I was so very unhappy. Now, I feel as if I could fly.* She giggled at the image of floating down the aisle to her groom.

Harriet gathered her up her skirts to climb the stairs and stepped into the church. As she crossed the small foyer, a hush fell over the room. She'd chosen to walk up the aisle alone instead of asking Mr. Cobb, the logical choice, to escort her.

Everyone turned to see her. She gave David, standing straight and proud next to his uncle, a fond smile, but then she only had eyes for Ant. Her husband-to-be waited tall and dark in the front of the church, wearing a new black suit and vest with a white shirt.

Elizabeth started playing Mendelssohn's "Wedding March."

Her heart lifted by the notes of the music, Harriet walked up the aisle, her eyes on Ant. His stunned expression, so full of love and pride, softened the angles of his face, rendering him handsome.

Harriet gave him a tremulous smile and couldn't wait to reach his side.

As she approached him, he took her hand. "You look beautiful," he whispered, bringing her hand to his lips.

The brush of his mouth on her hand sent shivers up her arm and down her spine. In his eyes, Harriet saw the promise of love for all the years to come.

Ant solemnly gazed into her eyes and gave her his crooked smile.

How could I ever have thought him frightening?

Then they turned and faced the minister. Reverend Norton's austere face softened with a smile of affection. "Dearly beloved, we are gathered here...."

THE END

Read on for an excerpt of *Montana Sky Christmas:*
A Sweetwater Springs Short Story Collection

As the campfire radiated warmth in the opening of the lean-to, Red Macalister crouched before the burning logs. He added more wood to the blaze, then rocked back on his boot heels, studying the flames, and decided the fire would do for the next few hours to ward off the cold winter night. He glanced up at the black sky dotted with diamonds. *A clear night.* Tomorrow, they'd be able to herd the straggling cattle back to the pasture near the ranch house. He scooted backward under the lean-to of pine branches and nodded at his two companions.

Curly Joe, named for his long brown beard, not the hairless head now covered by a brown knitted cap, sat cross-legged next to him. Jed, a thin, silent man, sprawled on his bedroll at the edge of their shelter.

Curly Joe stroked his beard. "I'll take first," meaning he'd wake up in a few hours to feed the fire.

"Second." Jed made the single word as terse as possible.

Red shrugged. That meant dawn and boiling water for coffee fell to him.

The men didn't really need to spell out the order. They'd worked together for ten years, two of them at their own Circle Three Ranch. They'd fallen into a familiar routine, rotating the chores each day.

But, as they often teased Jed, if they didn't play out their ritual each night, they might not hear a word from their quiet partner for days. They jested that his voice would dry up, and then what would happen if he needed it?

Red pulled off his boots and set them by the fire. Not too close, but near enough so the leather wouldn't freeze his feet in the morning. He wiggled his toes, grimacing at the widening hole in one of his red stockings. If he didn't wear another pair of brown ones underneath, his big toe would be flappin' naked in the chill wind.

Curly Joe looked over at Red's feet and guffawed. "That pair is plumb wore out. Might as well give 'em up."

Red clenched his jaw, leaned over, and picked at the hole, trying to pull the edges together, to no avail. Ignoring Curly Joe, he slid underneath his bedroll. When he got back to the ranch, he'd have their housekeeper darn the hole. It didn't matter that his stockings now had more darns than yarn on the heels. He needed his lucky stockings and wasn't about to give them up.

∾

Louisa Cannon walked back from the train station empty-handed. She'd prayed that there would be a letter from her brother waiting in the mailroom at the depot. But the empty slot had dashed her dwindling hopes.

Michael must not have received my letter. She didn't dare let herself think there could be a worse reason. *Please, God, may he be safe.*

As she walked down the frozen main street of Sweet-water Springs, the wind whipped around her, colder than when she'd set out. She passed the mercantile, decorated with a pine wreath and a big red bow, and spared a hope that the Cobbs managed to sell more of her knitted goods.

The white wooden church on her left contrasted with the saloons and the skeleton of two new buildings on the other side of the street. The sound of hammers rang out, the crew taking advantage of a clear day. Normally, she stopped to watch their progress, but today, she was so preoccupied with her worries that she almost ran into Mr. Livingston, the banker, who'd stopped to tip his hat. "Good day, Miss Cannon."

"Mr. Livingston." Louisa gave him a polite smile.

The thrill that usually tingled her spine at any attention from the handsome banker didn't affect her today. She couldn't even appreciate his polished Eastern manners, because his presence was a reminder that the rent on her little house was due to him by the end of the month.

Her fingers tightened on the front of her coat. She didn't have it, nor have any way to get the money short of...Louisa let her gaze slide toward Hardy's Saloon and had to repress a shudder.

I'd rather die.

The banker dropped his hand to his side. "I see the Cobbs have a wreath up for Christmas." He waved toward the store. "My sister and nephew put our tree up yesterday. How are your Christmas preparations coming, Miss Cannon?"

Just dandy.

Remorse crossed his face. "Excuse me. I'd forgotten about your mother. Christmas will be—"

"I'll have good memories," she interrupted, mostly to make him feel better, not because she believed her words.

He nodded and continued walking toward the mercantile.

No doubt he's eager to buy more presents to add to the pile rumored to already reside under his Christmas tree.

For Louisa, just eking out enough heat from the stove, burning the last of the candles and a small amount of oil for the lamp, and fixing a plain meal of beans would suffice as her Christmas. After that, her nights would be dark except for the glow of the stove, and she'd have to sleep in the kitchen because there was no extra wood or coal for a fire in her bedroom.

Perhaps I can walk to the forest and bring back an armful of branches.

Her mind replayed the familiar litany, struggling to find ways to survive, before discarding each idea.

Teacher? Harriet Gordon already had that job.

Washer woman? She'd gladly take in washing but Widow Murphy at the boarding house wouldn't appreciate Louisa encroaching on her territory. In fact, with the woman's propensity for nasty gossip, she could make life quite difficult. *More difficult,* Louisa amended.

Teach music lessons? Her brother had taken his violin with him when he'd headed to California three months ago to make his fortune. *How could he have been so selfish?*

She pulled back her resentment. Michael couldn't have known their mother would die suddenly. But he should have known that without his income they'd run out of money.

Seamstress? Louisa glanced down at her unadorned black dress and grimaced. She could do basic sewing, but not the kind of work she'd need to set up a business. And she didn't have a sewing machine.

Cook? Her cooking skills were not her strongest suit, but she could rustle up a basic meal.

Housekeeper? She'd made inquiries and hadn't yet found a place.

Wife? She cringed, knowing of an open position. Donny Addison had hinted he'd be glad to marry her. He'd said he'd give her a short time of mourning for her mother, but expected her answer in the New Year. Unlike his spare parents, Donny had grown up buff and hearty. Some might call him a fine figure of a man. But he had squinty eyes, and big, meaty hands, and stood too close to her when he talked, as if he already owned her.

I'd rather die.

Louisa rolled her eyes at her own mournful thoughts. *I'm not going to die, and I am going to find a solution that doesn't involve marrying Donny Addison!*

She could tolerate a loveless marriage with someone she liked and respected, someone she could bear to have touch her. But no other man had expressed interest, a circumstance that puzzled and hurt her, especially since men outnumbered women in these parts, and even the homeliest women found husbands.

Quickening her steps, she turned the corner and walked the blocks to her little house, feeling her feet and hands turn to ice. Her nose must be red, matching her flannel petticoat and knitted stockings—not that anyone could see the bright attire under her proper mourning gown.

Louisa trotted into the house. Inside was almost as cold as outside, but at least the walls stopped the chill breeze. She hurried to the kitchen, where she stirred up the banked coals in the stove and added a measly stick of wood. Standing as close as she dared, she held out her fingers to the heat, meager though it was, trickling into the air.

Once her fingers had warmed, Louisa placed a pot of beans that she'd soaked overnight on the surface, pulled the rocking chair next to the stove, and picked up her knitting. The Cobbs had bought a steady stream of scarves, shawls, mittens, and stockings from her these last months. The money had sustained her while she waited for word from her brother. But a few weeks ago, the shopkeeper had told her the store was overstocked, and they wouldn't need any more for a while.

But Louisa couldn't sit idle, waiting for a pot of beans to boil; not while she still had yarn left. And maybe a horde of cowboys would descend on the town and wipe out the inventory at the mercantile.

Louisa peeled off her mittens and had just started the stitches on a shawl, making a fancy edging, when the idea came to her. Most women could do plain knitting, but not the more elaborate patterns Louisa had learned from her grandmother. *What if I teach fancy knitting?*

The idea raced around in her head. Her fingers sped up, and she rocked harder. Even if her students couldn't afford to pay in cash, she could barter for food or firewood.

Louisa set her knitting on the table and rushed to her room. She pulled out some paper and ink and carefully penned a sign: **Knitting Lessons, Inquire Within**. Then she made a dozen flyers to distribute around town, describing what kind of stitches she could teach. Maybe she could even find enough courage to venture into the saloons and hand them out to the women. Many of the townsfolk would criticize her if she associated with saloon girls and prostitutes, but they weren't on the verge of losing their homes. *Or having to marry Donny Addison.*

ACKNOWLEDGMENTS

Thanks to all my readers who love the Montana Sky Series.

You have my warmest appreciation!

To Louella Nelson, my writing teacher and editor.

To Adela Brito, my copy editor.

To my copyediting friends: Walter Koenig, Tracy Suttle, and Linda McLaughlin.

To Claire Lazerson for the sailing poem.

To Amy Atwell and Rob Preese for their formatting work.

To Delle Jacobs for her beautiful covers.

To Linda Prine, who twice a week writes with me and helps keep me on track.

ACKNOWLEDGEMENTS

ABOUT THE AUTHOR

 *New York Times* bestselling author Debra Holland is a three-time Romance Writers of America Golden Heart finalist and one-time winner. She's the author of The Montana Sky series, sweet historical Western romance. In 2012, *Wild Montana Sky* (her debut novel) made the *USA Today* list. In February of 2013, Amazon selected *Starry Montana Sky* as one of the Top 50 Greatest Love Stories, and a few months later *Stormy Montana Sky* made the *New York Times* bestseller list.

Debra is also the author of The Gods' Dream Trilogy (fantasy romance). She has a nonfiction book, *The Essential Guide to Grief and Grieving*, from Alpha Books (a subsidiary of Penguin) and is a contributor to *The Naked Truth About Self-Publishing*. Sign up for her newsletter and receive a free booklet, *58 Tips for Getting What You Want from a Difficult Conversation*, on her website, http://drdebraholland.com.

Mail-Order Brides of the West is her latest book.

You can contact Debra at:
Website: http://drdebraholland.com
Facebook: https://www.facebook.com/debra.
holland.731
Twitter: http://twitter.com/drdebraholland
Blog: http://drdebraholland.blogspot.com